COMMON GROUND

Jeane Gilbert-Lewis

A KISMET® Romance

METEOR PUBLISHING CORPORATION

Bensalem, Pennsylvania

For "Boy" who wanted me to . . .
For Dudley who thought I could . . .
And for Don who knew I could.

With special thanks to Catherine and Terri
for those mind-boggling phone calls.

JEANE GILBERT-LEWIS

At fourteen and living in Crewe, Virginia, Jeane dreamed of being a writer. Life took her coast to coast, and along the way, she stockpiled a mountain of ideas but had little time for writing. Then she married Don who cherished that dream. She gave up the nine-to-five, bought a PC and dug into that stockpile. A dream is now a reality. Jeane, Don, and Phoebe the cat live in Jacksonville, Florida.

ONE

Black leather creaked in protest as Ben Trainham leaned back in his chair. Across a banker's desk piled high with the accoutrements of his business, he considered the composed expression of the lovely woman who faced him. *Rather unusual*, he reflected, *when you consider the bombshell I just dropped in her lap. Most women would be reaching for a hankie right about now.*

But then, he reconsidered. *No, not unusual for Leslie Braddock.* From the top of her head with its long flaxen hair to the tips of her toes, she projected elegance and good breeding. But Ben knew beneath that blue linen dress, almost the color of her eyes, beat the heart of a guerrilla fighter.

"I'm sorry about all this, Leslie," Ben said.

A tight smile curved her mouth. "So I'm another offspring about to be crushed by unsuspected familial obligations. How much do I owe exactly?"

Ben stated the balance outstanding on the sizable loan the late Corrigan Braddock had secured against the family property. Then he moved forward to rest his arms along the edge of the desk.

He'd dreaded this meeting even as he'd looked forward

to seeing her. All morning, he'd toyed with the idea of asking her to dinner. But it was obvious the topic of their conversation did not lend itself to amorous advances on his part. Besides, Ben knew there was a good chance she'd turn him down as she did everyone else who exuded the slightest romantic interest in her.

"Leslie, as I told you on the phone, out of deference to your loss, I let the payments slide as long as I could. But, dear, even a bank president has limits to which he can go for preferred customers. They'll have to be brought current or—"

His voice trailed off. His meaning was clear.

"Or the bank could foreclose on River's Edge." Les finished for him. "Well, you can strike that from the agenda because it won't be happening. Now, I believe you mentioned the possibility of refinancing?"

"I have the application right here." He explained the loan application in detail, and when he was finished, Les scribbled her signature on the designated lines. Then she opened her purse and crammed in her copy.

"Thanks for the good news," she said curtly as she rose to her feet, carelessly tugging the strap of her leather bag up over her shoulder.

"Perhaps your mother can be of some help in the event there's a problem with the refinancing," Ben suggested as he, too, rose from his chair. "I understand the two of you have remained in touch since she and your father split, and from what I hear, the man she married is affluent."

"Mother sends money each month to help with Aunt Josie's care," Les cut in as they moved toward the office door. "No one expects her or Frank to assume responsibility for property she hasn't lived on in fourteen years."

"Look, Leslie, why don't you simply sell that white elephant and buy yourself a little—"

"No."

Her words were like a thunderclap. Determination

burned in her eyes, heightened the color in her cheeks as she glared up at him.

"I am so tired of hearing that dog-eared solution. If it's not Mother, then it's every man I come across with an extra dollar in his pocket. Sometimes, I wonder if the whole world knows something I don't about my home. Like maybe there's a diamond mine behind the stable? Gold nuggets floating in the well? Maybe it's oil, not rust, clogging the water pipes?"

Les grabbed for the doorknob, in a hurry to quit the confines of this office, his condescending presence . . . grab a moment's respite from the problems that had been unearthed here.

"I'll give you a call as soon as the board meets," Ben offered. "Or maybe you can come up with another solution by the first of the month. Refinancing is an expensive alternative to catching up the back payments, you know."

"Yeah, maybe by August first, the money tree out in the backyard will have produced a bumper crop," Les interrupted. She raised her eyes to meet his and attempted a halfhearted smile. "Thanks for seeing me about this, Ben. I detest those god-awful letters you people send out."

"Well, in your case, you'd have dismissed it as a computer error," Ben said. He sensed a lessening of her anger. Maybe . . .

"I'm just sorry I had to be the one to tell you River's Edge isn't unencumbered as you thought. When your father's health started sliding, I advised him to apprise you of the lien since you were in line to inherit. But like all of us, he certainly wasn't anticipating an untimely death."

Her second attempt at smiling was even more artificial. What a stupid thing to say!

"No, Ben, I believe my father had better things to do than sit around worrying about his own demise."

Ben flushed and smiled weakly. Then he glanced at his

watch as though the idea hadn't been seething in his mind all morning.

"Say, why don't we go grab some lunch? It's about that time."

No more attempts at smiling, she told herself as she studied him for a long moment. Then she shook her head from side to side.

"Thanks, but no thanks."

Annoyance gave him a surge of courage.

"Tell me, Leslie. Why is it you turn me down every time I ask you out? Not only me, but from what I hear, every other man as well."

"I wasn't aware I was a topic of gossip," she said tightly. "But to answer your question, I haven't met a man in this area who didn't have his eyes on River's Edge, including the president of Williamsburg Bank."

"I don't deny I'd like to own River's Edge. It's a valuable piece of property," he said. "You can't blame investors for their interest."

"No, but I can blame investors for trying to secure what they want with a bottle of wine and a free dinner," Les retorted. "Isn't that the usual ploy?"

Ben ignored her question. "Leslie, you're a beautiful woman. That evokes an interest as well."

"Valuable land, beautiful woman. What a tempting combination," Les said flatly. Turning on her heel, she left him standing beet-red in the doorway of his office.

Outside in the July sunshine, Les stalked across the concrete lot to her car. A sizable insurance payment was looming on the horizon. Aunt Josie's glasses needed changing. Wayne, her head mechanic, wanted a raise and now this?

"Why me, Lord?" Les muttered as she crawled beneath the steering wheel and started the engine. Heap into one pile pride of business ownership, pride of home ownership, and a visiting mother with whom your rapport has been questionable since the divorce. Throw in plenty of money problems for good measure and what do you have? One mind-piercing headache all the aspirin in the world couldn't cure.

Blaise Hollander trailed a long finger down the column of black print under the heading "Automobile Repairing." Beads of perspiration slid from his thick black hair and down his temples. Absently, he brushed them away with his free hand. Eyes the color of India ink settled on an advertisement in bold block form. The Car Doctor.

Interesting concept, he mused. House calls or, in this case, a backwoods call.

He punched out the numbers and when the phone was answered by the brisk voice he assumed belonged to the receptionist, he stated the reason for his call.

"Have you any idea of the problem?"

"No, Miss," Blaise replied. "If I knew what was wrong with the jeep, I wouldn't have walked three miles in this insufferable heat to the nearest phone to call you, now would I?"

Though by nature he was a tolerant man, there were exceptions. Coastal Virginia humidity, the countless mosquito and bluefly bites on his bare arms, and an unexpected disruption in his day in the form of an inoperative vehicle had all combined to lend a decided growl to his deep tone of voice.

When asked for the location of the jeep, Blaise gave directions as best he could, though the feat was not easy. He was unfamiliar with the outlying area of Williamsburg, knowing only that he and Celia had traveled about thirteen miles along historic Route 5 before deciding to investigate a narrow dirt road slicing into the thick forests that edged the James River.

"The old Lancombe place," the feminine voice replied. "I know it. I'll have someone out within the hour."

"I'd prefer you send Les Braddock, the proprietor," Blaise instructed as he recalled the advertisement he'd found in the yellow pages. He was in no mood for inexperienced mechanics.

"I'll see what I can do" was the response. "Your name?"

"Blaise Hollander."

"And you'll be paying by cash or credit card?"

Blaise sighed with obvious annoyance. *No, with baskets of corn and dried catfish*, he thought, *just like in the days when your ancestors fought the Indians and the British for the right to say Hail Marys at will.*

"Cash," he replied. "And can you hurry it up a bit? It's ninety-three degrees outside."

This time, the audible sigh came from the other end of the telephone connection.

"Yes, it is a hot day," she said curtly. "I'll have someone there within the hour."

Blaise thanked the hovering matron who continued to eye him cautiously when his call had been completed. *Obviously a native of this historic community*, he decided after insisting she accept a dollar as payment for the call. *Leery of tourists even though the entire area depends primarily on that lucrative source of revenue for its continued existence . . . unless, of course, one was fortunate enough to be sixth-generation plantation owners with a cache of old family money buried in the root cellar.*

Five minutes later, Blaise was retracing his steps toward the stalled vehicle with its cooler full of ice-cold beer and his younger sister, who he knew would be extremely hot and irate by now.

Les brought her van to a halt behind a maroon jeep bearing Pennsylvania license plates and its share of road dirt. A man was standing at the rear of the jeep, arms folded across his chest and a scowl on his face as he peered at her through the windshield of the van.

Blaise, Les thought as she shut off the engine. *As in fire? Nope, there is absolutely nothing red about this*

*blaze, unless you considered the annoyance in his dark
eyes. He was definitely ebony, should one use color as
part of his description.*

Les slid from the van and slammed the door.

"Blaise Hollander?" she asked as she approached him.

He nodded as he shoved his hands deep into the pockets
of well-tailored khaki slacks. Muscles bunched beneath his
black pullover shirt. Short sleeves revealed the well-toned
arms of a man not afraid of hard work. Overly long,
windblown black hair matched the color of his eyes with
their twin arches of black brow and long, lush lashes for
which most women would be inclined to kill.

Bedroom eyes, Les mused.

His skin was deeply tanned. Les credited this to either
long hours in the sun or ancestry or perhaps a combination
of both.

Nice-looking, Les decided and then swept his physical
attributes from her mind. Not only was he just a man; he
was a customer.

"I'll get my tools," Les said as she turned and proceeded to the access door on the side of the van, Blaise
at her heels.

Nearby, a dark-haired woman lounged on a thick bed
of pine needles, fanning herself with a folded map.

Tourist, Les surmised as she reached for the door's handle. *But what the devil were they doing two miles off the
highway on private property? Old man Lancombe would
have a fit!*

She decided not to ask. There was an aura about this
twosome that spelled money. Two people with the where-
withal to do exactly as they pleased, no explanations offered. But weren't they just a bit old to be necking in the
woods? The posh Williamsburg Inn maybe.

"I thought I specifically asked for Les Braddock,"
Blaise snapped behind her.

"You got her," Les said over her shoulder.

Blaise stared in disbelief. This slender creature with flaxen hair and sky-blue eyes was a mechanic?

His eyes swept over her blue uniform with its mannish tailoring. If the original design concept had been to conceal, on Les Braddock, the effort was wasted. Though her curves were not as lush as was his preference, they were nonetheless noticeable. And she wasn't beautiful in the classic sense. More like arresting with her tawny skin, that cute nose, and her long hair twisted into a French braid.

Blaise felt his annoyance growing. Teenagers didn't own companies and this woman-girl didn't look a day older than eighteen.

"What kind of problem are you having with the jeep?" Les asked as she slid the door open.

"It won't start," Blaise replied flatly.

"Not much of a clue there," Les commented. She leaned into the back of the van and pulled the heavy metal toolbox toward her.

Immediately, inborn chivalry rose to the occasion. Blaise leaped to attention. "Let me get that for you."

Les turned in surprise . . . and wished she hadn't. She'd seen tall men before. She'd even noticed a few with shoulders as broad as his. But not recently had she encountered anyone who smelled so darned good. His was a masculine fragrance, an astonishingly provocative combination of pipe tobacco, expensive after-shave, and sweat.

For a second, she gazed up at him. But only for a second. Those seductive brown eyes were a dangerous enticement. Though they were chilled with annoyance, beneath that annoyance, she saw an unmistakable flicker of awareness . . . heard that primitive calling out, male to female.

Les diverted her attention, instantly sealing off that portion of her mind sometimes given to idle speculation.

"That's not necessary," she told him as she backed out of the van and then hefted the toolbox onto the ground. "I've been lugging these tools in and out of this van for quite some time now. Do you own the jeep or is it a rental?"

"It's a company vehicle. What difference does it make?" he asked as he stepped aside so she might proceed to the front of the jeep.

"An owner would know the condition of the engine," Les replied. Tools clanged as she placed the heavy box back onto the ground.

After raising the hood, Les peered at the jeep's motor. In her peripheral vision, she saw the woman rising to her feet. *Obviously,* Les thought, *I'm to have an audience while I perform a little magic on a vehicle that has seen its share of neglect.*

"When'd you last have this engine tuned?" Les demanded. "It doesn't look like it's seen a wrench since it left the factory."

"How should I know?" Blaise retorted. "I have a service department for that sort of thing. Is that what's wrong with it?"

Les tossed him a tolerant look and again wished she hadn't. He was much too close; she could see a faint pulse in his smooth tanned neck. She could easily have reached out and trailed a fingertip along his sexy lower lip . . . if she was inclined, which she wasn't.

"I haven't checked," she replied, and waving him aside, she proceeded to open the toolbox. "You might as well make yourself comfortable. Even we experts require a few minutes to operate. Are you related to David Lancombe?"

"Never heard of him," Blaise said and then he frowned as she withdrew a handful of tools. "Are you sure you know what you're doing?"

A familiar wave of annoyance rippled over Les, and from force of habit, she bit back a heated response. He was, after all, a paying customer. She was, after all, quite accustomed to the question.

"I assure you I've done this before. And in case you

didn't know, David Lancombe owns this property and he's been known to get nasty with trespassers." She began removing the air filter to get at the carburetor. It was hard not to notice his hovering presence or his seductive aroma that, totally involuntarily, was filling her head with unwanted imaginings. "Could you move back a little, please? I need room to work."

"Sorry."

For a moment Blaise watched in silence. But then, his natural curiosity got the better of him. "How'd you get to be the car doctor?"

Les glanced up at him, decided his question was born of genuine interest, and then smiled. She had neither the time nor the inclination to divulge to him her life story. She settled for a light quip.

"Aren't you glad I did? It's a long walk back to town."

Blaise shrugged and jammed his hands deep into his pockets. Not a man easily influenced by the invisible force between men and women, he was annoyed to find himself in a position of being just that. Totally against his will, there resided within him a ridiculous urge to bend over and press his lips to that vulnerable expanse of sun-kissed skin just below her earlobe, run his tongue over her flesh, taste her.

Far too many solitary nights in a cold king-sized bed, he decided just as Celia wandered up to him.

"How much longer?" she asked as she watched Les's deft hands in amazement.

"You guys are in luck," Les replied. "I just happened to bring along five gallons of gas."

"Gas? For what?" Blaise demanded.

"Most engines run on the stuff."

"We're out of gas?" Celia asked, peering up at her towering, scowling brother. "But you said—"

"Impossible," Blaise argued. "The needle indicates half a tank."

"Better tell the engine that," Les replied, and stepping

around him, she proceeded to the van once more. Blaise openly watched the unconscious sway of her hips.

When the contents of the gas can had been emptied into the jeep's tank, Les crawled beneath the steering wheel and in seconds the engine roared to life.

She smiled with satisfaction and then shut off the engine.

"There's a gas station down the highway," she instructed as she began replacing the air filter. "Maybe it'd be a good idea if you get that fuel indicator fixed."

"I'll do that," Blaise snapped, and when Celia chuckled, he shot her a withering look. Then he bent, closed the toolbox, and before Les could protest his help, carried it back to the van.

"How much do I owe you?" he asked as he started to reach for his wallet.

"Wait, there's grease on your hands." Les grabbed a rag from the bin installed for that purpose. Turning, she crammed it in his hand. "Don't want you to ruin your clothes."

He stared down at her own hands, frowning as he noted the grease beneath her short, though neatly filed nails. Les reached for another rag.

"Unfortunately, it's an occupational hazard. You owe me thirty for the road call and five for the gas," she told him.

After wiping away as much grease as possible, Les completed the work order. Blaise was still frowning when she handed him the clipboard for his signature.

"Is something wrong?" she asked. If he was a dissatisfied customer, she would certainly like to know why.

Inadvertently, Blaise's attention was again drawn to her slender hands and the grease embedded there. Why would a woman so young and so lovely choose such a grimy means of earning a living?

"Uh—no," Blaise replied. "Everything's fine."

He forced his attention back to the clipboard. It certainly

wasn't any concern of his and the grease beneath her nails did not, in any way, reduce either her femininity or his own reaction to her gravitational pull. But a man was inclined to wonder. And a man was inclined to believe he'd insist on a more ladylike occupation if this utterly appealing woman was his.

His scrawl was broad, completely overpowering the limited space on the signature line.

A lot can be surmised from handwriting, Les thought as the man handed the clipboard back to her. If a person was inclined to analyze . . . which she wasn't.

"I appreciate your help," Blaise said as he again reached for his wallet, extracted the money, and handed it to her. The brief touch of his fingers against her own sent a little shiver up her arm, and to cover her acute awareness of this total stranger, she flashed him a businesslike smile.

"The purpose of the business," she said briskly.

Blaise was on the verge of drowning in those captivating blue eyes, and before he could prevent his actions, he reached over and swiped a smudge of dirt from her chin.

Her eyes widened in surprise. Her lips parted. She had no choice but to label the crazy awareness for what it was. Though far from being a dispassionate woman, since her divorce, she suppressed sexual urges. She'd told her body that was the way it had to be. Until this moment, her body had accepted that dictate. Until this moment . . .

Boy, he was good-looking! So tall and so male and if the merest touch of his fingers could incite the urge to indulge in illicit ponderings, what would it be like to . . .

Damn, Blaise thought in disbelief as he sensed an involuntary awakening in the nether regions of his body. *If Celia wasn't standing there gawking like a twelve-year-old girl, I'd probably do something stupid like grab this wisp of a woman in my arms and the devil be damned!*

Les sucked in a deep breath of air and then stepped back from him as one from a fire that's too hot.

As she crawled up into the van, Blaise caught the door and closed it. His eyes clung to her face, indecision tugging at him. He was in town for only four more days. When the golf tournament was over, he'd be leaving. He had a life. He had responsibilities miles from this deep, sensuous forest and this blond-haired woman. But, God help him, he wanted her . . . desired her with a fervor that was unbelievable. It wasn't often it happened that way. At least, not to him. And the worst part . . . or maybe the best part, that combustible feeling was reciprocated. He'd seen it in her eyes only seconds ago. He'd seen the heat rise in her cheeks.

"What's your name?" he asked. "Besides Les."

"Leslie Joanne," she replied in little more than a choked whisper, and before he could detain her . . . before she allowed herself to be detained by this overwhelming man with the sexy dark eyes, she reached over and started the van's engine. Then, not trusting herself to look at him again, she shifted into reverse and backed slowly toward the highway, her heart thumping against her ribcage.

"I feel as though I just witnessed the seduction scene of the decade," Celia said with a brisk laugh. "Why didn't you just go ahead and rip her clothes off, brother dear?"

Blaise tore his eyes from the address and phone number printed at the top of his copy of the work order. He forced the crazy thought from his mind.

No, he wouldn't call her. What would he say? *Hello . . . I'm only in town for a short time . . . I'm not in the market for commitments but I sure would like to make love to you . . . how about it?*

"Yeah, sure," he muttered as he crammed the paper into his back pocket.

"She was pretty, brother dear," Celia persisted as they climbed back into the jeep. "A little young, perhaps, but youth is just what you need to clear the cobwebs out of your antiquated brain and steer you away from this workaholic binge you've been on for too many years."

Blaise made no reply. Instead, he feigned intense concentration on getting the jeep back to the highway.

Celia reached over and punched him on the shoulder.

"So, Mr. Cool, are you going to give the lady a call?"

"Stifle it, Celia," he growled.

"That's an affirmative if I ever heard one," Celia declared as she extracted a rubber band from her purse and then fastened an abundance of rich dark hair high on the crown of her head. "Jeez, it's hot here. And I thought Pittsburgh was bad. I saw you cram that paper in your pocket. But knowing you and your penchant for remembering numbers, you already have it memorized. Oh well, a man needs a diversion once in a while."

Blaise found it difficult to curb the smile now curving his mouth. His younger sister had the most delightful but equally frustrating habit of flipping from subject to subject with the ease of one turning pages in a book. Celia had been, was still, and would probably always be a royal pain in his backside.

Nearly fifteen years his junior, she'd hero-worshiped her only brother since toddler age. Now she worked for him . . . or with him, depending on Blaise's mood at the time in question. With this, he couldn't find fault. Though she gave the impression of being an air-headed piece of fluff when the notion struck her, Celia was smart, lightning quick in forming what he'd found were accurate opinions, and she had a sixth sense for making a buck. Her contribution to Hollander & Associates had been, thus far, beyond his wildest hopes. And besides, with the exception of his son Brandon, she was all that remained of his family.

"So, what do you think of this little tract of land?" Celia asked. "Interested?"

"Nope," he replied. "I'm thinking more and more of a place Dennis mentioned yesterday at cocktails. Seems the owners have neglected it over the years, and from what he says, they'll be glad to have someone take it off their hands. On this tract, we'd have to start from the ground up. But Dennis said, with a little renovation, that other place is exactly what I'm looking for."

"We're headed there now?"

"Nope. We'll check it out tomorrow afternoon. Right now, I need a shower and a decent meal."

"And a little privacy in which to make a phone call," Celia finished. "So, where is the other property?"

"According to Dennis, it's farther on down the highway. A place called River's Edge."

Later, in his room at the Williamsburg Inn with that privacy surrounding him like a thick cloud, Blaise stretched out on the bed and stared at the phone. True to Celia's words, Leslie Braddock's office number was imprinted on his brain.

Okay, so I'm intrigued, he told himself. *But I'm not an overzealous kid prone to tailspins every time I meet a spectacular-looking woman.*

Blaise closed his eyes and willed himself to relax. He'd taken this mini-vacation for that express purpose. But as usual, he and Celia were turning it into yet another work session, though scouting property could hardly be called physical labor. In truth, he was enjoying those treks along back roads, through forests thick with mysterious silences, along river banks tangled with ageless growth.

Damn, she WAS pretty, Blaise found himself thinking. But as Celia had mentioned, she was also young . . . probably close to Brandon's age. After a particularly troublesome relationship two years ago, Blaise had sworn off younger women. It would seem they were hell-bent on changing not only the world around them but a man's mind as well. He was satisfied with his mind as it was.

Okay, Leslie arouses your protective nature.

At this, Blaise groaned in protest and shoved himself

into an upright position. He rose from the bed and began pacing.

Protective nature, my eyeballs! Think again, fella. A few minutes in that woman's company and you know you've met one who doesn't need protecting. Call it like it is, man. She arouses all right, and it's not only your protective nature she arouses.

Against Blaise's will, Les's face materialized in his mind, warmth infused him, and his decision was made.

She was an interesting young woman. Inviting her to dinner was a far cry from the pursuit of a relationship. He'd enjoy her company, satisfy his curiosity about her, then dismiss her from his mind.

Blaise reached for the receiver, excitement leaping in his chest.

And seconds later, he replaced it with a heavy sigh of resignation and a healthy amount of relief. She'd already left for the day. Now he could push temptation out of his mind. Couldn't he?

TWO

With the wind through the open window withering her like a blast from an open furnace, Les turned off the highway and onto the graveled lane. Ahead of her, panes of glass in the upstairs windows caught the early evening sunshine. Les rather enjoyed this particular view of River's Edge. The reflection momentarily blinded her to the blistered paint on the front of the majestic dwelling.

She was hot and tired and dirty and her nerves needed a balm. If they kept the stuff in the house, Les knew, on this particular evening, she'd be tempted to seek the calming effect of a tall glass of bourbon. Since they didn't, she longed for the energy to throw a saddle over Windmere's broad back and race across the pastures until the horse was lathered with sweat and her mind was cleansed of the turmoil there.

Heretofore, she'd made certain that turmoil had nothing to do with a man. As for financial problems, they certainly weren't new animals in her personal zoo. Hence, no reason for undue stress. She'd simply deal with this new burden as she'd done in the past.

But the man on her mind?

His aroma still filled her senses and the unexpected

flame he'd ignited in her lower body burned hotter each time she allowed herself to dwell on those electrically charged moments in the woods.

Now this was turmoil . . . unwarranted, unwanted, and completely unexpected. She had to stop thinking about him. It was ridiculous. She'd never see him again . . . thank goodness! Dynamite was a dangerous substance.

It had been nearly two years since her last botch in the romance department. Tony, with a head full of bright visions and a pocket full of worthless checks, had wined and dined her straight down the road to disappointment. His and her own. His, because she was not the wealthy landowner to which he felt entitled; hers because she'd honestly liked the scoundrel. She referred to Tony as her last attempt to achieve some measure of happiness as one half of a couple.

But a man like Blaise could befuddle a woman's mind and encourage her to give it one more try. Fortunately, there was only one Blaise and she was now safely departed from his explosive powers.

Sherry was settled in a wicker chair on the wide screened-in porch off the kitchen, a tall glass of iced tea at her elbow, the *Richmond Times* spread open on her lap.

She glanced up as Les came out the door, freshly showered, her own tea glass in one hand.

"You're late tonight," her mother commented as she watched her daughter, fresh out of uniform and clad in wrinkled cuffed shorts, sink down in a matching chair and sling her long legs up over the arm.

"Wayne wanted another little conference," Les replied and then took a long drink from her glass. After dabbing at her lips, she continued: "He thinks he's entitled to another raise and I can't afford it. He's threatening to quit and I can't afford that either. Where's Aunt Josie? I didn't see her when I came in."

"Napping." Sherry carefully folded the newspaper and laid it aside. Then she took her time removing her reading glasses and returning them to their leather case. Irritation crawled in Les's stomach. She knew the signs. Sherry was missing the bright lights of Miami.

"You're going home," Les said, her blue eyes intent on her mother's face. Since it was the custom for Sherry and her husband Frank to take separate vacations once a year, Sherry came to River's Edge. She normally stayed a month with her daughter and sister-in-law. This visit bore the signs of being a two-weeker.

"I'm thinking about it," Sherry replied. "Country living gets boring after a while."

Sherry searched Les's face for a show of disappointment. But she found only the same implacable expression so characteristic of the Braddocks . . . of her daughter, when revealing inner thoughts might also reveal a chink in the armor. When Sherry and Corrigan's marriage had soured and they'd split fourteen years ago, Les had chosen to remain with her father and Aunt Josie. When Sherry had met and subsequently married Frank Weston, Les had accepted it . . . on the surface. But Sherry knew Les's suppressed resentment toward the divorce was a barricade against the closeness they'd once shared.

"I wish you'd reconsider and come home with me. You and Frank get along so well. And there's plenty of room for Josie, too."

"I'm not leaving River's Edge, Mother," Les replied. "It's my home."

"And it's falling down around your ears," Sherry scoffed and ran her fingers through her short cap of silver hair to fluff it, a gesture Les knew spelled annoyance. They'd had this discussion several times since Corrigan Braddock's death had placed River's Edge in Les's hands. And Sherry knew moving Leslie Joanne Braddock could be likened to moving the Rock of Gibralter. She'd inherited not only the family estate but also every bit of the Braddock obstinacy.

"And it needs a new roof and the plumbing's outdated

and thanks for telling me about that astronomical loan Dad took out when you two divorced," Les finished, her eyes intent on her mother's face. "No wonder the settlement was so impressive."

Sherry squirmed a little in her chair and then smoothed imaginary wrinkles from her skirt.

"At the time, Corrigan's choices were limited. He could either borrow money or sell River's Edge and split the proceeds. I was entitled to fifty percent, you know. Anyway, I assumed your father had repaid it by now," she told her daughter. "I have a little money if you need it."

What an understatement, Les thought angrily. The Westons were loaded.

"No thank you," Les replied. "It's my responsibility. But if you or father had told me about the lien on this place, I could have pulled in the reins a little tighter. As it is, I have until the first of the month to come up with a lot of money."

"That's why you need to sell this place and you and Josie come to Florida with us."

"No," Les replied in a stubborn voice. "And even should I consider a sale, it would only be to someone interested in living here. But everyone who wants River's Edge sees it as a prospective site for condominiums or another motel. I won't be a party to the destruction of a historic monument. I'll manage somehow. Braddocks always do."

The screen door creaked and both women glanced up as Aunt Josie scuffled out onto the porch. Her limpid gray eyes lighted on her niece.

"There's a phone call for you, Leslie," she said in her whispery voice as she lowered her petite frame into the chaise lounge. "It's a man."

Les rose, her mind racing ahead. Wayne was supposed to be taking the road calls tonight. And should he be overextended, Carl was next in line. This was Les's week to enjoy the nine-to-five routine for a change. In the kitchen, she reached for the receiver on the extension phone.

"Hello?"

"Leslie?"

Her heart dropped into her stomach. There could be only one person with a voice like that.

"How'd you get my number?"

Because it's my nature to persevere until I get what I want, Blaise thought. Relief made him almost light-headed. Her voice was as stimulating as before. Red flags of warning snapped in his mind. He ignored them.

"From the phone book," he replied. "Since there is only one L. Braddock listed in the Williamsburg directory, it was easy to assume it was you."

Les reached for one of the ladder-back chairs at the kitchen table, and pulling it nearer, she sank down. Strength had vanished from her legs. She was again seeing those seductive eyes with the sinful lashes, the sensuous curve of his lips, the breadth of his shoulders, and hearing, thanks to the inventive expertise of Alexander Graham Bell, that commanding voice that seemed to dare one to refuse anything he might ask.

"Will you have dinner with me tonight?"

On the tip of her tongue was the automatic response she'd been delivering to hopeful males for the past two years. Thanks but no thanks.

Mentally, she tested it for credibility and, for the first time, found it lacking.

"Blaise, I don't even know you," Les replied. She toyed with a loose thread in the cuff of her shorts. She studied the toe of her sneaker. She willed her body to resist the excitement flowing through her veins.

"I think you do, but if it'll help, I'll give you a few basic facts." Blaise replied. "Blaise Monroe Hollander, Twenty-twenty Wainwright Court, Pittsburgh, Pennsylvania, red-blooded American male currently lodged at the

Williamsburg Inn, Room One-oh-eight, social security number—''

Darn it, why was her body responding like this? So he was good-looking. He didn't have a corner on the market. So he was sexy.

''Yes,'' she cut in, her voice throaty. All desire to hedge was gone. She wanted to see him again . . . the sooner, the better. Tomorrow, she'd probably hate herself for this uncharacteristic submission, but after all, it wasn't that she hated men. She just hated an opportunist salivating over her property. Blaise couldn't be after River's Edge. He didn't even know about the place.

''Where shall I pick you up?'' he asked.

''I'll meet you.''

''I assure you my vehicle is fine now. I had the indicator fixed and the gas tank's full.''

Les ignored his argument. Though out of practice with the dating game, she nonetheless remembered a few of her own rules. Having one's own transportation could solve a multitude of problems should her initial judgment of the man be wrong and he turn out to be a first-class jerk.

''Do you like seafood?'' she asked. ''Captain George's is probably the best in town.''

Blaise's gut tightened. Food was the farthest thing from his mind. Even as he stood watching the normalcy of life outside his window and fought against it, desire wormed in his middle. Her voice was a promise of passions inspired and subsequently abated. It had been a long time since he'd allowed himself to hear that promise in a woman's voice.

''How about a picnic?'' Blaise suggested even as he wondered from where in the Sam Hill that idea had sprung. He hated picnics! Hated the fuss and the bother. Hated the insufferable insects.

''It'll be dark soon.''

The silence that lingered was fraught with innuendos. Les swallowed hard.

Blaise closed his eyes and willed the heat from his loins. The flags snapped again in his mind.

"I'll put together some food and meet you in Waller Mill Park in an hour," Les said softly. "Just go west on Sixty. The park will be on your right."

Weakly, she replaced the receiver, and for a moment, she sat in the silence ordering her heart to be still, her pulse to stop racing, the heat to leave her cheeks. Why hadn't she refused him?

Forget that question, Les told herself. *The answer could be disquieting unless you're ready for the truth, simple truth being you're attracted to Blaise Hollander.*

The screen door creaked, and as Sherry entered the kitchen, she frowned with concern.

"Leslie? Are you all right? You look a little pale."

"I have a date," Les said simply.

"You're kidding me," Sherry exclaimed. "After all these years, you've finally decided to participate in the pleasures of the living? Who is he? He has to be a paragon of perfection to measure up to your standards."

Les ignored her mother's quip. After all, Sherry had yet to be apprised of Les's last indulgence in the 'pleasures of the living.'

Rising to her feet, Les jammed her hands deep into her shorts' pockets. She really needed to reconsider this impulsiveness.

But, fortunately or unfortunately—she'd decide which later—it was too late to reconsider. She'd already accepted.

She glanced up and then smiled weakly.

"You don't know him, Mother. Look, I'm in a bit of a hurry. Could you slice off some of that roast pork while I change? Make it enough for three sandwiches. And some cheese. Maybe some fruit."

"But Les," Sherry exclaimed, "you've already had dinner."

"Yes, but I didn't have dessert," Les said and then she laughed huskily. "By the way, his name is Blaise."

*   *   *

The sun was just beginning to settle into the dense forests across Waller Mill Lake when Les pulled into the parking lot at the park and shut off the Datsun's engine. Twisting the rearview mirror around, she made a cursory inspection of the minimal makeup she'd decided upon after finally selecting the blue floral skirt and matching T-shirt from her closet. Taking a brush from her purse, she ran it through her windblown hair and then shoved the thick mass back over her shoulders. As she tucked the brush back into her purse, she heard the crunch of his footsteps on tiny pebbles beside the car.

"You look just fine," Blaise said as he reached down and opened the car door. "In fact, you're beautiful."

Les slid from the car. Blaise bent to extract the picnic basket from the back seat. It was a struggle not to notice the smooth play of muscles beneath his gray cotton pullover . . . or the snug fit of his black jeans . . . or the cloud of aromatic enticement surrounding him when he straightened and turned to face her.

"This is crazy," Blaise growled softly, his dark eyes threatening her innate composure, which was already in danger of showing a few cracks. "I haven't stopped thinking about you since you drove off in that dusty van."

"Good mechanics are hard to come by," she replied, and when the evening breeze lifted a lock of hair and tossed it across her cheek, he reached over and brushed it aside, his fingertips barely grazing her skin.

"Is that why you're nervous?"

"Not exactly," Les assured him. "I'm just a little out of practice with this dating routine. Where shall we go?"

If I had any sense I'd go straight back to my motel room and forget this crazy attraction, Blaise thought as he linked his arm through hers and urged her in the direction of the lake. *The sooner the better*, he added silently, as he studied her in his peripheral vision. Silky blond hair tumbling onto her shoulders . . . unbelievably blue eyes and a smile that revealed, yet hid too much. Beneath her shirt, soft curves moved provocatively as she walked beside him, long legs enabling her to easily match his stride.

Lush grass provided a soft padding beneath the blanket he spread on the ground at the base of a sprawling oak tree. They chose a spot well removed from the picnickers who had chosen sites nearer the water.

"So what are we eating?" he asked as they settled down on the blanket.

"I think I brought roast pork sandwiches," Les replied. "Aunt Josie did the cooking and Mother fixed the basket. I'm not very domesticated."

"Makes two of us," he said. His eyes drifted over her face, caressed her lips, moved on, and finally paused when his gaze found the dimple in her left cheek. Reaching out, he pressed a forefinger against that girlish indentation. "I can't help but wonder if you have gorgeous children with a dimple just like that."

"No, and it's not on my list of things to do tomorrow either," Les murmured. "Maybe the day after."

She was glad when he moved his finger from her skin. She'd already decided this thing between them—whatever it was—had to be digested in bits and pieces. Obviously, Blaise was not of the same mind.

Broad, sun-bronzed fingers made short work of opening a chilled bottle of wine he'd extracted from the small cooler he'd brought along. He filled a glass and handed it to her.

Blaise noticed her hesitation, but he had no way of knowing her thoughts were on the remark she'd made to Ben about a fine dinner with a bottle of wine. Well, this wasn't dinner; it was a picnic. And thank goodness, River's Edge wasn't even in the picture.

"Just like in the movies," he said, watching her closely. "Corny, huh?"

"A little," Les agreed. "Especially when Williamsburg has some wonderful restaurants."

"It's hard to get to know someone in a restaurant unless you spend four hours toiling over a piece of charbroiled meat while a tip-hungry waiter hovers at your elbow," Blaise replied, his eyes again intent on her face as he raised his glass. "To the car doctor."

Les touched her glass to his and then took a sip of the wine. It was tart and fruity and soothing to her tight throat.

"Okay," Blaise said as he adjusted his position, now sitting cross-legged to face her, elbows resting on his splayed knees. "What do people on a first date talk about these days?"

"Oh, the usual, I suppose," Les replied, wishing for the world she could relax. "Your bank balance, your astrological sign, whether or not you prefer the missionary position in bed."

Jeez, why in the world had she said that!

Blaise frowned handsomely, decided her quip was intended to be humorous, and then grinned.

"With an approach like that, I'm not surprised you're out of practice dating."

"Believe me, that one gets saved for special occasions," Les exclaimed. Thank God, he had a sense of humor.

She took another sip of the wine, savored the taste, and then reminded herself that her tolerance was not to be tested in this, an ideal setting, with this, a most appealing male.

Blaise watched the muscles working beneath the satiny flesh in her slender neck as she swallowed. *Satisfy your curiosity, banish the intrigue, and get the heck out of Dodge*, his common sense warned. His body wasn't listening. Nothing was listening anymore.

"You aren't married, of course," he said abruptly.

"Would I be here with you if I was?" Les asked in surprise.

"My ex-wife didn't find a husband a hindrance to romantic involvements," he replied. Though his words were blunt, his eyes mirrored satisfaction with her answer.

"Well, neither did my ex-husband," Les said. Then she laughed. "Thanks for telling me you're not married. You just wasted one of my reasons for driving my own car."

"Let's try for a few more. What are the others?" Blaise asked.

"I'm accustomed to being in charge," Les replied. Turning, she dug into the picnic basket and retrieved strips of cheese wrapped in cellophane. Slowly, she unwrapped the cheese and extended it in his direction.

"You didn't have me fooled for a moment," Blaise said as he took a piece. "It's like a banner across your chest." Even white teeth bit into the cheese, and as he chewed, he nodded in approval.

"You don't object?" Les asked. "Most men hate that quality in a woman."

"I'm not most men. Besides, would it matter if I did?" Reaching behind him, he picked up the wine bottle and refilled her glass. "I admire strength in a woman."

"Well, when you've been in charge of the show half your life, it pays to be strong," Les said. "When my father and mother separated, he just leaned over, placed the reins in my hand, and I've been driving the carriage ever since."

"And you were how old?" Suddenly, he was ravenous to know everything about Leslie Braddock and annoyed with the fact he had such a short time in which to do it.

"I think I made my first major decision when I was fourteen," Les mused and then she laughed, her face soft with secret memories. "Our cook kept disregarding Daddy's special diet because it was easier to throw a roast in the oven and then go home. So I fired her and hired the caretaker's wife in her place. For days afterward, I was afraid to sleep for fear Millie would come back looking for revenge. Of course, she didn't."

Les paused and laughed sheepishly. "And I think I'm talking too much."

Blaise's eyes narrowed as he studied her for a moment. He had the distinct impression there was beneath her words an undercurrent of sadness. He had an immediate vision of a wide-eyed little girl with an overload of responsibility on her thin shoulders. He didn't care for the vision.

Les pretended concentration on smoke boiling up from a charcoaler down by the lake as she tried forcing herself not to ask the question uppermost in her mind at that moment. But her efforts didn't work. Besides, didn't she have a right to be inquisitive about the possibility of a girlfriend? A traveling girlfriend?

"Where is your lovely companion?" she asked casually.

"My sister is haunting the lounge at the inn." His emphasis on the word "sister" made her pulse rate escalate.

Damn, she's pretty, Blaise thought as his guard slipped another notch.

"Why a mechanic?"

"Why not?" she said lightly. "It helps to pay the bills. What do you do?"

Reaching into his rear pocket, Blaise extracted his wallet, flipped it open, and removed a business card that he pressed into her hand.

"Hollander & Associates," Les read aloud. She raised her eyes to meet his. "And that is?"

"Contracting, engineering. Whatever pays my bills," he replied. Stretching forward, he returned the wallet to his pocket. "And to fill in the rest of the gaps, I'm here for the golf tournament, a spectator this time."

His eyes narrowed as he contemplated her.

"You're staring," she said inanely.

"Yes, I am. I'm trying to figure out how old you are."

"Honest, aren't you?" Les teased. Then reaching over, she patted his shoulder. "I assure you I'm past the age to vote. Are you?"

"A couple of decades past it. I'm forty-four. Is that too old?"

"For the Boy Scouts, yes."

Blaise threw back his head and laughed. Good looks and a wit to match. It was a combination he'd always found attractive in a woman.

For a while they munched on the cheese and watched the antics of two little boys trying to get a kite up on the other side of the park.

"I don't believe the wind's strong enough," Les commented. Then she turned to Blaise. "How long are you in Williamsburg?"

"Four days," Blaise replied, and merriment danced in his eyes. "Unless I run across something too compelling to leave. In that case, my stay would be for an indeterminate period of time."

Les smiled slightly and lowered her gaze.

"If you mean what I think you mean, then it'll be four days," she assured him. "I took my name off the availability roster a long time ago."

"Why?"

"Shortage of interest on my part, I guess. Maybe we should eat while it's still light enough to see."

"Are you hungry?"

"No," Les admitted. "Are you?"

"No, but I'm impatient," he replied, and suddenly, he was on his knees, his arm looping around her neck, drawing her closer until she could feel his warm breath on her face. "If I had more time, I'd wait for this. But since I only have four days . . ."

He gave her no time to think and for this Les was thankful. She would need that time later when the mental ramifications struck home. But absolutely no time was needed to decide if she wanted the same thing he did.

The touch of his mouth was cool like the man himself. But his kiss was in direct contrast to what she was learning of his nature . . . persuasive but not demanding . . . insistent but not commanding, and as easily as though she'd practiced all her life for the touch of this man's lips, Les melted and parted and molded herself into the moment. Her breath caught and warm pleasure spilled over her.

Beneath his mouth, her lips moved open, inviting the gentle exploration of his tongue. The dam around her suppressed feelings broke and she was flooded with need, the intensity of which was frightening.

And just when she was beginning to enjoy the reawakening of that feeling, he pulled away. Her eyes clung to him, her heart racing madly. A vein throbbed in his neck, his breathing was as labored as her own, and the unmistakable gleam in those ebony depths that studied her brought reality crashing down around her.

What she was sampling here had all the earmarks of danger. Who she was sampling had all the expertise necessary not only to shake but also to demolish her protective wall.

"I had a feeling you'd kiss like that," Blaise murmured.

Les laughed shakily.

"If I ask, will you come back to my room?"

"No," Les said. "Did you think I would?"

"No," Blaise replied and then he smiled sheepishly. "Actually, I'm relieved."

"Afraid I'd steal your virginity?"

"Afraid you'd steal my Timex watch," he corrected, his eyes warm on her face, his hand dropping down to grip hers. "After all, I don't know you that well. But I intend to rectify that."

The pressure of his warm fingers was comfortable . . . too comfortable. And she was sorry when he released her hand.

Reaching over, Blaise pulled the picnic basket closer, and together they spread out the contents.

Les's mind was far from the tantalizing array of food her mother had provided. *Yes,* she thought, to paraphrase his words, *this was crazy . . . utterly insane.* She'd known him a scant few hours and yet she felt as though she knew him from the soul outward. That he'd asked her to his room did not insult her. Nor did it surprise her. It was as though, by mutual accord, parameters had to be set around the instantaneous attraction that had been there between them since she'd crawled out of her van earlier in the day. Now that those parameters were set, albeit temporarily, she felt the tension between them begin to dissipate.

She watched him unwrap a sandwich and then stop to straighten the lettuce before he took a bite.

"Can't stand it drooping over the edge," he explained as he caught her staring at him. "Want me to fix yours?"

Les laughed, happiness warm in her veins. This was how it was supposed to be. Simple enjoyment. Nothing heavy. This was safe.

"I've been eating droopy sandwiches for years. One more won't hurt. Here, have a pickle."

Dusk was gathering by the time they finished with the food and placed the basket aside. Les could not believe how relaxed she'd become, even though conversation had gone from the casual banter between strangers to the inquisitiveness of two adults who like what they've found. And like him? She did . . . too much. But then how could she not like a guy who'd assured her Taylor had gotten what he deserved when Les had related the time she'd stomped the neck off his new Gibson guitar when she found him in her bed with another woman.

"I can't believe you gave your wife a monogrammed bag of horsefeed when she divorced you," Les exclaimed for the third time since he'd told her his own story of ridiculous revenge.

"Yep, I carried it right into the courtroom. A mere token of remembrance for fourteen years of marriage," Blaise reiterated with a sheepish grin. He poured the last of the wine into their glasses and handed one to her. "Image was important to her polo-playing lover. I made it possible for her to carry that image into the stables she admired so much more than what I had to offer.''

"Sounds to me as though you were bitter," Les commented.

"Then, perhaps. But now, I'm simply resigned," Blaise replied. "She wanted out. I let her go. That was seven years ago and believe me, Angel Eyes, the bitterness is gone and God gives people this miraculous ability to forget pain. So what we have here is a normal male who's wondering if now there's a hopeful Romeo on the sidelines of your life.''

He balanced his wineglass on a folded knee and peered at her. It didn't make sense. Leslie was not only a lovely woman, but she also had a mystical quality about her that would intrigue any man in his right mind.

"Nope," Les said. She stretched long legs before her, crossing them at the ankles, and then leaned back on her elbows. "And believe it or not, it isn't my approach that's responsible as you said. It's a well-practiced withdrawal based on some well-learned lessons since my divorce. What about you?''

"I assure you there's not a single Romeo on the sidelines," he teased. "Or even on the front lines. All that's left of the Hollander family per se is a keg of dynamite called a sister and a tower of brawn and brains for a son named Brandon. When Elaine split for Brazil, her parents disowned me for chasing away their lovely daughter, and my parents are dead. Truly shortens your Christmas card list.''

Blaise raised his glass and drained the contents. Les stretched leisurely.

Resisting the urge to gape as her altered position pulled her shirt tight across her breasts, Blaise set his glass aside and rose to his feet. "Let's pack this stuff in the car and go someplace nice and private. Sitting on the ground is fine for a while, but then my knees begin to protest.''

In truth, it wasn't his knees that were protesting. The

two boys had given up on the kite and had decided the vicinity beside Blaise and Leslie was perfect for a game of Frisbee. He didn't mind when the disk accidentally sailed onto their blanket more than once. In fact, he rather enjoyed the excitement on the kids' faces when he picked it up and sailed it back, each time throwing it a bit farther than the time before. But he did mind the lack of privacy.

"I'd like to, but I really need to be getting home," Les advised when he reached down and clasped her hand in his warm grip. "A five o'clock alarm demands at least a ten o'clock curfew during the week."

As they started toward the car, one of the little boys came running up to Blaise, his flushed face mirroring disappointment.

"Heh, mister, we thought you'd play with us some more," he said. "My dad's got a bum arm and he can't."

Blaise grinned and ruffled the little boy's hair. "I'd like to, little man. You throw a mean Frisbee, but right now I'm baby-sitting this young lady."

"She can play, too," the boy insisted. " 'Sides, she's too big for a baby-sitter."

"Maybe, but you see, she's got a wooden foot. Tell you what. If your parents don't mind, I'll spring for a couple of sodas to cool you guys off."

"Oh, they don't mind," the little boy exclaimed, his interest in Les's foot gone as he held out his hand for the change Blaise was taking from his pocket.

"A wooden foot?" Les exclaimed as they moved on.

"Did the job, didn't it? But most important, they left happy," Blaise replied quietly.

Les knew she wasn't imagining that his mood had darkened. She glanced up at his slight scowl. She stopped and gazed up at him, her expression playful.

"Heh, if you want to play, I don't mind."

"Hum-m? Oh—no, I don't want to play," Blaise said with a chuckle. His hand closed around her upper arm as he urged her forward. "I want to be with you. It's just that little boys are my weakness, I suppose. I missed most of Brandon's early years. Workaholics have a habit of letting their priorities get out of whack.''

He glanced down at her. His words trailed off. She was so lovely with her hair fanning around her face and that look of innocent curiosity. That sexy dimple. His eyes drifted down to her mouth. He couldn't wait until his hands were free and he could grab her and hold her and feel her mouth go pliant beneath his.

Wait? Why should he? He'd wasted enough time already, and with Leslie time was a commodity he did not have. His footsteps quickened; Les had no trouble keeping up.

When they reached the car, Blaise plopped the cooler and the blanket on the hood and then reached for the basket she carried.

Strong arms impatiently folded her against his hard length. Her head tilted back. Her breath caught.

"I love being with you, Leslie," he murmured.

But it was not his words that immediately set her heart to racing. Nor was it his chest, warm and solid against her breasts. Nor was it the intimate pressure of his maleness as splayed fingers dug into her back, urging her to curve against him.

No, it was an honest fear of the fiery feelings raging inside her. In such a short time since she'd met him, so many desires had crawled out of the closet just as so many ghosts had reared their warning heads. So much determination was in danger of being slaughtered by his appeal. She had to resist this appeal. She had to think, for Pete's sake!

"Blaise, I think—"

"Don't think," he ordered. When his urgent mouth finally settled perfectly over hers, strength vanished from her legs.

For a lifetime, he kissed her and then kissed her some more, each talented capture of her mouth more devastating than the one that preceded. And when, finally, Les thought she could not refrain from a response another minute, he raised his head. Dark, sultry eyes bored deep into her own.

"I'm sure there's a logical reason why you're holding yourself like you had a ramrod in your back," he whispered roughly. "And if it helps, keep on doing it. Just remember I warned you, it won't do a piece of good."

Les said nothing, not trusting herself to be as articulate as he seemed to find no difficulty in being. Did he really want to hear that for the past couple of hours, common sense had been waging a terrible war with her growing interest in him? Did he really need to know that she had decided Blaise Hollander was only a temporary diversion who'd stumbled into her quiet life? Did he need to be reminded of the fact that for all his masculine persuasions, Blaise Hollander would be leaving in four days?

He'd surely laugh if she confessed her abhorrence for a broken heart or even a cracked one. And given the way her body already cried out for him, a few more days of this and she'd suffer the loss when he was gone, albeit a light case. She was just that kind of person. Somehow, she'd never learned to love'em and leave'em with everything completely intact.

Oh, in truth she had to place him a little higher in the category of heartbreakers than that slot reserved for her ex-husband Taylor. But in so many ways, Blaise Hollander was far worse than Taylor would ever learn to be. Blaise Hollander was dynamite, and the sad fact was, no matter how she argued with herself, she was already in danger of his explosive charms.

Oh, for Pete's sake, give me a break, Les silently screamed at the vexatious voices in her head. *I just need to think this through.*

"I'd give my favorite pair of jockey shorts to know exactly what you're thinking right now," Blaise said as he noted the ambivalence flitting over her lovely features.

"No, Blaise," Les said with a wry laugh. "I don't think you would."

"Okay, then I'll chance a guess," he murmured as he bent to nuzzle his lips against her neck. "You have that 'He's just a man out for a good time' look on your face, which was preceded by that 'vacationer wanting to sow some wild oats' grimace, and just now, I saw the real clincher. A frown called 'It's time to throw some cold water on this rutting dog.'"

He raised his head, merriment now dancing in his eyes. "How many points for a perfect score?"

Les laughed and pulled free of his arms. "Okay, so I have a few misgivings." She opened the car door and shoved the basket inside.

"A few I can handle," he replied. "It's those barrels full I might have a little difficulty with."

In truth, his accurate perception made her feel a little silly about all those misgivings. *Jeez*, she told her nagging common sense, *give the man a chance*.

He caught her hands and squeezed them tightly. "We'll start work on those doubts of yours tomorrow. How about taking the day off and—"

"I'd love to, Blaise, but I can't," Les interrupted. "This is one of our busiest times of the year."

"Then tomorrow night?"

"Okay," she breathed. "I'll meet you here at six-thirty."

"Now that we've established that I'm safer than your resident granny, why don't I pick you up this time?"

"Sorry, it's resident auntie in this case," Les said lightly as she returned the pressure of his hands. "And I wasn't aware we'd established anything."

"We haven't?" he asked huskily, and as his hands released hers to slide up her bare arms to her shoulders, Les closed her eyes in readiness.

His mouth was warm and only slightly insistent against her lips; his obvious control was almost disappointing.

"Okay, so you got an A in kissing," Les murmured when at last she could breathe easily enough to speak.

His ebony eyes flashed hidden messages as he gazed down at her. For a second, Les anticipated more of his delicious mouth. Instead, he squeezed her shoulders and then released her.

"Thanks for a lovely picnic, Angel Eyes," he murmured. "Dinner's on me tomorrow night."

Curfew or no curfew, it was nearly midnight when Les, exhausted and wired at the same time, finished mentally listing and examining all the reasons why she should not see Blaise again. Unfortunately, none seemed strong enough to quiet the excitement flowing like liquid heat in her veins. Not even the fact that he was transient. She was a big girl now. She'd enjoy him and then she'd forget him. It happened to other people all the time.

THREE

After watching nine holes of golf with the temperature hovering at a brain-baking ninety-eight degrees, Blaise had had all he could take. Turning, he surveyed the crowd. Celia was easily spotted in her red Panama-style hat and oversized dark glasses. Blaise wormed his way to his sister's side.

"Look, I'm heading out of here," he said. He shoved his own dark glasses up into his thick hair and then wiped the perspiration from his high cheekbones. "We can meet for a quick drink at the inn around five if you like."

"Meet, my buns," Celia exclaimed. "I'm coming with you. Golf, I love. Sunstrokes, I don't. Where's Dennis?"

Blaise smiled and nodded in the general direction of the posh clubhouse.

"Another one?" Celia said with a laugh as she fell into step beside her long-legged brother. "I swear, that man's got the stamina of a bull. Which one this time?"

"I think he's with the blonde in the green shorts," Blaise replied. "Feel like a drive or would you rather grab a drink first?"

"The nearest convenience store for a quart of ice-cold

44

cola will do just fine," Celia assured him. "Where to, this time?"

"That place Dennis was telling me about. He got some directions from one of the locals last night so we shouldn't have any trouble finding it."

"You do have gas this time, don't you?" Celia teased.

"Ha, ha. Very unfunny, kid."

Later, Blaise pulled the jeep into the parking lot of a convenience store, secured cups of cola for the two of them, and then headed down Route 5, excitement leaping in his chest. When his friend and contracting superintendent Dennis Farlow had first mentioned the esteemed golf tournament in Williamsburg, Blaise had been on the verge of declining. When Dennis had mentioned combining the pleasure trip with a little scouting expedition, his interest had perked up. And when he'd read the sales figures for the condominiums recently built by a competitor on the grounds of one of the area's smaller plantations, he'd started packing his suitcase. If Wyler Industries could make a fortune in historic Williamsburg, why couldn't Hollander & Associates? True, high-rise office buildings were their specialty, but he hadn't gotten rich adhering to form. Now, if that parcel of land Dennis had mentioned proved to be as enticing as it sounded and Blaise could come to reasonable terms with the owners, Hollander & Associates would be on the road to realizing yet another astonishing success with their innovative ideas, flawless construction, and ingenious sales tactics . . . Celia and her crew deserved thanks for the latter.

Mountains of white clouds hung in silent suspension in the afternoon sky as Blaise and Celia reached the bridge at the Chickahominy River. Below the span, a gentle breeze wrinkled the flat gray waters and irate seagulls screamed in protest as the jeep's progression across the bridge disturbed their roosting on the guardrails.

"So, how was your date last night?" Celia asked.

"Okay," Blaise replied.

Picking up on his reticent mood, Celia lapsed into silence, seemingly content to watch the passing scenery, which consisted of trees, trees, and still more trees.

"It's like another world here, isn't it?" she said abruptly.

"Humn? Oh—yeah, it's quiet all right," Blaise agreed. "The perfect setting for spacious, ultra modern condos nestled beneath the trees, facing out onto the river, bay windows catching the evening breeze, wide decks to bring life out into the open air. Et cetera. Et cetera."

"Well spoken, just like one of my brochures," Celia said. "Where are we going for dinner tonight?"

"Waller Mill—" He glanced at her and grinned sheepishly. "Sorry, kid. You're on your own tonight. Unless you can corner Dennis."

"Again?" Celia exclaimed, turning in the seat to gaze at him in wonderment. "This must be one hot cookie you've hooked up with, brother. And if I'd have known the two of you were coming down here to do a charm number on the local female populus, I'd have brought Keiffer along."

"Batting zero in the lounge?" Blaise teased. He was well aware of his beautiful sister's popularity with men and the ease with which she could remedy a solitary status if the notion struck, even if that notion was for a fair amount of conversation. For the past year, Celia had been devoted to a Yale graduate, bespectacled Keiffer Woodson, for reasons Blaise had yet to determine. They were about as mismatched as salt and sugar. But when Keiffer had joined Hollander's legal department, Blaise had corrected his summation to incorporate the fact that both salt and sugar were equally essential in the scheme of things.

"Are you kidding? The tourists are here en masse and the locals don't seem to care for those born above the Mason-Dixon line. I'm afraid my accent throws the fear of God into them."

At this, her dark eyes twinkled with merriment and then she sighed with contentment.

"But then, I don't mind living on the periphery of my brother's love life. It certainly hasn't happened in a long time."

"No love life, Celia," Blaise assured her. "She's simply a nice woman."

"And you're simply attracted and I'm simply overjoyed and even more simply speaking, where in tarnation are we going? Richmond?"

"We should be getting close according to Dennis' directions."

And even as he spoke, the sign, affixed by what appeared to be broken plow chains to a cedar frame, loomed several yards ahead. Below the sign, a neatly tended cluster of shasta daisies swayed in the breeze. Slowing his speed, Blaise pulled into the graveled driveway and braked to a halt.

"River's Edge," Celia read aloud. "Interesting name anyway. Who owns this place?"

"I haven't the foggiest idea," Blaise replied as he started along the curving driveway, his eyes intent on the rooftops he could see in the distance. Excitement began leaping in his chest as towering chestnut trees, a thick stand of pecan trees, and oak trees that had to be close to two hundred years old proclaimed the authenticity of this plantation's ties to an era in history never to be forgotten. Stately names flashed to mind . . . George Washington, Thomas Jefferson, Captain John Smith, Pocahontas, Jamestown—and now, River's Edge.

Blaise's decision was made even before he braked to a halt in the circular driveway fronting the H-shaped structure standing proud and somewhat tired beneath the thick curling limbs of several huge oaks.

This was the place. This was what he wanted. This was what he had to have, regardless of who he had to cajole, bargain with, argue with, or even fight to lay claim to this magnificent relic from days gone by.

Neglect abounded, both in the main house and in the outlying buildings, although the grounds surrounding the house indicated at least a love of gardening. In the distance, he could see a well-tended pasture in which three black horses grazed in the dazzling afternoon sunshine.

"This is gorgeous, Blaise," Celia murmured, awe in her voice as they crawled out of the jeep and stood for a moment, absorbing the mysterious serenity that encompassed them.

In answer to his heavy knock on the front door, hinges creaked and a tiny face appeared in the slight crack when the door was partially opened.

"Hello," Blaise greeted. Instantly, he noted a flicker of alarm in the small, surprisingly alert eyes of the short, plump, elderly lady who stared at him in unabashed curiosity. "Sorry to disturb, but I'm looking for the owner. Would that be you?"

"No," the woman told him in a high-pitched voice, at the same time shaking her head slowly from side to side. "She's at work."

"You see my partner and I are looking for some land to buy in this area and this place might work out fine if the price is right and they're willing to sell. Would you mind if we have a look around?"

Again, the eyes showed a flicker of alarm, this time coupled with a slight pursing of the lightly rouged lips.

"Maybe you'd better not" was the reply.

"Do you know how many acres you have here?" Blaise asked, striving for his most patient tone of voice, even as he fought against the urge to be more persistent. Never had he known such an overwhelming desire to finalize a deal on the spot. It was as though he feared all that surrounded him was a figment of his imagination, brought on by his intense longing to acquire that ground on which he now stood.

"No, but we have a lot of land."

Blaise smiled and raked his hand over the back of his head, his eyes momentarily downcast.

"All the way to the river?"

"Yes. And down to the crossroad. That way."

Again, he smiled and glanced at Celia.

"Maybe we'd better come another time," Celia suggested.

Blaise had to agree, although the delay was not to his liking.

"Well, would you do me a favor and tell the owner I dropped by? Look, can you give her this card for me? Tell her I'd like to talk to her whenever it's convenient."

Blaise removed his business card from his wallet and stuck it through the narrow opening the woman had allowed in the door.

"Okay," she murmured with a brisk nod. "Bye." Immediately, the door snapped shut.

"Good-bye," Blaise and Celia called out in unison.

And back in the jeep, Blaise sighed in agitation.

"Patience, brother," Celia urged as she reached over and gave his thigh a pat. "Besides, you didn't bring your checkbook."

"You want to bet?" Blaise growled. He took one last look around, experienced a strong swell of elation, and then started the engine.

On a good-day rating scale of one to ten, this has been a minus three, Les decided as she ground to a halt and leaped from the van. The road calls had been more than her limited crew could handle; she'd pitched in and made her fair share; the heat had been unmerciful; her anticipation for the evening ahead tended to stretch each hour into an eternity of waiting.

As she bounded in the front door of River's Edge, Aunt Josie rushed toward her, her plump face flushed with excitement.

"Some people came," she exclaimed in her breathy voice. "A tall man and a pretty woman. They wanted to look around."

"That's nice, Aunt Josie," Les said as she patted her aunt's arm in passing. "Where's Mother?"

"She's taking a bath. I didn't let them look around though, because you said I should not encourage strangers. But the man gave me a card and he said for you to call him when you were convenient."

"You mean, at my convenience," Les corrected. Love for her slightly backward maiden aunt deemed it essential she pause for a quick hug.

"Yeah, that's what I mean," Aunt Josie replied. "I'll go get the card."

"No, never mind. I'll see it later," Les said. "Right now, suppose you and I have a nice cold glass of tea and you can tell me about your day. Then I have to shower and dress."

"You have another date?" Aunt Josie sat primly at the wide kitchen table and watched as Les prepared two glasses.

"I sure do," Les exclaimed, excitement dancing in her eyes. "And he's something else, Aunt Josie. Very handsome and enough charm for ten just like him."

"That man who came today was very handsome and I bet he had charm, too."

"My goodness, Leslie," Sherry exclaimed from the doorway as she knotted the belt of her terry robe around her trim waistline. "Am I actually hearing you laud the attributes of one of the male species? Why, I was beginning to believe you'd lost your vision in that department."

Les reached to take a third glass from the cabinet. "Could be I'm suffering from heat exhaustion."

"Some people came to see Leslie today," Aunt Josie said. "I think they want to buy River's Edge."

Sherry glanced at Les, only to find her daughter standing at the sink, her eyes riveted on the scenery visible through the double windows.

"Did you hear that, Leslie? Maybe this is your chance to get out from under this place."

"I've had ample opportunities to get out from under this place if that was what I wanted," Les replied, turning from the window. "If that's the reason for those people coming here today, then it's just as well I wasn't here. At the risk of sounding repetitive, family dear, I'm not selling my home. Aunt Josie, you can throw the card away, and if they come again, you tell them I said to hunt elsewhere. River's Edge is not for sale to anyone, at any time, at any price."

Sherry sighed with annoyance. "I would think a person in your financial situation would welcome the relief of a sale."

"Mother, you're starting to sound like a worn record."

"Perhaps you might consider letting Bernie and Willa go, thus negating that monetary outlay."

"Fire them, you mean," Les said in a voice more curt than she intended. "No, Mother. Bernie's been the caretaker here since Grandfather was alive. And what do I pay them anyway? A mere pittance. Besides, I need Bernie if for no other reason than to give me advice and Willa keeps an eye on Aunt Josie when we're gone."

"Aunt Josie doesn't need a baby-sitter and my advice is free," Sherry replied. "Sell this place and if you're bound and determined to be a homeowner, buy yourself a little five-room house somewhere. Something you can afford. You're spitting into the wind trying to hang on to River's Edge, Leslie, and for what reason? An overabundance of ridiculous pride in heritage. You're worse than your grandfather."

"Probably so," Les said lightly as she rose from her chair and took her glass to the sink. Taking her time to empty out the ice cubes and rinse the glass, she willed away the annoyance always conceived by her mother's heartless disregard for the Braddock estate.

"Anyway, you two will have to excuse me," she said lightly as she turned back to face them. "In the midst of all this financial upheaval. I have a more pressing problem. What does a lady wear when she doesn't even know where she's going?"

An hour later, Les faced her reflection in the full-length mirror she'd hung on the back of her closet door. Apropos, she decided as she adjusted the thin gold belt encircling her narrow waist. She then turned to make certain the hem of the circular black silk skirt hung evenly. The shirtwaist dress with its seductive whisper when she moved could, according to the sales clerk who'd eagerly stuffed her dollars into the cash register, go easily from the office to evening cocktails with the appropriate accessories.

Well, Les wasn't at all certain what accessories would be appropriate since she had no earthly idea what the evening held in store. So she'd settled for the gold belt and a simple pair of gold loops in her ears. Her soft blond hair had been swept up and secured in a careless topknot. All in all, she decided less would have to be better.

Her heart was thundering in her ears as she drove into the parking lot of Waller Mill Park. After pulling into a parking space and shutting off the engine, she looked around for the maroon jeep. Then she glanced at her watch. No, she was not early. It was precisely seven o'clock and unless he'd folded the jeep into a compact wad and then stuffed it into his back pocket, Blaise Hollander had not arrived.

Les settled back to wait, fervently hoping she had enough gas to enable her to occasionally run the engine and the air-conditioning. She'd readily discovered on the drive over that the sales clerk had neglected to mention that black silk and summer evenings in Williamsburg did not easily jell.

At seven-thirty, with still no sign of the maroon jeep,

Les considered some rational excuses. Perhaps the tournament had run overtime.

Nope. No good. He could have left at any time he chose.

Perhaps he'd lain down for a nap and had fallen asleep.

Nope. No good either. Inns have wakeup calls for those with appointments to meet and the desire to be on time. There were also such objects as travel alarm clocks.

And then the most logical excuse of all. Perhaps he'd simply forgotten.

No, that was not logical at all, Les told herself with growing concern. It was absolutely inconceivable. Unless, of course, she'd been drawn into his magnetic web only to discover the man was not as interested as he had seemed to be. If that was the case, Les had been stood up.

The thought made her queasy in the pit of her stomach. Not that it hadn't happened to her in the past. Taylor had made the habit almost an inherent part of his character. And Les had forgiven. But that was the past and that was an ex-husband and that was a Les who had long since grown up and learned to appreciate good manners and a healthy amount of consideration.

At ten after eight, Les started her engine and drove slowly from the park. A portion of her heart was on the verge of freezing into a solid block. But what could she say? He was a stranger she'd met only yesterday. Though their insane attraction for each other had felt so right, obviously she should have followed her initial instincts.

See where susceptibility gets you, Leslie, that strident voice nagged.

Okay, I see, but at least my pride won't suffer. How was he to know I hadn't stood him up?

With that thought in mind, Les's spirits rose somewhat. If she should ever be fortunate enough to have an opportunity to speak with Mr. Blaise Hollander, she'd lie through her teeth and tell him she'd had a change of heart about seeing him again.

But just as she was about to make her right hand turn out onto Route 60, a maroon jeep with a very harried, very sweaty, very distraught driver roared up to her side and slammed on the brakes. Thick black locks of hair clung to his forehead and the neck of his white polo shirt was damp with perspiration. A five o'clock shadow of beard defined his jawline and upper lip. And he was, undoubtedly, the most delectable piece of humanity she'd seen in her entire life.

Les's heart leaped into her throat, the ice immediately thawing beneath a flood of warmth as those beguiling eyes locked with her own.

"You were leaving," he said gruffly, resting one arm along the window ledge as he regarded all he could see of her.

"It certainly looked that way," Les replied with a tight smile.

"I'm here now."

"An hour and fifteen minutes late."

"Don't you want an explanation?"

"I won't beg," she replied. She pursed her lips in a fashion reminiscent of her dear aunt. "But if you have one handy, I'd listen for the sake of curiosity."

At this, Blaise grinned sheepishly. "I overslept. Okay?"

Les waited.

"That's it," Blaise said. "I was tired, I lay down, I overslept. Now if you'll back up so I can turn around and then follow me to the inn so I can get cleaned up, we can get on with our plans. Damn, Leslie, you look sensational in black. And I like your hair up like that."

"Have you run the gamut yet?" Les asked with a teasing smile curving her mouth. "Of compliments, I mean?"

"No, but I can apply the brakes any time if it's in my best interest," he replied. His smile was heartbreaking even if he did look grubby.

"Could be," she murmured. "No, Mr. Hollander, I won't follow you to the inn. But I will wait for you at the Coppertop Lounge just up the road. I didn't get dressed up to sit on the grass in the park. And you'd better make it quick because my patience is running dangerously thin.''

"You haven't eaten, have you?"

"They don't have room service in the park, remember?" Les replied. She shifted into reverse, backed up enough to get into the lefthand turning lane, and then, with a wave in the rearview mirror, headed for the lounge, blood thundering in her ears at a tempo which was almost deafening.

It had taken him little more than a half hour to complete the transformation from grubbiness to sensuous elegance. Every female head in the room had turned when he'd entered the lounge. His pale gray slacks, soft blue silk shirt, and navy blazer blended well with his expression of casual indifference to the attention he was receiving.

Les's heart had literally stopped for half a second as she contemplated her handsome date for the evening. And then, she'd experienced a rush of confidence when his eyes mirrored appreciation for the effort she'd put forth in her own appearance.

"Are you too mad to drink a gin and tonic?" Blaise asked when he'd managed to signal a passing waiter.

"I'm sure you've heard the old adage—dogs get mad, people get even," she teased.

"Yeah, many times," Blaise said with a chuckle. "But you I honestly believe."

"Good. I appreciate a man with intelligence."

"Honestly, that's what happened," Blaise told her as he leaned back in his chair and crossed one leg over the other in a posture of total relaxation. "Celia and I were out in that sun all day. We had a flat tire on the jeep forty miles from nowhere, which, by the way, I managed to change myself. So by the time I got back to the inn, I was zapped. I laid down for a quick nap and next thing I knew it was seven-thirty."

He reached over and took her hand in his.

"Thanks for waiting, but if you hadn't, I'd have rung the phone off the hook until I found you." Les was all but dissolving beneath the compelling look he was giving her.

The drinks were served and the bartender had turned on the artificial logs so that in the fireplace on the opposite side of the room, gentle flames added to the room's ambience. As if in this man's presence, ambience was a necessity. A respirator was more like it.

"That jeep isn't one of your better friends, is it?" Les commented. She took a sip of her drink, noting that the liquid sloshed slightly in the glass as a result of her shaky hand. Hoping that Blaise did not notice was in vain; his dark eyes glimmered with amusement as they slid from her face to her hands and then back again.

"Should I have ordered a double?"

"Only if you'd get a perverse thrill out of carrying me out of here," Les replied.

"Perverse or otherwise, I'll order a triple if that's my reward."

The look he was giving her could have melted stone. Heat rose in her cheeks. Goose bumps skittered along her backbone. Frantically, she dug into her repertoire of small talk . . . and came up empty-handed. The fire burning just below the surface of those incredible dark eyes was just too hot.

"Let's get out of here," he mumbled, his voice husky. He dropped some bills onto the tiny tabletop, and reaching for her hand, he moved to his feet.

The moment they'd cleared the doorway and were out in the balmy night air, Blaise's arms were around her. He drew her in line with his taut frame and yet carefully maintained enough air space so as not to elicit her withdrawal. His lips were warm, almost frantic as they covered hers. Instantly, the embers of need that had remained smoldering since the night before burst into flame. Warning bells clanged in her head. Les ignored them. It was far nicer to savor the divine pressure of his knowledgeable mouth as it tested and teased and captured. Her senses were reeling.

"I've been waiting all day to do that," he murmured. His lips trailed down to the warm, silky flesh along her jaw. Gently, he bit and then tenderly kissed where he'd bitten. "Celia thinks I've lost my marbles. I think you've bewitched me, Angel Eyes."

"And I think we're necking in a public parking lot," Les whispered.

She hated to leave the perfection of his arms. But if propriety was to be maintained, that was exactly what she had to do.

"And it's the most dissatisfying thing I've done all day," Blaise murmured in a sultry voice.

His mouth molded again to her own. Temporary insanity swept her mind clean of everything but his nearness. Against her splayed hands, his heart thudded double-time. His breath was hot on her skin, his fingers clutched her back, and against her stomach, she felt the warm pressure of his need.

"Blaise, this is happening too darned fast," Les gasped, and her glazed eyes fastened on his own flushed expression. "I feel like I'm on the highest peak of a roller coaster, getting ready to plummet straight over the edge. And not only am I afraid of heights, but I detest that falling sensation, especially when I have no idea how far it is to the bottom."

"You don't strike me as either a coward or a negative person," Blaise said softly as he wiped the moisture from her lower lip with the tip of his forefinger.

"Nor am I impulsive in situations like this," Les replied firmly. "I think it's time to slow the pace just a little."

Blaise's eyes were intent on her face as he thought of the limited amount of time he was scheduled to remain in Williamsburg.

"Leslie, I hate to sound like a man on the make, but I have to remind you time isn't something I have a lot of right now. And I've never been guilty of possessing the tiniest amount of patience."

A car pulling past them silenced his declaration for a moment. The two female passengers made no effort to withhold their verbal appreciation for the tall, broad-shouldered man with his thick hair feathering in the breeze. Blaise frowned handsomely and then tucked his arm around Les's waist.

"I hate analyzing. Come on. Let's go have dinner and be happy we complement each other so magnificently."

His words lightened her heart. But the knot of rationality tightened in her stomach. A whirlwind romance. A four-day whirlwind romance with only three days left. Could she handle this?

Carefully, Les breathed silently. *Very carefully*.

Those illicit fingers gripped her stomach as he settled her into the passenger seat and then closed the door, his eyes black and filled with undisguised want. As he moved around the front of the jeep, Les decided once again he was the most attractive man she'd ever met. When he climbed in and closed the door, she tallied her own inadequacies when it came to keeping him at arm's length. One was hard pressed to do what one had no inclination to do.

He glanced around at the dusty confines of the jeep.

"We could drive your car," he said. "This jeep isn't exactly a golden chariot."

"Please, Blaise," Les exclaimed as she peered over at him. "Don't tell me you're worrying about image. You don't seem the type and it's for sure I'm not."

She settled more comfortably in the seat. "Besides, I'm almost out of gas. Come on. It's been hours since I had that peanut butter sandwich for lunch."

And obviously it's going to be a while longer, Les thought with a sinking sensation in the pit of her stomach as Blaise turned the ignition switch. A dull, almost taunting click rewarded his actions. Muttering something that sounded like an Italian oath, Blaise tried once again to start the engine.

"I honestly don't believe this," he protested as he tossed a fiery glare in her direction.

"Well, they say three strikes and you're out," Les said with a sigh. "Dead battery, do you think?"

"How should I know? I'm no mechanic."

"That's obvious," Les replied, smothering a grin. "Would you like me to try?"

"No," Blaise retorted, availing Les of a portion of what could be a very explosive temper. "And you can forget your profession, Miss Braddock. If I can't get this thing started, I'll worry about it in the morning. I won't have you out there in a black silk dress tinkering with a filthy engine while I sit here looking like an incompetent jerk."

"Chauvinism," Les murmured as she folded her arms across her breasts and watched his futile attempts to start the jeep.

Finally, she reached over and halted his hand. "Look, you're wasting your time, Blaise. Your battery doesn't have enough power to turn the engine over. If you insist on driving this pile of misfortune, then we'll have to jump start it. I have some jumper cables in the trunk of my car."

Blaise sighed heavily and rested his forearms atop the steering wheel.

"I haven't had this much car trouble in thirty years of driving," he muttered. He turned to face her, annoyance etched on his face. "I'm sorry about this, Les."

"Heh, it's people like you who keep people like me in business," Les said lightly as she reached for the door handle. "I'll make a deal with you. I'll stand back and supervise. You do the labor. That way you won't feel like a jerk."

At six three, he would have had to find a pretty deep hole, but at the moment Blaise knew he'd love to find one and crawl in it. He'd waited all day for a delicious evening with the most enchanting woman he'd met in his entire life and he'd had first a flat tire and now a dead battery.

Slowly, Blaise crawled from the jeep, his jaw taut, and with an exaggerated jerk, he raised the hood.

Les brought her car around and parked it nose to nose. It was with difficulty that she managed to keep a straight face as she handed him the jumper cables.

"Just be sure you connect positive to—"

"I know how to jump start a car, Leslie," he snarled, and taking care to keep his jacket from brushing the dusty jeep, he connected the cables.

Les climbed into the jeep, and in moments, the engine was grumbling noisily.

Though Les found the incident far from catastrophic and even amusing, she'd been around enough men in her life to recognize a healthy case of injured male pride. Nevertheless, it was vital to be practical even if it further offended.

"We'll drive to a service station and leave your battery for a short charge," she said after the cables had been stowed and her car reparked. "That way, you can be sure of getting home tonight."

Blaise took his time cleaning the grime off his hands with a handkerchief he'd removed from his back pocket. His brow was furrowed; his disposition almost surly.

When he'd cleaned his hands as much as was possible, he folded the handkerchief and then, reaching inside, he tucked it on the dashboard of the jeep. Turning, he contemplated her bland expression.

"Okay, go ahead and say it," he demanded gruffly.

"Okay, I will," Les replied. "It's almost nine o'clock. Suppose we forget dinner."

"You said you were hungry."

"So, I changed my mind. Besides—"

"Why don't you say what's really on your mind," he challenged.

"Blaise, do you really need me to tell you your jeep is in a state of outrageous neglect? You already know that."

Les reached up and tucked a stray strand of hair back into her topknot and fought against another impulse to laugh at the grim expression on his handsome face. Her effort was wasted.

"Oh, come on, Blaise," she exclaimed with a chuckle. "You look like a little boy with the wheel off his wagon."

Companionably, she tucked her arm beneath his and urged him away from the jeep's door so that she might reopen it. "There's a station a few blocks from here. Follow me and we'll leave your battery for a charge. Besides, as I said, I need gas anyway."

"I love authority figures," Blaise growled as he crawled beneath the steering wheel and moved his arm aside so that she could close the door.

"Really?" Les teased. "That's odd. I could have sworn your old-fashioned interpretation of my help was making you rather angry, Mr. Hollander."

With that, she flounced away.

A reluctant smile curved his lips and his heartstrings tugged slightly as Blaise watched the soft night wind swirl her skirt around her knees and pull playfully at her tousled topknot. And when he was afforded a glimpse of her thigh as she slid into her car, quite a different feeling swept over him.

"Chauvinistic, huh," he murmured as he shifted into gear in preparation for following the red glow of her taillights. "Miss Braddock, I don't think chauvinism frightens you the least bit."

When the jeep had been turned over to an attendant at the service station, Blaise reached for her car keys.

"Come on. The aroma from that seafood place over there is driving me nuts. Let's go eat."

At Captain George's buffet tables, they piled plates high with a variety of both fried and broiled seafood, concocted a simple salad, and then retired to a table. Blaise ordered wine and then they lapsed into compatible silence as they tackled the mountain of food on their plates.

"I thought you weren't hungry," Blaise teased as he used the corner of his napkin to wipe a dribble of drawn butter from her chin.

"So did I," Les exclaimed. "But crab legs have a way of turning me into a glutton. How's your shrimp?"

"Wonderful. Have one."

At the dessert bar, Blaise took a sampling from several of the offerings and scoffed when Les spooned only a small portion of chocolate mousse onto her plate.

"It's a wonder you aren't big as a house," she told him when, back at the table, she watched him consume the last bite of the rich desserts and then plop back with a sated groan.

"Right now, I feel like I just ate a house," he assured her as he rubbed his taut waistline. "More wine?"

"No, but I'd love a brandy," Les said. "How was the tournament today?"

"I enjoyed what I saw of it," Blaise replied as he turned and motioned for a waitress. "Around noon, my sister and I left to look at some property—"

His voice trailed off.

"You look surprised," he said.

"I am," Les replied. "I wasn't aware you were thinking of moving to Williamsburg."

"I'm not. But this area is prime for investment property. Out on Route Five, we've seen numerous tracts that would be perfect for—"

His words again trailed off as a shadow moved over her features.

"Heh, why the cloud of gloom?" he asked as he reached out and tenderly traced the curve of her lower lip.

It was an effort, but she managed a slight smile.

"No gloom. Just curiosity. Perfect for what?"

"Condos, houses, whatever." He watched her closely.

What had he said to cause that shadow? To bring that gleam to her eyes, a gleam that almost looked like anger?

"And have you decided on any particular place?" Les asked as she idly turned a spoon over and over on the tablecloth, her eyes intent on her mundane task.

"No, not really," Blaise replied. "Les, are you—?"

"May I help you, sir?"

Blaise glanced up at the waitress he'd signaled. He ordered the brandy, asked for their check, and when the woman had left the table, turned back to Les.

"Okay, tell me what's wrong," he commanded softly, and reaching over, he laid his hand over her own to stop the monotonous turning of the spoon.

"Not a thing," Les said lightly and then she flashed him a smug smile. "If the rest of the property owners feel as I do, you'll be wasting an incredible amount of time out on Route Five. That's a historic area and condominiums don't belong."

"Ah so," Blaise exclaimed, nodding his head in understanding. "Me thinks the little lady is chock full of that Southern pride of heritage."

"No, there's still room for a little old-fashioned anger toward big businesses that would try to destroy that heritage with their steel and glass creations. I know that's the nature of your business and I'm sure you're quite good at what you do. But there's plenty of room north of Williamsburg for your condominiums."

"I take it you live out Route Five?" Blaise said.

"All my life with the exception of a few years in college and to try my hand at marriage."

"Look, you don't need to get yourself in a dither. If destruction was my business, which it isn't, you can bet I've better sense than to attempt to destroy anything belonging to a woman with a scowl on her face like you have on yours right now. You do take things seriously, don't you?"

"Just about everything," Les replied, and when the

brandy was served, she gulped hers down and reached for her purse. "I'm ready if you are."

In silence, Blaise paid the check and they left the restaurant. At the service station where they'd left the jeep, Blaise shut off the engine and turned in the seat.

"Okay, why don't you tell me what's wrong?" he demanded quietly.

Les opened her mouth to speak. Then she shut it again. She simply didn't have the courage to ask about properties around the area in which he was interested. Was River's Edge one of those properties? Did he know she owned it? Was that the reason for his interest in her? It had happened before, hadn't it?

She thought of the man who'd left a card with Aunt Josie. *Coincidence*? she wondered.

"Are you going to answer me?"

"I was just thinking how your idea of tearing down historic landmarks to build condos could be compared to Sherman's burning Atlanta. Downright heartless desecration. Now can we drop the subject? And it's getting late."

"Okay," he said with a sigh of resignation. "Will you see me tomorrow night?"

"I can't," Les replied. She struggled hard to shove aside the troublesome thoughts . . . to keep reminding herself she really had no reason to distrust Blaise. Plenty of businessmen carried cards. "I keep Friday nights open for my Aunt Josie. We have a standing date for pizzas."

"Is your Aunt Josie opposed to party crashers?"

"You want to come along?" Les asked in surprise.

"Sure," Blaise exclaimed. "I'd love to meet the rest of your family."

Les considered extending the invitation and then she considered the manner in which Aunt Josie was ill at ease with strangers. Friday night was her highlight of the week. Perhaps it would be better if Aunt Josie was forewarned of a third party.

"I think not," Les said. "Another time perhaps."

"Well, suppose you keep your date with Aunt Josie and, when your obligation is fulfilled, meet me in the lounge at the Williamsburg Inn."

A shivering sense of anticipation washed over her as she immediately calculated the short distance from that crowded lounge to the room where he was staying. An inner voice dictated she select a less suggestive meeting place; a much more strident voice dictated she stop re-acting like an adolescent and realize the practicality of his suggestion. After all, why should he hang around some strange locale when she couldn't even tell him for certain what time she'd be arriving?

"Well?"

"Okay," Les said.

It had been his intention to hold her tenderly . . . kiss her gently . . . ensure his forthcoming solitude would not be plagued with intermittent heat waves that would rob him of sleep. But when his arms wrapped around her softness and he drew her against him . . . when he felt the hard press of silk-covered breasts against his chest . . . felt the heat instantly rise in her flesh . . . heard her breath catch, logic fell beneath a lightning bolt of raw hunger.

"Leslie," he groaned, and then he was kissing her in wild abandonment, his fingers digging into her back as he urged her still closer to his awakening body.

Les saw colors explode behind her eyelids, and involun-tarily, she clung to him . . . he wantonly tempted her last bit of restraint until she was quivering with the impatient need for all of him. He filled her mind . . . he filled her thoughts and now she longed for him to fill her body with his urgent maleness . . . love her . . . possess her . . . leave her gasping with delight.

Her fingers threaded into his lush hair and she meshed her womanly curves with his hard angles . . . relishing the heat waves coursing over her from head to foot until, with a groan of frustration, he released her.

Blazing eyes burned down into her face as she gazed up at him, her breathing harsh and erratic.

"I don't know why I don't haul you back to my room and satisfy this itch we both have," Blaise mumbled as he reached out and smoothed the backs of his fingers along her cheek. "Maybe because we need to give this thing some serious consideration. I'm forty-four years old, Leslie, and summer flings with dazzling blondes grew boring a long time ago."

"Well, if it makes you feel any better, I don't do the summer flings routine myself," Les said inanely. "And I'm already considering. Things like time and distance and the emptiness when—"

"Time and distance can be corrected. Emptiness can be eradicated and, Leslie, I'd never hurt you," Blaise said quietly. Then he opened the car door and stood waiting as she slipped across the seat and took her place beneath the steering wheel.

"Is that a last-minute pitch for my consent?" Les asked boldly, peering up at him.

"Nope," he said emphatically. "It's just a simple truth. You drive carefully, Angel Eyes."

Later, as she stood at her dressing table removing the pins that held her hair atop her head, she noticed the business card. Slowly, she traced the delicate black lettering that spelled out his name, involuntarily reliving those torrid moments in his arms and feeling, once more, the ache of frustration.

And when she finally settled into bed, Les realized she didn't even remember taking the card he'd given her from her purse and placing it on the dressing table.

FOUR

"Those people came again today," Aunt Josie announced the moment Les entered the house after another grueling ten-hour day.

"Oh? And did you give them my message?" Les asked absently. She riffled through the accumulation of mail that Aunt Josie had stacked on the foyer table. One return address in particular brought a frown of annoyance. Tidewater Insurance Company. Les tore open the envelope, noted the figure, and then stuffed the bill back inside.

"Yes, but that man just smiled." Aunt Josie fiddled with the buckle on her belt and carefully considered her next words. "I think he really wants to buy our house."

"Well, unless he's dense, he'll get the message soon enough. We aren't selling." Les laid aside the stack of envelopes and turned to her aunt. She fastened a smile of enthusiasm over her tired features. "Are you ready for pizza?"

"Yes," Aunt Josie replied, excitement dancing in her eyes. Les gave her a quick hug.

"Let me wash off the day's grease and then we'll go," Les told her.

As Les attempted to adjust the water pressure in her bathroom, a tired groan emanated from the old pipes.

"Just keep the water flowing a little longer," Les muttered. "I haven't forgotten you need some TLC, too."

New plumbing and a new roof. The magnitude of the figures that bounced through her mind made her stomach ache. How she'd wade through it all, Les had no idea. But it was for sure she couldn't neglect River's Edge forever. She simply had to take some time off for deep thought. She'd come up with something.

Later, dressed in a yellow cotton skirt that skimmed her knees and a matching cotton sweater, Les flicked a brush over her hair and then went downstairs to find her aunt waiting patiently.

As they drove toward Williamsburg, Aunt Josie told her of the bees' nest she'd knocked out of an apple tree in what had once been a thriving orchard along the river bank. And then Les listened to Aunt Josie's rendition of Willa's latest gossip. But it was the description of the couple who had come to visit again that fully captured her attention.

Driving a jeep? Dressed in nice clothes? Good-looking?

"What was his name, Aunt Josie?" Les asked as her eyes narrowed in speculation, a chill settling in her stomach. Coincidence . . . again?

"Something like—oh, I don't remember," Aunt Josie replied. "I put his card on your dresser where I put the other one."

Les's breath caught. So that explained what she'd found the night before. No, she hadn't remembered removing it from her purse because the one Blaise had given her was still in her purse.

The excitement with which she'd begun this evening with Aunt Josie—an evening to culminate with a few hours in Blaise's company—instantly vanished. *So,* Les thought with a mixture of disappointment and anger, *here we are, back to the same old song and dance. It would seem Blaise Hollander's interest in me might be in direct correlation with his interest in River's Edge. Why in the world didn't I listen to my own instincts? I knew this was too good to be true.*

It was with supreme difficulty Les managed to keep her mental disturbance from overshadowing dinner with her aunt. And by the time Les had driven Aunt Josie back to River's Edge, she'd made up her mind. If her supposition about his misplaced interest was correct, then it was best to nip this thing in the bud before they went another step.

In the kitchen, Les picked up the telephone extension and dialed the Williamsburg Inn. When there was no answer in his room, she had Blaise paged in the lounge.

"Hollander" was his gruff greeting.

Involuntary awareness stirred deep in her mid-section, followed by an eradicating coil of anger. Sucking in a deep breath, she forced herself to sound cool and impersonal. One thing was for sure. This time she had managed to learn the true motivation behind a barrage of torrid kisses before she got burned, not after it was too late.

"I won't be meeting you tonight, Blaise," Les said bluntly. She closed her eyes and bit hard on her lower lip. How easy it was to visualize the frown surely creasing his brow. How easy it was to visualize him shoving his free hand deep in his pants' pocket as he studied his shoes while trying to figure out why she'd changed her mind.

What if she was wrong about his interest in her property? But then, there was little possibility of that being the case. Hadn't he been out on two occasions to hound her poor aunt?

"Why not?" he finally asked. The disappointment in his voice almost brought about a change of heart. But Les stood adamant. *Remember his ulterior motives,* she told herself. *Remember the excruciating pain of a broken heart.*

"Blaise, I just think you and I are a waste of time.

Vacation romances are appealing to some people, but not to me.''

Blaise chuckled, cutting off her words.

''I could have sworn we'd already had this conversation,'' he mused, his husky voice arousing chills along her spine. ''Or maybe it's familiar because that's exactly what I've been telling myself for the past two days. Fortunately, one of us doesn't always listen to the voices inside our head. If you won't come here, then I'll come there.''

''No,'' Les argued. ''Blaise, look, I'm tired. I'm going to bed.''

''It's only nine-thirty on a Friday night and I want to see you.''

Tell him the truth, common sense raged. *Corner him. Stop hedging.*

And suppose she came right out and asked the question for which she already knew the answer? Blaise wanted River's Edge. Did he want her, too? Was he looking for a bargain package? Hardly! He was a vacationing Romeo dangerously armed with the best of nature's endowments, and by some cruel twist of fate, she was the target.

Damn you, Blaise. Why couldn't you have been different?

''No,'' Les said. ''I've had a long day and I plan to rest.''

''Fine, hardhead,'' Blaise said, obviously as nonplussed as she was enraged with him. ''Just tell me where you live. I'll be there first thing in the morning. It's time you and I had a little talk, Leslie.''

''About what?'' she demanded. No more stalling. It was time to have the cards out on the table, face up. ''River's Edge? Don't tell me you have a few more subversive methods to try. Well, you can save your—''

''What are you talking about?'' Blaise cut in. What the devil did River's Edge have to do with the annoyance— no, downright anger!—in her normally sultry voice?

Les bit down on her lip again and then winced against

the sharp pain. Why couldn't he have been different? And how in the heck had he learned she owned River's Edge in the first place?

Oh, come on, girl. That would have been easy for Blaise to discover.

Against her will, she thought of his expertise in setting her on fire. She thought of his gentle touch. She thought of the honesty in his eyes.

And she thought of Tony.

Okay, so she'd been fooled once. And she'd taken it literally lying down. This time, she'd stand toe to toe with this greedy opportunist. This time, she'd level both barrels of opposition right between his beautiful dark eyes and blow his determination to possess what was hers all the way to the South Pole.

God, please let me be wrong about him, Les silently prayed.

"Okay, Blaise. Come on out here. I suppose we do have a few things to say to one another."

"I need directions," Blaise repeated. What the heck had he done? She was obviously mad enough to spit oranges.

"Oh, I think you know the way to River's Edge quite well," Les muttered, and without waiting for further comment, she replaced the receiver.

Well, at least he's punctual, Les thought as her hand curled around the doorknob the next morning.

Glancing down, she made a quick assessment of her final choice for an outfit appropriate for ending on an up-note what had seemed to be a promising relationship. A green ribbed tank top emphasized the unbound breasts of a woman confident of her sexuality. A full white cotton eyelet skirt suggested a measure of nonexistent fragility. Her hair floated freely over her shoulders, enticing one to touch . . . if he dared. Barefoot sandals hinted at innocence. A head-to-foot picture of contradiction. Let him guess which was the real Leslie Braddock while she told him to take a flying leap.

He was dressed in faded jeans and a bright red cotton shirt with the cuffs turned back. In the morning sunshine, his hair gleamed blue-black, he smelled of soap and masculinity . . . and the somberness of his expression could not have been more unexpected.

" 'Morning, Leslie," Blaise greeted when she beckoned him into the foyer and then turned to close the door. White lace floated around her knees. Blaise didn't even notice.

"I'm afraid I don't understand," he said.

"Don't you?" Les asked sweetly. "Well, perhaps you'd like to be enlightened over a cup of coffee. I'd offer breakfast but, unfortunately, we've already eaten."

Her monologue carried them along the carpeted hall of the massive structure and into the kitchen at the rear of the house.

"Uh—coffee's fine," Blaise said absently as he gazed around the thoroughly refurbished, totally modern kitchen, quite in contrast to what he'd been able to glimpse of the rest of the house as he'd followed Les's precise steps. Though River's Edge boasted of its fair share of priceless antiques, the beautiful hardwood floors needed resanding, walls cried out for fresh paint, and the handrails on the twin curving stairways leading to the second floor were scarred and dented.

Perfect, he thought with excitement growing in his chest.

Les noted his surreptitious interest in his surroundings as he pulled a chair out from the long, well-worn kitchen table and sat down. She swallowed back the sudden rush of annoyance as she envisioned the renovations running through his mind should he have the good fortune to con her out of this property.

"We remodeled this area some years back," she explained as she brought a tray from the counter on which she'd already arranged the silver coffee service. "That's when the money ran out. But it's home, and if your morning shower isn't all you'd like it to be because of outdated plumbing, you simply consider the alternative . . . bathing in the river."

She leveled her blue eyes in his direction for just a moment. "And it's not for sale."

Her hands were steady as she filled his cup, placed it in the saucer, and then passed it to him. The hands receiving were not so steady and some of the steaming liquid sloshed into the saucer as he placed it on the table before him. Les was almost giddy with elation. So Mr. Cool wasn't so cool after all.

Ideas were running rampant in Blaise's mind.

"So you own River's Edge," he said simply, staring at her in disbelief.

On the tip of her tongue was the proud proclamation of affirmation. But then, she remembered the little matter of a lien with payments outstanding.

"Myself and the bank," Les replied. "The title was free and clear but I understand my father had to borrow some money."

Her voice faltered and Blaise's eyes narrowed in speculation as he watched a variety of expressions play over her features. She'd said the money had run out. Leslie and River's Edge were in dire straits? Just how dire?

Blaise knew he should not ask such a personal question, but the answer was written all over her lovely face.

"But I'll be able to pay it off in another five years. I hope," Les said brightly.

But Blaise was not listening to her financial planning. On one hand, he was a man totally infatuated with the beautiful creature standing before him. On another, far more practical hand, he was a businessman. He wanted River's Edge. River's Edge was in trouble. River's Edge could, no doubt, be had for a song and dance, no matter her declarations to the contrary. He simply had to go to the bank and purchase her loan.

Blaise grimaced as he considered the monstrosity of his speculation. It was a feat that had been accomplished several times in the course of his business dealings, but no, he couldn't do that to Leslie. Should she default on her loan, he would have no better choice than the bank. He'd have to foreclose.

"You own this beautiful estate with unlimited potential and you run a garage?" he demanded, angry with himself for this turn of events and his mercenary considerations for personal gain.

"I wondered if my occupation was a thorn in your side," Les said with a tight smile.

"No, it's no thorn but I am curious."

"I told you. The Braddocks are broke but not broke enough to sell their heritage for a few kisses in the moonlight."

Her blue eyes were again intent on his face, her expression unrevealing. Blaise sat in silence, digesting what he'd learned in the past five minutes. Suddenly, he raised dark eyes to meet her gaze as the meaning behind her words sank in.

"And just what's that supposed to mean?" he demanded quietly.

"I think you know very well what it means," Les retorted. "But it won't work for you any better than it worked for your predecessor."

For a long moment, he stared at her, anger roiling in his middle. Boy, for a woman, she had a left hook that went straight for the gut.

"I think I'm getting the picture," he said curtly. "And you're dead wrong, Leslie. I had no idea—"

"You could have asked about the ownership the first time you came by, Blaise. My Aunt Josie is a little slow, but she's perfectly capable of answering a direct question."

At this, Blaise felt heat in his cheeks. Yes, Les assumed

correctly. He had wondered about Aunt Josie's senility when she'd shoved her reticence between them like a guard dog.

"I'm sorry if I've offended you where your aunt's concerned," he said inanely. He plopped back in his chair, his eyes flitting around the spacious kitchen before coming back to light on her stony expression. "I guess I've muffed it, huh?"

"That would depend on what it is you were trying not to muff," Les replied. "If wining and dining for the purpose of cajoling me out of River's Edge was your modus operandi, you're in line for the Muff of the Year award. Otherwise, what we have here is a lack of communication and one fact carved in stone. River's Edge is not for sale."

A frown again creased his brow, and reaching for his coffee cup, he pulled it nearer. Les noticed his hand no longer trembled.

"And if the bank forecloses?" he asked quietly.

"Why do you assume that's in the cards?" Les demanded.

"Two and two is four in anyone's book, Leslie," Blaise replied as he raised his eyes to meet hers. "You said you were broke."

At this, Les made no comment.

"I could help you, you know," Blaise said quietly.

"Oh, I just bet you can," Les retorted. "By taking this white elephant off my hands." She bounded to her feet and carried her cup and saucer to the sink. "Put your checkbook away, Blaise. The answer's still no."

"I could loan you—"

"Absolutely not," Les broke in, color flaring in her cheeks.

"Excuse me. Leslie?"

Les turned as Sherry poked her head into the kitchen, her eyes intent on first Les's face and then Blaise's dark scowl.

"My mother, Sherry Weston," Les said flatly. "This is Blaise Hollander. What do you want, Mother?"

"I forgot to tell you the bank called earlier," Sherry explained. "Said there's a little problem with your loan request. Apparently, the board seems to think—"

"Mother!" Les exclaimed. Grabbing her mother's arm, she urged her out into the hall. "Do you have to air the laundry in front of a stranger?"

"Well, I thought you ought to know," Sherry defended. "Anyway, Ben wants you to come to his office around ten this morning."

"Oh, I just bet he does," Les muttered. She shoved her hands deep into her skirt pockets and considered the wallpaper while struggling not to notice that Blaise had followed her and was now watching her closely. Sherry discreetly left them alone.

"Seems as though everyone has solutions for my problems these days but me," Les stated flatly. "I just wonder if Ben's tactics are as subtle as yours, Blaise."

"Ben is your banker?"

"Well, he sure isn't the gardener."

"Would you like me to come along?" he offered. "I might be of some help since—"

"Since your interest parallels his?" Les demanded. "No. I have nothing to discuss with Ben Trainham."

"I think you should go," Blaise insisted. He stood watching her for a long moment. "Just how bad is it, Leslie?"

"My money problems?" she asked, turning cool eyes to meet his. "You've heard about having your back against the wall? That's me. I applied for refinancing to cover the back payments on the loan. Ben assured me the board would have no problem with it. Apparently, he doesn't know his buns from his hairline."

"Then go listen to what he has to say," Blaise said. "He's holding the ball, Leslie. Not you."

Les narrowed her eyes. Her chin jutted forward. "You'd have no way of knowing this, of course," she said icily. "But there are three things in life that I can't stand. One is being told what to do."

"I figured that one out for myself, but even you, Miss Braddock, don't know everything there is to know about everything," Blaise replied.

"I don't claim to," Les shot back. "But I've been doing a pretty good job of faking it since I was fourteen."

"Would you like me to come with you?"

"And watch me squirm as he lays out my options?" Les scoffed. "Not in this lifetime, Blaise. You're welcome to wait here if you like. Running down my list of quote, unquote, options shouldn't take more than a few minutes."

"I'll wait. Do you mind if I have a look around River's Edge while you're gone?"

"I don't believe in waving a bone in a starving dog's face," Les told him as she started for the door. "But if that's what you'd like, feel free. I'll introduce you to Aunt Josie and I'm sure she'd be glad to show you around."

Then she turned back to him, her eyes flashing with pride.

"I'm not ashamed of my home, Blaise. It's just that I've had no money for repairs and such and the place is not exactly what I'd call a tourist attraction. But if you can overlook that, I'd love for you to see what I love so dearly."

Just as she opened the front door and was about to leave, Blaise called after her.

"You said there were three things you hated," he drawled. "You gave me one. What're the other two?"

For a moment, Les contemplated the tall, outrageously handsome man lounging against the door frame, hands shoved deep in his pockets. Then she decided she had nothing to lose by honesty. He was leaving anyway.

"Long-distance romances and a blatant opportunist," she replied and hurried out before he could offer a comment.

* * *

Blaise reached up and plucked one of the leaves from the tree and stood rubbing his thumb absently over its smooth surface, his eyes downcast. Aunt Josie had shown him through the house and then she'd gone to take her nap while he roamed the property at will. His trek had brought him to the old apple orchard flanking the river bank.

Now as he stood with the sun burning hot on his back, his heart felt as heavy as though it was cast in stone. Such a beautiful place, filled with the silent trappings and ghosts from days long gone. Would he, in her place, feel the same fierce loyalty to the memories of ancestors? Blaise knew he could not honestly say. His own heritage lacked the excitement; his roots were not bound up in the rich tapestry of early American history.

He glanced up when he heard the sound of a vehicle pulling into the yard. And then his heart leaped as he watched Les climb out of the car and head toward the house. Moments later, she was making her way down across the lawn to the orchard.

With myriad emotions flitting through his mind, not the least of which was compassion, Blaise regarded her as she moved toward him until she was standing only a few yards away. The light summer breeze teased her flowing blond hair, and the sun forced her to squint against its harsh glare as she contemplated the dull gray waters of the river flowing silently toward the ocean. Maturity was in her stance, but clad in a T-shirt and cotton skirt, she was youth and femininity with a subtle arrogance that did a good job of concealing her vulnerability to the casual onlooker.

But Blaise was no casual onlooker. He was involved. His heart had opened and he was in danger of finding her inside. And he wanted desperately to help her with the financial dilemma she now faced. But how, when two of her most desirable characteristics that classic arrogance and her pride, would frustrate any attempt on his part.

"Seen enough?" Les asked as she turned to level her blue eyes on him.

"River's Edge is a beautiful place," Blaise said quietly as he tossed the leaf aside and moved toward her, aching to hold her in his arms, somehow convince her his shoulders were broad enough for her problems, no matter what they were . . . his heart big enough to house her inside. But as he reached out to grasp her hand, she smiled a little and turned away.

"So how did it go at the bank?" he asked, hoping his husky voice did not reveal his disappointment in confronting the wall she'd erected between them.

"The bank isn't going to allow me to refinance," she said flatly.

"Why not?"

"Because I'm not cooperative," Les replied.

"I don't understand, Leslie—"

"You know, it's amazing how a bad case of the hots can cause a man to perform some miraculous things," Les interrupted. "Like convince the board of directors at the bank to allow me the financing I need for, shall we say, a little friendship in return? You know, I never realized my kisses could hold such potential."

"You kissed that Trainham guy?" Blaise demanded, moving to her side and grasping her arm. His eyes were pools of anger as he glared down at her surprised expression.

"Of course I didn't kiss him," Les retorted, jerking her arm free. "But if I had, would I have been any bigger a bastard than the next guy for using sex to get what I want?"

With that, Les turned away, her breath coming in heated gasps that had nothing to do with exertion. She was so angry with Ben Trainham it had taken all her emotional fortitude to refrain from bashing him over the head with one of the crystal wine goblets so conveniently positioned on the corner of his desk, along with a bottle of Chianti.

Immediately, Blaise was behind her. Strong hands closed around her waist, spinning her around.

"I wasn't trying to get anything from you, Leslie," he growled, his dark eyes boring deep into her own. "I saw this place and I wanted it long before I had any idea you owned it. And if I was the bastard you think I am, I'd simply go to the bank and buy your loan. Then I'd sit back and wait for you to default. And I could have done all that without ever putting my hands on you."

Les contemplated the anger on his face, in his eyes, and for a moment, she fluctuated between crawling into his arms and jerking free of him again.

"No, you didn't have to touch me but, unfortunately, you did," she said inanely as her confusion grew in equal proportions to her realization that he was being honest with her. No, he wasn't Ben Trainham. Blaise Hollander would never have to coerce sexual favors from a woman. He had only to ask. And at that exact moment, she wondered what would be her answer should he come right out and ask.

Perhaps she should follow her gut instinct, give full rein to the fires between them, and then send him on his merry way. There was no future for the two of them, so the sooner they parted company, the better for her peace of mind, to say nothing of her heart. And the sooner he was out of her mind, the sooner she could concentrate on the financial dilemma facing her now.

But then, when in her entire life had she ever even considered casual sex? To involve herself in an affair with Blaise could only be for that reason. They were literally strangers drawn together by a simple call of the loins.

With that thought uppermost in her mind, Les regarded him for another long moment, felt that ridiculous tug on her heartstrings, and decided she was most definitely fooling herself. Something far stronger than her loins was screaming out at the top of its lungs for this incredibly magnetic male who stood so tall and arrogant before her, the wind making havoc of his thick hair, the sun on his bronzed face, and a determined set to that powerful jawline.

Hot tears of frustration burned behind her eyelids and she turned her back to him lest he construe them as a plea for compassion.

"Ah, Leslie," Blaise murmured. He wrapped his arms tightly around her narrow waist, pulling her back against him. His chin rested on the top of her silky hair, his dark eyes fixed on the river just yards away. A barge floated silently into view, its dark bulk moving effortlessly through the dull gray water.

Blaise felt as helpless as ever in his life. True, women's tears had always made him uncomfortable. But just the threat of Leslie's tears had an entirely different effect. He ached for her plight and yet, with her stubborn pride standing like an immovable object in his path, what could he do to alleviate her problems when even his better suggestions met with her disapproval? Bide his time maybe?

"If it just wasn't for that note," Les muttered as she recalled the one cloud threatening to obliterate those golden rays of happiness she'd been feeling since he'd come into her life, limited though his stay would be. "It hasn't been easy, but up until now, I've managed to keep this place afloat." She stopped and sighed heavily. "I sound like a walking plea for commiseration, and believe me, that's not the way it is, Blaise."

"I know that, Leslie. Not with your pride. I also know your responsibilities here go far beyond simple bank payments," Blaise said and immediately Les stiffened.

"Is this the scene where you again whip out your checkbook and offer to bail me out with flourish of your pen?" Her voice was hard; apparently, her desire to cry had vanished.

"Are you kidding?" Blaise retorted. "And get it stuffed down my throat? No way. You've made it plain you don't intend to sell. But what about taking on a partner and turning this place into a profitable business?"

"Oh sure," Les scoffed. "I'll open a fruit stand or sell homemade preserves. I ought to make a fortune, huh?"

"Well, I wasn't exactly thinking of a fruit stand—"

"Come on, Blaise, I've already got one business that's more than I can handle."

Les closed her eyes and forced the tension from her body. Her head sagged back into the curve of his neck as she swallowed around the lump of misery.

Against her back, she could feel the beat of his heart. His breathing was slow and regular; the arms that bound her were strong and fraught with the promise of a safety she'd never had before. But what good was that safety? Theirs was a fleeting romance in its broadest terms.

"I like it when you hold me," she said softly.

"I like holding you."

His arms tightened imperceptibly, and against her backside, she felt the slow birth of his arousal. His breathing grew deeper.

"There are plenty of times a person has to seek financial help," he murmured, his breath fanning her earlobe as he forced his mind away from the ache growing in his lower body. She was so good in his arms . . . against him. "I just hope you make the right decisions when you do your seeking."

Les did not answer immediately. She simply closed her eyes in a senseless attempt to quell her body's intense reaction to the intimacy of his nearness.

"Damn, I want you," he whispered as his hands moved to the curve of her waist. His hold tightened and, involuntarily, Les pressed back, loving the feel of his fullness against her. Her eyes closed to savor the heat flaring in her middle. The only partnership she wanted at that exact moment was the union of his body with her own. She wanted him with a hunger that bordered on desperation and to heck with tomorrow.

Blaise swore beneath his breath and then he turned her in his arms. His dark eyes were slumberous as his gaze drifted over her upturned face and settled for a moment on her parted lips.

"You make my blood boil so easily," he muttered. His fingers were strong on her waist. A tiny pulse throbbed in his neck. "And you do it in some of the most inconvenient places."

"Is it unheard of to think about making love in an apple orchard?" Les whispered as she slid her hands up to clasp around his neck.

"Don't tempt me, Leslie," he growled as his heart tripped over in his chest. "We were supposed to be having a serious conversation."

"Then why don't we talk about something else?" Les asked softly. "Or maybe not even talk at all? Maybe we should just kiss."

She tugged lightly, and rising on her tiptoes, Les fastened her mouth over his warm lips, gently molding her mouth to fit his contours.

Blaise groaned deep in his chest. His arms whipped around her, clutching her tightly against his heated condition. His tongue sampled the inside of her mouth, teasing and tempting. His fingers clutched her taut buttocks. Desire was an enraged demon inside him.

Her fingers laced into his hair, nails digging gently.

"Love me, Blaise," she murmured against his lips. "Right here, right now."

"Leslie—" But his words were caught beneath her demanding kiss. Firm breasts pressed tighter to his chest, and when she arched against his throbbing hardness, Blaise stiffened.

"Damn, woman," he growled as he forced her from his arms. His breathing was labored, his eyes deep pools of need as he held her away from him.

"Do you know how much I want to lay you down here in the grass and make love to you?" he demanded.

"Do you know how much I wish you'd do just that?" Les challenged, a mental image forming in her mind, the effects of which were weakening.

"At the moment, maybe," he replied as he jammed his hands deep into his pockets and sucked in a deep breath. "Until you got around to considering how easy it would be for your Aunt Josie to meander to a window and see us. Or, worse still, decide to come in search of us."

His voice trailed off as a guilty smile curved her mouth.

"What's funny?" he demanded.

"We are, Blaise," she replied, tilting her head to one side and studying his serious expression. "Like two kids with a bad case of the hots and no place to go."

His eyes bore deep into her own. "I wouldn't test that theory for accuracy if I were you. My room at the motel is completely private and chain locks from the inside."

"A room you'll be using for one more night," she reminded him . . . reminded herself with a sinking sensation in the pit of her stomach. So little time they had left before he'd be returning to his own life, his own world so far from her own.

Her blue eyes drifted past him to watch a butterfly that had settled on the head of a daisy, its gossamer wings flitting in the warm wind. Yes, and when he was gone, she'd have to face her folly in throwing caution to the wind . . . letting down her guard . . . letting him into her heart.

He could feel the sadness in her thoughts . . . the finality. But then, Leslie had no way of knowing he'd made some decisions about her. Perhaps if he told her about a foolproof plan that had come to mind the moment he'd entered River's Edge, the warmth might return to her blue eyes.

But then if he acted precipitously, she'd more than likely turn on him like an enraged she-cat. Perhaps it was best he keep his mouth shut and wait for a more appropriate moment. Leslie Braddock wasn't the easiest person in the world to sway or to convince. It didn't take brains to recognize these facets of her character.

"Are you ready to calm down?" he asked quietly as he reached out and cupped her cheek in his warm palm.

It was time to start working on that moment.

"Maybe if you relaxed a little, things wouldn't seem quite so bad," he added, a thumb moving over her lower lip.

"That worn-out adage that makes no sense whatsoever," Les murmured, hoping for the world he could not read the feelings she knew were so obvious in her eyes as her body responded to his delicate touch on her mouth.

"Okay, how about my asking you to play tourist with me? Any sense there?" he teased. "Come show me Jamestown."

In the Jamestown Festival Park, Blaise held her hand in his as they strolled beneath sprawling oaks to view the re-created James Fort with its log homes furnished as they had been in the days of the first settlers.

Out on the river, Blaise took his time prowling the full-sized replicas of the three ships that had carried 104 settlers from England in 1607. With the brisk wind making a mess of his thick black hair and plastering his shirt against his strong back, he looked rakish and so handsome that Les leaned against the ship's roping and simply watched him, her heart in her throat.

"Can you imagine going to the Bahamas on one of those?" he said with a chuckle when at last he'd had his fill of the ships and they were once more on land.

"Not today," Les replied. Bending, she scooped a flat white pebble from the sand, and after dusting it off, she pressed it into his hand. "A souvenir from the place where it all began."

Blaise grinned, shoved it into his pocket, and then encircled her waist with one arm, his hand resting just below her breast.

"Shucks," he said in a crude rendition of a Southern drawl. "A fella could get real attached to a gal like you."

"Then suppose we find you another rock," Les teased as she gazed up at him. His dark eyes registered a flicker of surprise and, imperceptibly, his arm tightened.

"Would that a rock was all it would take," he murmured as he considered her earlier suspicions about his true motives.

They strolled through a Powhatan Indian village that represented the native American culture encountered by the English colonists in those days of old. Costumed staff members on the ships, in the fort, and in the Indian village interpreted life in the early seventeenth century, and by the time their tour had ended, Blaise had settled into a subdued silence.

"No wonder you feel such pride in River's Edge," he remarked as they crawled back into the jeep and began the five-mile ride that would take them out onto Jamestown Island.

"It's my home," she said simply. Turning in the seat, she studied him for a moment, suddenly realizing how little she actually knew about Blaise, beyond the fact that he was the most appealing male she'd yet to meet. "Tell me about your home, Blaise."

"What? My overcrowded two-bedroom apartment?" he replied. "Move closer. I can't touch you."

"You have bucket seats, dear," Les replied, and stretching her arm across the gap, she laid her hand on his shoulder. "Okay, Big Man. We're touching now. You live in an apartment?"

"Yep. Surprised?"

"Well, actually, yes," Les admitted. "I had you pictured in one of those ultra modern condos you like to build or in some sprawling glass-walled house crammed full of expensive furniture."

"Hate to disappoint," Blaise replied. "Besides, what

does a single man need with all that? As long as I have a bed to sleep in and a place to shower, I'm happy."

Les had a very clear vision of Blaise in both locations . . . sprawled nude on a rumpled bed, his hair obsidian against the pillows, lashes brushing his cheekbones as he slept . . . beneath a spray of water, his corded muscles glistening and slick with soap. Inadvertently, her fingers curled, and as heat infused her cheeks, she realized she was actually clutching his shoulder. Immediately, she dropped her hand back onto her lap. If Blaise noticed her momentary retreat, he gave no indication as he slowed and braked at the first of the informative markers set up along the narrow road. In his deep, reasonant voice, he read aloud to her as though she had not made this drive countless times in the past.

When they moved on, he chuckled.

"Don't you hate people who do that? As though they assumed you couldn't read it yourself?"

"Either that or they are frustrated tour guides," she added playfully.

Thick forests hugged the road on either side, obliterating the sun. The summer wind murmured in the lofty pines and brought the pungent aroma of the marshes into their surroundings. And through it all, Les pretended a nonexistence of the tension growing like wild fire as recurrent thoughts of the night ahead played havoc with her concentration of the moment.

As they left the park, Les leaned her head back against the headrest and sighed heavily.

"I'd forgotten how tiring it is to be a tourist."

Blaise smiled, and reaching over, he capped his hand over one warm brown knee and squeezed lightly. Goose bumps skittered up her backbone.

"I enjoyed the heck out of it," he said quietly. He'd miss her so badly when he pulled out of Williamsburg in the morning. Why did life have to be so complicated? Why couldn't he have met her in Pittsburgh? Why did she have to be so tied to home and family that she couldn't simply pack her bag and come back with him? The absence of answers made him clench his teeth in silent anger.

As they drove up Route 31, Blaise spotted the little tavern.

"I'm hungry," he said as he whipped into the parking lot of the Williamsburg Shopping Center.

"Polo Club is good," Les replied, still struggling against the heat rising from his personal and yet impersonal touch on her leg.

Inside the informal tavern with its trappings of polo gear and late Saturday afternoon patrons sipping beer and watching a game on the wide-screen television, Blaise leaned back in the hand-hewn, highly polished booth and regarded his companion as they waited for tall glasses of iced tea.

The tension had not left her face; she was finding it difficult to meet his eyes.

"Dammit, Leslie," he muttered as he leaned forward and grabbed for her hand. "I can't stand seeing you worry like this. And you've been doing it for the past two hours."

"Then look the other way," she said quietly as she studied his thick fingers with their blunt nails. A man's hand, she thought. And a man's rationale.

"I'll loan you the money you need."

Les's head shot up and she jerked her hand away from his warm grasp.

"Thank you, Blaise," she replied. "But, my financial problems aren't even on my mind."

"Then what is?" he demanded.

Les toyed with the edge of a cocktail napkin as she considered a generalized answer that would satisfy his curiosity. But was there a general manner in which she could tell him that she was already dreading the moment he'd tell her good-bye? No, there was only the truth. And this pride prevented her telling him . . . pride and a fear of looking like a kid with a schoolgirl crush. He'd said nothing to make her believe his feelings were the same.

"I've enjoyed your company," she finally replied with a tight smile. "I'll miss you when you're gone. Can we leave it at that?"

"Hardly," he muttered, and picking up the menu, he slapped it open on the table before him. "I might remind you, I haven't even packed my bags and you have me on the highway already. A man would be inclined to get the idea you were in a hurry to ditch him."

"I gave it serious consideration," she replied honestly.

"Like you really believe that would work," he murmured, and then her blue eyes were locked with his ebony gaze. Shivers ran up her spine, heat flooded her middle, and nervously she licked her dry lips. As clearly as though it was scrawled on the tabletop, the tension was labeled. Oh yes, he might be leaving, but still ahead was the night. Cause for tension!

"One of the things I admire about you, Leslie, is the fact deep down you're no coward."

After giving her hand a tight squeeze, Blaise slid to the edge of his seat and then rose to his feet. "Order me a crabmeat sandwich, would you? I have to make a phone call."

She hardly remembered eating the sandwich, so loudly was her heart thundering in her ears . . . so strong was the magnetic pull of him . . . so hot was the anticipation flowing in her veins. Did he intend taking her back to his room now? Was she ready to lay down her guard and enjoy his lovemaking? Oh, dear gussie, how quickly they'd arrived at the moment of decision.

On wooden legs she followed him back out into the sunshine, constantly stealing glances at his enigmatic expression.

And when they were once more in the jeep, whatever

she'd been expecting certainly did, in no way, prepare her
for his casual question.

"How long will it take you to pack?"

"I beg your pardon?"

"Pack, as in throw clothes in a suitcase," Blaise said
noncommittally as he reached over and started the engine.
Well, if she turned into a raging she-tiger, he'd suffer
through. He'd made the reservations and now he'd deliver
the information. Besides, he couldn't leave her . . . not
yet . . . not like this.

"For what?"

"We're going to Tampa," Blaise stated as he shifted
into reverse and directed his concentration to turning the
jeep around. "There's something I want you to see. We've
got reservations on the six-thirty flight out of Richmond."

FIVE

"I can't go to Florida with you, Blaise," Les protested, her eyes widening in horror even as excitement coursed through her.

"And why not?" he asked casually. He pulled out onto the highway and headed for River's Edge, a satisfied smile playing over his lips. "I believe you told me you've reached the age of consent."

"Why, I don't—I mean, we aren't—why Florida? You have a perfectly good motel room if shacking up is all you have on your mind."

Blaise's eyes darted in her direction and then he laughed boisterously.

"You sure can be blunt when you want to, Angel Eyes," Blaise drawled. "What I have on my mind is spending every minute possible with you, during which time I hope to convince you of an idea that can help you with River's Edge. So I told Celia she and Dennis could go on back to Pennsylvania without me and I called the airlines. And why Florida? Well, for one thing, I have a son there I'd like you to meet. And for another, I want you out of the forest so you can see the trees."

"What in the world are you talking about?" Les demanded. "I have responsibilities, obligations. I can't just pack up and head out on vacation like I haven't a care in the world."

"Leslie, do you trust me? Just a little, maybe?"

"Well, yes, I suppose I do, but—"

"Then stop babbling like a frustrated little girl." Reaching over, he grabbed her hand and gave it a tight squeeze, his own excitement growing almost uncontrollable.

Sherry made no effort to conceal her surprise when Blaise informed her it would be necessary that she arrange for someone to cover for Les at the Car Doctor on Monday. Their return flight wasn't until Tuesday afternoon.

"I don't know, Leslie," Sherry hedged as she followed Les upstairs to pack. "Are you sure you know this man well enough to go off with him?"

"No, Mother, I'm not sure at all," Les replied as she stood in the middle of the bedroom and stared at the closet door. "He could be Jack the Ripper for all I know. But I've been living on my gut instincts since I was fourteen. It's a little late to start distrusting them, wouldn't you think? What in the world do I pack?"

Sherry plopped down on the side of the bed to watch her daughter.

"This just isn't like you," she finally stated.

Les turned and stared at her mother for a long moment.

"Mother, you don't even know me," she finally said quietly. "But on this point, you're right. I'm not impulsive and it's for sure I'm not clairvoyant. I like Blaise, and in the past four days, I've seen nothing about the man to make me fear for my life. So suffice it to say, I'm going with him to see his son. Now go downstairs and treat him like a guest in our home."

Les had never in her life had so much trouble packing a suitcase. An off-white linen suit for the trip down, a cocktail dress for their dinner with Brandon Hollander, and clothes to travel home in posed little problem. But when it came to selecting a nightgown, her hands froze above the assortment of pastel lingerie in her drawer. Hotel accommodations had not been discussed. Would they share a room? Would she be spending the night with Blaise?

Finally, closing her eyes in childish deliberation, she dug deep into the drawer and withdrew a gown at random. As she slipped it into the suitcase, Les had a mental image of herself clad in that froth of peach lace with her breasts all but falling out of the plunging neckline, her long legs revealed by the thigh-high side slits.

With icy shivers of frightful anticipation racing up her spine, she tossed in her most conservative, demure to the point of being boring terry robe.

Aunt Josie could not fathom the fact that dinner would be served on the plane; she insisted on packing the picnic basket and had even tossed in a quart of milk.

At the motel, Les waited in the jeep and fidgeted with the clasp on her bracelet while Blaise went for his own suitcase. When he appeared ten minutes later, her breath caught at the sight of him. He'd changed into navy slacks and an open-neck cream sweater. The anticipation grew.

"I can't believe I'm doing this," she exclaimed when, at the airport, he handed her the ticket envelopes to slip into her purse.

"Come on, Nervous Nelly," Blaise murmured with a chuckle as he slipped his arm around her waist. "We've got plenty of time for a calm-you-down cocktail. In your case, I'd suspect a double."

In the cocktail lounge, he settled her into a booth, and instead of taking the seat opposite, he slipped in beside her.

"You might as well get used to close proximity," Blaise whispered huskily as he tilted her head up and gazed deeply into her eyes. "For the next twenty-four hours, at the very least, you've got a shadow, lovely lady."

He kissed her lightly and the butterflies in her stomach

went into tailspins. This would never do. She'd be in coronary arrest until she learned the answer to one simple question.

"Where are we staying, Blaise?"

Blaise smiled and motioned for a passing waitress.

"What you mean is, wherever we're staying, will there be a room for each of us? Well, at the Hollander House, there are fourteen rooms, including the bridal suite, and since it is not officially open for business yet, you, Miss Braddock, may have your choice."

"Hollander House?" Les exclaimed in disbelief. "Don't tell me you own a hotel."

"To coin a phrase, the bank and I do," Blaise replied. "And it's a bed and breakfast inn."

He flashed the waitress a smile that positively radiated happiness as he ordered their drinks. When she'd left to fill their order, he turned back to Les.

"My son is graduating from college next June and he'll be managing the Hollander. Besides, this venture was his own idea and he's spent the last couple of years looking for just the right place. Even though it's pretty much ready for business, we've decided to wait until Labor Day for the grand opening."

"Expensive graduation present," Les commented.

"No, it wasn't a gift," Blaise corrected. He collected her hands in his and idly ran his thumbs over her flesh.

"Brandon had some money of his own. We invested together." His expression grew thoughtful for a moment as he considered his son's rather lavish life-style as opposed to that of the woman who was coming to mean so much to him. He'd taught Brandon responsibility but it had never been forced upon him before he was ready as, apparently, it had been on Les.

"Whatever made you become a mechanic?" he asked as he raised his eyes to meet hers. "You could have pursued a thousand other careers. You're certainly bright enough."

"And it doesn't take brains to be a mechanic?" Her tone was more defensive than she'd intended.

"I didn't say that. I asked why is all."

"No complicated or deep-seated reason," Les replied as she toyed with the heavy ring on his finger. "It's honest, dirty work that pays good money and besides I inherited the love of fixing things."

Blaise said nothing. Somehow he knew the reason went deeper. He also knew from the look on her face she was going to tell him the reason.

"My dad," Les murmured and then she smiled sadly. "He was supposed to be a farmer like my grandfather. Fifth-generation Braddock and all. But Daddy just wasn't built that way. He was a dreamer, always envisioning himself in some exotic locale, doing great things. At one time, he even thought about going to Las Vegas and opening a nightclub. But, of course, he knew he couldn't afford to make those dreams a reality."

The waitress approached and Les grew silent. She extracted her hands from his and moved her arms off the tabletop so their drinks could be served. When the woman had again left their table, Les reached for her gin and tonic, took a sip, and replaced the glass on the napkin.

"So I suggested he lease out the land and open a garage," Les said quietly. When Blaise said nothing, she raised her eyes to meet his. "No, that wasn't another of my strong-arm maneuvers. He liked fixing things. He'd lie all day under a tractor dreaming his dreams and tinkering."

Blaise sipped his scotch and said nothing.

"He liked the garage, but he wasn't a manager. So when I finished college and marriage, I came back home, kicked out the mechanics who were robbing him blind, and together we built the Car Doctor."

"You loved your father a lot, didn't you?"

Les smiled and nodded.

Suddenly, Blaise had a very disquieting thought, so disquieting in fact he visibly stiffened under the impact.

Les glanced up, her brows arched. Then she smiled again.

"No, Blaise, I'm not looking for a father figure. Just an honest man with honest intentions."

"How did you know I was thinking that?" he asked in amazement.

"I honestly don't know," Les said with a giggle. "Maybe it was the way you turned a little green around the gills or the fact that my age bothers you. I saw the expression on your face that day in the park when you asked my age."

"It doesn't. Not that much, anyway," Blaise argued. Then he grinned. "Okay, it doesn't bother me anymore. How's that?"

"Why should age be a factor in the first place?" Les said.

"Brandon's only twenty-two."

"Jeez, what a child," Les teased.

"Not hardly."

"I rest my case, Hollander." Les finished off her drink and glanced at her watch. "Well, mister, if you're taking me to Florida, I think we'd better get on the plane."

"Ah, Leslie," Blaise said with a deep sigh. He was filled with an exuberance that was astonishing in its intensity. "You look so beautiful with that flush in your cheeks and your lips parted like that. Almost as though—"

He leaned forward, his lips hovering just above her own, his eyes sparkling with delight.

"Do you have any idea how happy I am?" he whispered, his breath warm on her flesh. "How glad I am you're with me?"

"I think so," Les murmured, and closing her eyes, she waited for the soft brush of his mouth against her own . . . a kiss to chase away the misgivings about this trip with a man she hardly knew.

* * *

Situated on sparkling Tampa Bay, the Hollander House was a monstrous three-story white wooden structure built in the Southern colonial fashion with six white columns adorning the front. Generous screened porches skirted out on either side, and green shuttered windows stared out at a sandy beach only yards from the spacious, neatly manicured lawn with its boxwood hedges intermingled with lush tropical growth and towering palm trees.

Blaise parked the rental car in the carport at the side of the house and then assisted Les out into the warm night air. A brisk wind whipped off the bay, carrying the sweet fragrance of bougainvillea and roses from the lavish gardens that were in abundance.

Les could only gaze around her in mute appreciation when they entered the massive domicile with its sweeping display of Early American furnishings. Thick braided rugs were scattered over the polished mahogany floor, subdued lighting spilled down into the parlor from a sparkling chandelier, and on the massive stone fireplace along one wall, thick logs lay waiting to provide the final statement of warm, rich comfort.

"Like it?" Blaise asked as he noted the look of awe on her face. His own expression was one of pride.

"It's gorgeous," Les exclaimed.

"We had to pay a handsome price for it, but we figure in two years, we'll see a profit," Blaise said as he urged her down the long hall that bisected the building.

"No one lives here, permanently, I mean?" Les asked as she caught fleeting glimpses of spacious bedrooms with plush trappings.

"Brandon is considering moving from his apartment but at the moment, no, it's strictly for guests."

He halted and grabbed her shoulders to draw her close to him.

"You could do the same thing with River's Edge, Leslie," he murmured as he gazed down at her.

"Sure," Les scoffed. "On what? My looks."

"Heh, I didn't say something like this was easy." He indicated their surroundings with a broad sweep of his hand. "But isn't it worth the effort?"

"Darling Blaise, if I had your money, I wouldn't have my problems," Les said as she reached to give his hand a quick squeeze. "Now did we come to sunny Florida to wage a full-scale debate or for me to have the privilege of a guided tour through the Hollander House?"

Blaise sighed. Well, he hadn't exactly expected her to grab onto the concept and run with it . . . not at first. She needed convincing and that was precisely why he'd insisted she come with him. Plant the seed, nurture it, and then stand back and watch it grow.

Bending, he kissed the tip of her nose and urged her forward.

"Tour gets under way as soon as we find my son and give him the privilege of meeting Virginia's most beautiful female. Come on."

They found Blaise's brown-haired son seated at an oversized desk in a spacious, dark-paneled office that reeked of Early American. Drapes at the tall, deep-silled windows had been opened and sunshine spilled over his shoulder as he bent over a stack of work orders.

"Well, you did make it," he exclaimed, rising from his chair as Blaise ushered Les into the room.

"Leslie Braddock, my son Brandon," Blaise said, and one quick glance was enough to surmise the pride Blaise felt in this tall, slender, but broad-shouldered, younger version of himself. Dark eyes assessed her and apparently Blaise's son liked what he saw, for immediately a warm smile widened his mouth as he extended his hand in greeting.

"Welcome to Hollander House, Miss Braddock."

"I'll show Leslie around, get her settled in, and then you can fill me in on what's going on," Blaise said.

His enthusiasm was contagious as he led her through the house, describing each room and its lavish trappings. Yes, Hollander House would draw hordes of guests, and though she wanted to ask the nightly charges he would be imposing, common sense told her the accommodations would not be cheap. He'd chosen an ideal locale in the third largest city in Florida. A mild winter climate made it an ideal tourist resort and he'd been quick to inform her that, so far, motels far outnumber the bed and breakfast concept.

"What made you decide to pursue this endeavor?" she asked.

"Actually, it was Brandon's idea," he confessed. "And after doing a little informal surveying, I discovered how popular an establishment such as this is among discriminating couples. All the comforts of home without any of the responsibility."

And you could do the very same thing with River's Edge, he wanted to repeat but decided later would be time enough. Later, when she'd soaked up a healthy dose of the atmosphere he was confident Hollander House afforded visitors. He'd bring her back for the grand opening, let her sample the culinary delights of the two chefs who'd already been hired, let her mingle with guests, make her hungry for her own success.

By the time Blaise had finished lauding the diligent efforts of the decorator who'd done the bridal suite in which they now stood, a strange excitement was racing in her veins. His intelligence, his cool confidence, the way his eyes danced with excitement all combined in a man with enough charm and good looks to dazzle any woman. Was there known an antidote against the powers of a man like Blaise?

He'd saved the bridal suite for last and the moment they'd entered the pale blue room with its lavish comforts awaiting some future occupants, Les had an immediate vision of Blaise and herself in that very role. She trailed her fingers over the plush velvet spread covering the wide four-poster bed, her eyes downcast lest he read the illicit thoughts coursing through her mind.

Waning sunshine filtered through the lacy sheers and gleamed in his ebony hair when he turned from her to gaze through the window at the courtyard below. Les sensed his momentary withdrawal, and when she glanced in his direction, delicious and totally unexpected waves of heat slid over her. Mentally, she stripped away his sweater. Her hands tingled as she imagined sliding her palms over his satiny flesh . . . coaxing him to that tempting bed . . . taunting him . . . seducing him until the troublesome urges coming to life inside her were echoed in his own body.

She'd known him less than a week, and yet, how quickly they'd traversed to this point in time where nothing stood between her growing need and the sweet satisfaction she knew she'd find in his arms. The setting was oh so conducive. Her overwhelming attraction to him oh so disturbing. Why not just open her arms and draw him inside? It had been so long . . .

And you'd better grab hold of some control real fast, her self-imposed moral structure warned. In accordance, Les closed her eyes for a moment, drew a deep breath, and forced from her mind the torrid images so capable of shredding that moral structure.

"It's absolutely beautiful," she said and hoped he'd mistake the husky quality in her voice for reverence and not simple, basic desire for him. "The entire house is breathtaking. Thank you so much for showing it to me."

For a long moment, Les wasn't certain he'd heard her. Or perhaps he'd decided no comment was necessary. Then, he slid his hands deep into his slacks' pockets and turned to face her.

Oh dear Lord, Les breathed silently as his dark eyes clung to her own . . . dark, sultry eyes, now smoldering with a passion of his own. Even from a distance, she could see the vein throbbing in his neck and it was no mystery at all the reason he'd shoved his hands into his pockets. He wanted her! Their thoughts paralleled in this sensuously romantic room. While she'd attempted to make conversation, he'd been standing at that window facing his own lascivious thoughts.

"I'm glad you like it," he replied. *Oh, woman, I want you,* his lusty mind cried. *Right now, right there on that bed with your hair tumbling over the pillow, your lovely body stripped bare for my enjoyment . . . your own need giving you the courage to let me love you like I've dreamed of loving you.*

"Blaise—" she took a step back from the bed.

"Leslie—" He took a step closer to her.

She laughed and folded her arms tightly across her breasts, almost gasping as the pressure on her hard nipples incited yet another wave of longing.

"It's the room, I guess," she managed. "So perfect, so . . ."

"Or us?" His intense gaze dared her to differ.

"Maybe we should go back downstairs."

"Is that what you really want?"

Les closed her eyes and exhaled loudly. A direct challenge if ever she'd heard one or, better yet, a perfect opening. A lesser woman would not grab the bait. But then, when had she ever been a lesser woman? She opened her eyes and visually drank in the man who waited for her answer, even though they both knew no answer was necessary. The tension between them crackled . . . a red-hot sexual tension that needed no romantic room for inspiration.

"You know darned well what I want," Les murmured. Moving purposefully, she came around the bed and joined him at the window. "I want you to hold me and kiss me."

"And do you promise to kiss me back?" he asked softly as his hands settled on her hips, drawing her closer until her tingling body was melding to his hard frame.

"Try me," she whispered. Her hands clung to his shoulders, fingers digging into the ridge of muscle there, and she closed her eyes in delicious anticipation.

His lips were warm and moist, his tongue immediately invading her mouth. For a heart-stopping moment, caution vanished, leaving only the intense desire to lose herself completely in the magic of his mesmerizing nearness, his wondrous kisses. His arousal was tight against her lower stomach, and involuntarily, she arched until she could feel him at the junction of her thighs.

Instantly, his hands slid to cup her buttocks, lifting her and molding her tighter to his need.

"Oh, Blaise," she moaned against his mouth. His breath was hot on her face, his expression almost a grimace as he alternately pressed and released until they were both quivering from head to foot.

"This is getting us nowhere real darned fast," he panted, his grip tightening, freezing her against him while he throbbed with impatience.

Les sagged against him and pressed her face against the heated flesh of his neck.

Slowly, his hold slackened as he struggled to quell the dangerous fires leaping nearly out of control.

"Leslie, baby, I'm too old to play like this," he finally said with a hearty sigh.

"And who's playing?" she exclaimed breathlessly and then she leaned back in his arms to gaze up at him. "Blaise, I've never wanted a man in my life like I want you. I just wish—"

Instantly, his fingertip was against her lips, silencing her.

"Don't qualify that statement," he urged, his intense gaze encompassing her flushed features, the slight smudge of lipstick at the corner of her mouth, the sexy dishevelment of her hair. Gently, he dabbed away the lipstick smear. "Unless that wish has something to do with that bed over there."

Les laughed shakily.

"It does." Slowly, she pulled free of his arms and smoothed the front of her skirt. Her limbs had the consistency of gelatin; her legs threatened at any moment to give way beneath her weight. She turned toward the door.

"You'd better give me a moment or two," Blaise suggested. Les glanced at the front of his slacks.

"Or three," she murmured, and reaching up, she ran her fingers through his tousled hair in a manner she'd seen him do many times. "There, handsome. You look exactly like a man who's trying not to look like he's been up to mischief for the past few minutes."

"Oh, baby, mischief isn't at all what I've been up to," Blaise corrected as he looped his arm around her waist and urged her out into the hallway. "Try enticement enough to drive a man to drink. Care to join me?"

"I think I'll unpack and freshen up a little," Les said. "I'm sure you and your son have a few things to discuss. Why don't I join you later?"

"Okay, Miss Braddock." He paused outside the guest room where they'd stowed her luggage. "Hurry up, though. I promised you undivided attention for thirty-six hours, remember?"

Standing on her tiptoes, she pressed a light kiss on his lips.

"Oh yes, Blaise. I remember all too well. And again, I love your house. If I was of weaker character, I'd confess to an envy beyond all comprehension."

"She's young, isn't she?" Brandon commented later.

"Twenty-eight," Blaise replied as he sifted through the work orders on which Brandon had been working when they arrived. Since Brandon had only two courses left to complete for his degree, he was going to school in the mornings and then working at the inn in the afternoon, getting it ready for the grand opening.

"She's a knockout, I'll say that," Brandon added as he

noted the scowl on his father's handsome features. "Where'd you meet her, Dad?"

"In the middle of the woods," Blaise replied absently as he scanned the billing for the new rugs in the dining room.

"And?"

Blaise glanced up, his expression quizzical.

"Is it serious?" Brandon persisted.

"Life is serious," Blaise hedged and went back to the papers in front of him.

Brandon chuckled and drew his chair closer to the desk. "Well, I suppose you're old enough to know what you're doing."

"I am," Blaise replied. He glanced up at Brandon again. "Am I reading you right, son? Are you giving me approval?"

"Sure, like Blaise Hollander has ever needed someone else's approval in his entire life or would have stood around long enough if they'd been inclined to give it. She's nice. Good luck to the two of you. You've been alone too long."

"Humph," Blaise growled, his brow furrowed in feigned annoyance. He bent his concentration once more to the bills he was perusing. "Did you get estimates on the rugs before you had them laid?"

"Sure did," Brandon assured him. "Good price, huh?"

"Very good," Blaise agreed as he laid the bill aside and then rose to his feet. "Well, I think I'll have myself a drink and then get ready for dinner. How much longer are you planning to hang around here?"

"Oh, I've finished for the day," Brandon told him. He recovered his jacket from the coat rack and shrugged it on. "I made reservations at Cleo's since our kitchen is lacking a staff at the moment. Hope that's okay."

"Cleo's is fine. Are you still getting discounts for being their daughter's number one?"

"Miss Shannon and I called it quits," Brandon told him

as they made their way toward the lobby bar. "Right now, I've got too much to do to cater to some spoiled female and Shannon took the cake. Now, find me one like your Leslie and I could be persuaded to turn off the midnight oil a little sooner."

"Keep your nose to the grindstone, son, and leave Leslie alone."

"Can't stand the competition, huh?" Brandon teased as he looped his arm around his father's broad shoulders.

"Sure can't," Blaise replied. "Now tell me what you've got lined up for the Labor Day opening."

The two were deep in conversation when Les finally joined them. She'd spent a leisurely half hour soaking in a fragrant bath and doing her level best to collect her thoughts. To no avail. And in that lavishly furnished room with the satin-draped king-sized bed, floor to ceiling windows overlooking a free-form swimming pool set in the middle of a lush, tropical courtyard at the rear of the house, she faced the futility of her own ambivalence.

Now as her attention riveted on the tall, dark-haired man draped over the mahogany bar, his attention fixed on his son, she faced another truth. Something was happening to her . . . had happened to her where Blaise was concerned. She'd known it all along and yet she'd persisted in ignoring that warm fluttering in her heart. Oh sure, lust was a part of it. There could be no denying she wanted him with a need bordering on desperation. But there was something else . . . something far more disquieting. She was falling in love with him and it was probably the stupidest thing in the world she could be doing . . . not counting this impromptu trip that would only serve to deepen the feelings growing by leaps and bounds within her.

Brandon glanced up as he heard the muffled sound of her footsteps and immediately flashed her a smile so like his father's. She returned his smile and then, as though drawn by an incredibly strong magnet, she locked eyes with Blaise for a heart-stopping moment as he watched her over the rim of the glass he'd just raised to his lips. Electricity sizzled between them.

"What is your pleasure, Miss Braddock?" Brandon asked as he stepped behind the bar and encompassed the gleaming bottles with a wave of his hand.

"A white wine and, please, call me Les," she said huskily. She slid onto a leather-covered stool beside Blaise, her heart thundering in her breasts.

"You look just about good enough to eat," he whispered as he reached out and tucked a tendril of hair behind her ear, his finger brushing feather soft against her earlobe in the process. Les said a silent thanks to her mother for insisting she buy the black lace concoction she now wore. Sherry had assured her it was pure man bait. She'd assured her mother she didn't want men noticing the manner in which the handkerchief points at the hemline called attention to her lovely legs nor did she want a man salivating over the creamy rise of breasts visible above the scoop neckline. At least, not at that particular time! Now, she was honestly basking in the warm gleam of appreciation in his dark eyes.

"All settled in?" he asked.

Les nodded.

"And how's the room?"

"Big," she exclaimed. Heat rushed into her cheeks as she recalled her earlier imaginings as she'd perched on the side of that enormous bed.

Blaise laughed huskily.

"Just don't get lost in there all by yourself," Blaise said, his eyes assuring her of his meaning. He'd made yet another decision. He was leaving it all up to her. He'd sensed her hesitation when he'd mentioned the trip and he'd known the cause. He'd known her passion—her torrid response—when he'd held her in his arms.

But he had not brought her to Tampa for the purpose of seducing her. As much as he wanted her, he wanted more than the possession of her body, mind-boggling as he knew that would be. And he knew he had to convince her of this if there was to be more than a simple affair with one independent, completely hardheaded Leslie Braddock.

The relief she derived from his simple statement was almost heady. For a second, she could only gaze at him in surprise . . . and a mixture of disappointment.

"Thank you for finally answering THE question," she teased.

"Well, at least now you can quit worrying about it," he replied, his dark eyes warm on her face. Then he glanced up as Brandon approached with her drink and a cup of coffee for himself. Just before he was within listening range, Blaise added: "Unless it's you who either walks in her sleep or changes her mind, I'm in the room next door to you."

Since Brandon had plans for later in the evening, it was agreed they would drive two cars to the restaurant with its glass-walled dining room overlooking Tampa Bay. Miniature waves slapped the shore below; seagulls swooped and soared just beyond the window and a crystal vase of gardenia blossoms adorned the white linen–clothed table. Perfect, Les thought as Blaise settled her into a chair and took the one beside her. A woman could easily become accustomed to elegance . . . and Blaise Hollander!

Beneath the table, Blaise's knee brushed her own, and when her eyes darted in his direction, Blaise laughed softly and gently increased the pressure. A thrill shot up her thigh; her hand froze in the process of reaching for the water glass.

It was going to be a very long evening, Les told herself as she finally managed to lift the glass. She took a dainty sip, all the while inhaling the warm, masculine aroma of the man who was now ordering a round of drinks . . . feeling his heat . . . wanting him.

And if I somehow manage to survive his intoxicating

nearness without melting into a puddle on the seat, then
we'll worry about the night ahead.

When the drinks arrived, Les contented herself listening
to the easy ebb and flow of conversation between Blaise
and his son as they discussed the upcoming grand opening
of the Hollander House. The sound of his voice was as
soothing as a violin concerto. The light pressure of his
hand resting over her own was a silent proclamation that
she was in no way out of his thoughts.

"Dad tells me you have a beautiful colonial estate,"
Brandon said. Les jarred herself back to reality, shoving
away the tantalizing memories of that session in the bridal
suite. Lordy, was making love to Blaise the only thing on
her brain here lately?

"Yes," Les replied. "Of course, it's in need of a lot
of work."

"Do what we did," Brandon said. "Make it pay for
itself. You'd be surprised how popular those old estates
are, especially if you restore—"

He halted as he caught sight of Blaise's scowl.

"Okay, wrong subject," Brandon said with a reckless
smile and the undaunted confidence of his youth. "Sorry."

Les laughed and patted his hand in a fashion she'd always called motherly. To Brandon? He was scarcely more
than a few years younger than she herself.

"It's all right, Brandon," Les assured him. She winked
at Blaise before continuing, "I'm not supposed to know
this trip down was a calculated move on your father's part
to lay some groundwork for an idea he has."

Blaise frowned and shook his head. Was the woman
clairvoyant? Or was he more gifted at subtle coercion than
even he believed?

"Actually," Les continued. "It's not a bad idea. In
fact, given time, I could probably even learn to like it.
However, in my case, there is one monumental problem
that I refuse to discuss because I would love to enjoy my
dinner."

For the remainder of the meal, conversation remained on an impersonal level, deviating only slightly when an overly dressed blonde with too much mascara undulated past their table, winking at Blaise in the process.

"He draws 'em like flies," Brandon commented as he polished off the last bite of his cheesecake. "And never pays the slightest attention. Me? I'd already be chasing her for a phone number."

"With your date sitting at your elbow, no less," Les teased.

His smile was an exact copy of his father's. It made Les's heart turn over, and inadvertently, she reached over and lightly squeezed Blaise's arm.

"Well, on second thought, maybe I'd do just like Dad. Nothing," Brandon confessed boyishly. Then he sobered. "But, he's blind like that whether he's with a date or not. Actually, Les, I think you're the first date I've known him to have in years."

"Or at least a few weeks," Les corrected with a wide smile. "It's all right, Brandon. Your father and I are just friends."

Les did not see the scowl that darkened Blaise's face for a moment.

"Friends, huh?" Blaise challenged when, later, they had walked Brandon to his car, said their good nights, and were debating a drive as opposed to dancing in the lounge.

"The drive sounds wonderful," Les said, deliberately avoiding his taunt. "And what would you call us if not friends?"

Blaise made no reply; he'd made his decision as to whether to rectify their status.

"He's a terrific boy," Les commented later as they drove through the sultry night air.

"Brandon hardly thinks of himself as a boy," Blaise replied. "More like my business partner, my baby-sitter, and he has monumental aspirations of one day being my personal confidant. And he likes you, too, Miss Braddock.''

"Does he see his mother often?"

"Brandon flies down about once a year, but he's not all that enthused about Raoul, her husband."

"The polo player."

"I suppose that's a nicer label than the one I have in mind," Blaise said with a chuckle. They'd pulled off the highway and were now traveling slowly through a residential area. Soon, Blaise whipped into a parking lot and shut off the engine. Ahead of them, white brick condos faced out onto the bay and the twinkling skyline of Tampa shone on the other side.

"Nice place," Les commented as they left the car and made their way down to where concrete ended and white sand spread out before them. Les bent and removed her high-heeled sandals. She knew she'd probably ruin her panty hose, but they were cheaper by far than a pair of leather shoes.

Blaise took them from her and stuck one in each of his jacket pockets.

"It should be," Blaise said proudly. "Hollander & Associates built them."

Les glanced back over her shoulder as though to envision the actual construction, this tall giant of a man, complete with hard hat, thundering out orders to a crew every bit as efficient as he himself.

"And this is what you wanted to build in Williamsburg?" she asked quietly.

"Initially, it was an idea," he replied, indicating a park bench nestled in the sand. "But then I had a better idea."

"Yes, like turning River's Edge into another Hollander House," she said.

"I heard a very good rule once," he said as he drew her down on the bench beside him. "When in the moonlight with an enticing woman, never introduce controversial subjects." With that, he cupped the back of her head in his broad palm and kissed her soundly.

"I heard one, too," Les murmured when she could speak around the tightness in her throat as desire infused her from head to foot. "When in the moonlight with a compelling man, thoroughly examine your options."

"And?" His fingertip brushed her damp mouth. Dark eyes burned down into her own.

"I forget what they are," she whispered as her arms slid around his neck.

SIX

Les had never been so disappointed in her entire life! Or so confused. Long after she'd crawled between the smooth, satiny sheets, she lay staring up at the ceiling, painted in wavery shadows by the diffused light cast up from the lamps in the courtyard below.

Had she figured Blaise wrong or what? With desire burning her alive, wasn't it reasonable to assume he was suffering from the same malady? Hadn't he given her every indication this evening would culminate in mutual satisfaction for the hunger they felt . . . she felt? What had gone wrong?

Mentally, she reviewed the scenario. They'd sat in the moonlight; he'd told her bits and pieces about his married life; he'd gone into minute detail about his relationship with his son; he'd kissed her twice more. And then they'd come back to the inn. He'd told her good night and that was it.

Flipping onto her stomach, Les buried her face into the pillow. But the thoughts would not cease and desist. Not since she'd suffered disappointment at the hands of one very immature husband named Taylor had Les known this kind of blow to her pride. Again, she questioned her own intelligence. How had she figured him so inaccurately? Had he been playing with her?

By the digital readout on her travel alarm, Les calculated the few hours remaining before she must rise from this sinfully comfortable bed and face the man responsible for the first case of insomnia she'd ever experienced. Damn him, Les fumed as she shoved aside the covers and leaped to her feet.

At the window, she gazed out into the night . . . and then down to the crystal blue waters of the pool two floors below. How inviting it looked out there in the gentle lighting from the gas lamps. How invigorating a swim would be.

Turning, Les considered her impulse. She'd brought no swimsuit, but then it was two in the morning. The hotel was empty of guests. Brandon had returned to his apartment, and Blaise, the only pair of eyes that might be privy to the fact she intended swimming in her underwear, would be sleeping. Why not? The courtyard and the pool were completely sequestered from prying eyes by the lush gardens and, behind that, the privacy walls surrounding the house.

Darn it, she'd do it. She'd come to Florida at his invitation. He'd made a jackass of her and, in her opinion, himself as well. She'd go for a swim if she darn well pleased. Who'd ever know?

A black lace bra and bikini panties are as concealing as any swimsuit I've ever worn, Les rationalized as she pulled on the undergarments and reached for her terry robe. And *I won't be out there that long.*

At first, Blaise considered an overwrought imagination. But the scene below was too realistic.

Reaching for the cord, he opened the bedroom drapes a little wider and leaned closer to peer down at the pool area from his vantage point two floors above.

His annoyance at having to get out of bed for aspirins

dissipated as he watched the lone, lissome form moving silently through the aquamarine water, her long golden hair trailing out behind her. Underwater lighting clearly revealed a body only partially concealed by a very brief, very clinging black two-piece swimsuit. Slender, well-formed legs scissored in perfect coordination with her arms as she breast-stroked to one end of the pool and then slithered over onto her back.

Blaise's breath caught as her breasts rhythmically swelled to the water's surface with every breath, her nipples in sharp relief against the black fabric of her top, and white heat surged into his groin when she finally raised her face to the lamplight.

"Leslie," he groaned. For a moment, he closed his eyes against a strong chaotic flood of indecision. All evening, he'd known her tension, though she'd tried so hard to conceal it. He'd read her thoughts so easily. She was expecting him to pressure her into bed. They both wanted it desperately, but her latent discomfort with the idea, for who knows what reason, had been the ice water to cool the fire in his veins. He'd weighed the advantages of satisfying his desires against the disadvantages of having her do a 180-degree turnaround when it was over. Because he wanted so much more than sex from Leslie, he'd taken his libido in hand and had treated her as a gentleman would; he'd made no advances beyond those kisses that had almost been his undoing.

And now? Down there in the moonlight? She was so beautiful . . . so slender, so perfectly formed, so enticingly revealed, her skin slick with water, every sensuous curve bathed in soft light.

Since when had voyeurism ever held any appeal to him? And wasn't that exactly what he was doing, standing here in the darkness, giving free rein to lusty thoughts that rendered the front of his shorts uncomfortably tight?

Blaise glanced down once more and sighed with honest relief. She was moving slowly out of the water, up the steps, and reaching for a towel. In the dim lighting, her hair clung like wet satin to her shoulders, and as she leaned slightly forward to wrap the towel around her head, ripe curves strained up and out of the brief top, until only her nipples were concealed from his hungry eyes.

Les's heart leaped into her throat as she caught sight of the movement at the window . . . the window of the room next door to the one she'd recently vacated. *Oh jeez*, she breathed silently as she appraised the man watching her and wearing nothing but a pair of briefs so skimpy he might as well have been nude. Even given the distance and the inadequate lighting, Les knew she could quite easily rate his most intimate male attributes extremely high on a scale of one to ten. And there was no doubt remaining in her mind . . . Blaise Hollander was a most impressively built male with wide shoulders, well-formed biceps, and a tapering waistline that drew her hungry perusal down to that portion of him for which her body had again burst into demanding flames.

There was no more indecision. Whirling around, Blaise grabbed for his slacks, and after jerking them on, he hurried from the room. His heart thundered in his chest, his mind spun with illicit longing, his body throbbed for fulfillment.

Against a backdrop of lush, tropical foliage with the moon a seductive halo over his head, Blaise stood frozen in his tracks as he realized what he'd mistaken for a swimsuit was nothing more than a very sexy lace bra and panties, the brevity of which made his mouth go dry. His eyes moved slowly along the length of her, visually drinking in the temptress who stood only a few yards away, her blue eyes burning with a passion that he knew equaled his own.

Slowly, Les stripped the towel from her hair and shook the long mass down over her shoulders, her heart thundering as she contemplated the masculine splendor of the man who stood watching her, the look of hunger on his face echoing the demanding voices in her head.

Fully clothed, Blaise was startling good looks and elegance with an untouchable air that challenged. Now, bare chested with the flickering light from the gas lamps playing across his bronzed chest with its covering of dark curling hair, he was brute strength and raw sex appeal. Ridges of muscles defined his broad shoulders, accentuated his arms, and crisscrossed his flat stomach, so enticingly revealed by the unbelted slacks that hung carelessly low on his lean hips. He was a powerful animal with untamed eyes and flared nostrils, poised and ready to strike . . . and everything in her that was woman instantly responded to his silent primitive call to mate.

"Well, I'm caught," Les murmured, her husky voice sending shivers along his spine.

"Yes, you are," he replied, moving purposefully toward her, his eyes never leaving her face. "In more ways than one."

Her head tilted back, her lips parted as he reached for her . . . drew her cool body against his hot flesh. Her arms automatically locked around his hard torso, and rising on tiptoes, she pressed to him, molding her soft compliance into every burning ridge and valley from his knees to his shoulders . . . arrogantly offering a body too long denied relief.

"I see you've changed your mind," Les murmured, her fingers clinging, her nails digging into his shoulders as she filled her senses with him . . . the smell of soap on his neck, the elusive fragrance of expensive after-shave, the traces of brandy on his breath . . . his strange, yet familiar flesh beneath her fingertips.

"I had help in that department," he mumbled. His ebony eyes raked her face as he fought against the urge to rip away those enticing garments that did so little to conceal her womanly attributes . . . plunge himself into the mysterious depths of her . . . make her his own.

"This was not done for the sake of tempting you," she said inanely.

"What makes you think it does?"

"Nothing, unless you consider your physical condition, your rapid breathing, your thundering heart, the heat of your skin and then employ just a smidgen of plain old common sense." Her eyes danced playfully over his taut features. "I guess you've figured out I want you, too."

"That's why you're out here in the darkness and not in my bed?" he drawled, his heart flooding with elation as he realized how foolish he'd been in prolonging what he knew would be heaven on earth.

"I have a bed in my room, too," Les whispered. Reaching up, she delicately smoothed his unruly brows with the tip of her finger. "A very empty bed."

Against the warm press of her body, his maleness surged with impatience. A grimace, attributable to the delicious pain of wanting, flitted over his handsome features.

"Not any longer," he promised. His hands dropped down to cup her buttocks, urging her into perfect alignment with his rigidity. "I promised you constant companionship, remember?"

"And what are you promising me now?"

"Everything I've got," he murmured raggedly as the heat swelled to almost unbearable proportions.

"From what I saw at the window, that's more than enough for any woman."

Les's hands drifted around to his back, and with nails light as a feather, she trailed their tips over his velvety smooth skin, gingerly tracing the ridges of his backbone and finally settling at the band of his slacks.

"Care to try it on for size?"

"Try and stop me, Hollander," she murmured. "I'm afraid you played your last ace when you dared venture outside the protection of a closed door."

"Yeah, I know," he said as his eyes moved over her flushed features and down to the ripe swell of her breasts, now pressed tightly to his chest. "Damn, these slacks are choking me. If I release you long enough to take them off, do you promise not to vanish like a figment of a very disoriented imagination?"

"Oh, I assure you, Blaise Hollander, I'm going nowhere," Les whispered. She released him and stepped back, uninhibited in her intent to enjoy his disrobing and relishing the immediate burning sweep of his eyes over her own bare flesh. "I believe in people keeping promises."

"And I believe in doing a job lying down if at all possible," he growled, and sweeping her up into his arms, he carried her into a shadowy sanctuary, created by a thick canopy of vines and beneath which had been placed an assortment of chintz cushioned lounges for those choosing distance from the pool area. He placed her down on the lounge and then towered over her, visually devouring the ripe promise awaiting his greedy enjoyment.

Lord, she was beautiful lying there with the shadows enhancing her basic mystique, the lush green growth enhancing erotic fantasies growing so easily in his mind. He'd envisioned countless ways of loving her . . . endless places, but nothing like this. Somehow, it seemed so in keeping with the incongruous manner in which they'd met, even though palm trees replaced oaks. But the melodious chirping of crickets and the mysterious scurryings in the shrubs could well have been accompaniment to their love whether the locale was Virginia or Florida.

"Is this what you call getting back to nature?" Les purred as though reading his thoughts.

"Seems appropriate, don't you think? We wanted to that day, remember? It was in your eyes. Besides, I honestly don't think I can wait till we get back upstairs."

He reached for the closure on his slacks, his hands trembling in the process.

Les swallowed hard as he slipped out of the slacks and tossed them aside. Then he turned to face her, proud and confident in hip-hugging black briefs, now strained by his magnificence. She felt the total impact of this man who had taken her common sense, her inhibitions, her rationale and sailed them into the ozone layer while neatly tucking her heart into his back pocket to do with as he would.

Oh, Blaise, I love you, she silently whispered as the warm night breeze bathed her flushed features. *Please let this mean as much to you as it does to me.*

Then, he was beside her, easing his bulk down on the side of the lounge, bracing himself with hands planted on either side of her shoulders.

"You're like something out of a dream," he murmured as he bent over her. "A beautiful erotic dream."

His lips were warm and masterful . . . totally possessive as he covered her mouth in a kiss that left no doubt as to the end result of the fires they were fanning. Strong hands closed on her shoulders, fingers kneading as his kiss deepened, daring her to return his kiss . . . join him in complete abandonment. Willingly, she complied with his silent entreaty, and as their tongues hungrily danced a primitive enactment of the joys to follow, the last of her grasp on propriety fled, leaving only the intense desire to satiate the hunger that had grown out of control since they'd first met.

Reaching up, she clutched him, urging him.

"Lie with me," she softly pleaded. "I want to feel you against me."

Blaise lowered himself until he was stretched out beside her, his long length, with its hot, bare flesh, resting along her side. Les immediately turned facing him, and with a deep moan, she moved closer, wantonly pressing toward him, until only a few scraps of cloth prevented her knowing the ultimate insanity of total union.

"I want you, Blaise," she whispered urgently. "So badly, I want you."

"And you'll have me," he replied. Rising onto his elbow, he rested his bare hand on the curve of her hip, his eyes drifting lazily along the length of her sun-kissed legs. "But not to rush, Angel Eyes."

Warm lips touched her neck, moved to her shoulder as his fingers trailed lower to close over the rise of her hip . . . undulating her . . . pressing and releasing . . . teasing her with the hard pressure of his maleness . . . leisurely taking his time to drive her slowly insane.

Les moaned with impatience, and in answer, he pressed his mouth to the throbbing pulse in her neck, his teeth lightly nipping.

"Right now, I just want to touch you," he murmured. "I've thought of this so many times . . . wanted it to the point of obsession."

And the moan grew louder . . . the want grew stronger as his hand coursed upward, trailing feather light along her torso until he found the firm crescents of her breasts straining above the black lace. Delicately, he traced an invisible pattern over her satiny flesh, dipping into her cleavage, his breath fanning her face as he murmured words she could not understand. Only the exciting intonation of his voice in conjunction with his erotic fingers left no doubt as to his meaning.

"You're speaking in Italian," she accused raggedly, her head sagging back as she writhed in delight. "What are you saying to me?"

"Love words," he whispered. "From a song. And, Leslie, you are a song to me, do you know that?"

And when his mouth moved over her ripe curves in search of the throbbing tip of her breast, Les closed her eyes and eagerly arched toward his mouth.

"Beautiful breasts," he murmured as his lips began sliding whispery smooth over the wet fabric. Instantly her nipples hardened and spidery fingers of delicious want slithered down over her body, accentuating the ache between her legs.

"Oh, Blaise, that feels so good," she moaned, her body writhing beneath his skillful mastery of her senses.

"But this will feel even better," he promised as his fingers found the front clasp on her bra. He unsnapped it and shoved aside the lacy fabric, releasing her creamy curves with their pale brown peaks.

Warm hands caressed her, lifted her, molded her; his thumbs moving across her tips brought a strangled cry to her lips.

"I've never wanted anything like I want you," he whispered, dark eyes, glazed with passion, boring deep into her own as he reached down to urge the scraps of lace from her hips.

"Then love me, Blaise," Les gasped as she trembled beneath his expert caresses on that most intimate portion of her body, so long denied the satisfaction of a caring man's attention.

His hands moved along her inner thighs and then upward once more, slowly and surely drawing her toward insanity.

"Oh, Blaise, you're driving me crazy," she cried out as a delicious tension began building where his fingers touched.

"Touch me," he murmured, reaching for her hand and drawing it down to the front of his briefs. "I want to feel your hands on me."

"Like this?" Les whispered as she cupped her hand over the hard ridge of his desire. "Or like this?"

As she stroked him through the fabric, Blaise throbbed and bit hard on his lower lip to control the urgency of his body. At this rate, it could end so quickly and he didn't want it to end.

"All of the above," he groaned.

The last of her inhibitions vanished as she realized the pleasure she was giving him. Now she wanted only to make him feel as good as he was making her feel with his knowledgeable caresses.

"Take these off," Les urged. She slipped her fingers beneath the tight band and Blaise moved away only long enough to urge his underwear away from his engorged flesh. And then her hands were caressing, stroking, skillfully imitating the act for which they both ached.

"Ah, baby," he moaned, his grip on control slipping. "Much more of that and it's all over."

Reluctantly, he drew her hand away from his rigidity, kissed her palm and then her lips.

"Now's a heck of a time to mention this," he whispered, his voice ragged, his breath coming in short gasps. "But I didn't exactly expect us to—what I mean is, I'm not prepared."

"The calendar couldn't be better. Oh please don't make me wait any longer."

Her words were the keys to the lock around his restraint. Blaise was power unleashed, a storm on the verge of breaking. His lips were hot as they crushed down on hers. His bare flesh was fevered as he moved over her, his hands beneath her hips, raising her legs to cup his hips, urging her into alignment to accept all he had to give.

Les closed her eyes and moaned with ecstatic anticipation.

"No, Leslie, open your eyes," he said hoarsely. "I want us to share this moment."

Wide blue eyes, glazed with passion, locked with his ebony gaze, and when his hardness touched her, her breath caught.

"Now, Blaise," she pleaded, her hands gripping his hips, urging him.

"Oh yes," he groaned. "Now."

With a sigh of relief, he plunged deep . . . filling her.

Her muscles screamed in protest of his invasion, and when he sensed her involuntary withdrawal, Blaise hesitated, his eyes boring deep into her own, silently questioning.

"It's been a long time," she gasped, closing her eyes against her own slightly diminishing passion and clinging to him, reluctant, even in her temporary discomfort, to have him move away. "Just—just give me time."

"I'd never hurt you," he mumbled, trembling with the

power of the need tearing at him that demanded appease-
ment. "Just relax, sweetheart. Just lie still till you're used
to me."

Bending, he sought her lips, silently willing them back
to compliance, and when they parted beneath his, he
strove with reassuring kisses to bring her back to that
euphoric plateau where her body was a writhing invitation.
And when at last he heard her low moan of pleasure, his
hands tightened on her hips and he resumed his slow,
deliberate capture of her senses.

"All right?" he murmured, his voice hoarse, his body
on the verge of exploding from the pressure of denial.

"Oh, Blaise, yes," she cried out as, again, the demon
inside her demanding satisfaction fought to the forefront
of her mind, erasing her momentary reluctance and render-
ing her incapable of but one thought . . . the man who
possessed her so fully and so completely.

Instinctively, she found his driving rhythm, felt his impatient throbs deep within her . . . knew again the volcanic fury of her own desire. She'd wanted before, but never
had every nerve in her body been on fire, screaming out
for more of this captivating man who loved her in a way
she'd never realized she needed. Strong, sure strokes
turned her into his lustful, demanding counterpart . . .
encouraged her to answer his fury with a matching one of
her own. And when she knew she could no longer endure
the sweet agony, his own body tensed in readiness.

"Let go," he gasped as he surged deep into her. "Let
it happen to you."

Needing no more persuasion than the exquisite perfection of his body mated with her own, Les arched and
clung and soared toward the crest. Beneath her hands, his
flesh grew damp; his labored breathing was hot on her
face; his eyes narrowed in ecstasy. Her legs gripped him
until, with a strangled cry of release, they knew the incredible wonder of fulfillment.

*   *   *

Warm tropical night air caressed her bare flesh. The wind murmured softly in the palms, and as she drifted slowly back to reality, Les was filled with wonder. She'd come to him an experienced woman and yet, in his arms, she'd discovered how limited was her knowledge of the true satisfaction of lovemaking. He was perfect . . . they were perfect together. It had to be symbolic. Was there actually that one special man for every woman . . . that one special someone who fit in every sense like the matching piece of a puzzle?

His lips moved against her shoulder and involuntarily her arms tightened around him, drawing his weight even closer to her tired body. Tears burned behind her eyelids and valiantly she fought them away. He'd never understand if she cried. Why should he when she dared not verbalize the reason?

I love him, Les told the dark night that surrounded them. *Simply and truly, I love this man.*

Blaise felt her silent retreat, and rising on his elbows, he peered down into her flushed face. Her blue eyes were a little too glassy; that tremble in her lower lip, telltale evidence of encroaching tears. And he knew her anxiety.

"I hope those are happy tears," he murmured as he stroked the damp hair back from her face.

"They are," she lied.

His lips were warm and almost desperate as they kissed her eyelids, her cheeks and then settled over her mouth.

"Wonderful," he whispered, his hands cradling her face. His thumbs moved tenderly over her lower lip.

"Not bad for a Southern girl?" Her attempts at levity deserved an A for effort even though the concern in his eyes evidenced his lack of belief in her lighthearted state of mind.

"Not bad at all. But then, you and me? I knew it would be like this."

Again, he kissed her. Then, he moved onto his side and drew her tightly against him.

"There's no time like the present to clear up one thing," he murmured as he stroked her damp hair, his fingers feather light. "It'll work out for us, Leslie. You can rest your mind on that."

"You're leaving soon," she reminded him in a soft voice.

"I have to go back some time, whether I want to or not."

"I rest my case."

"But I'll be back," he insisted.

"Great," she exclaimed, shifting her position so as to peer into his eyes. She had to make him believe she had no regrets. After all, she'd walked into this with all faculties intact. Now to face the consequences of falling in love with a man she'd known only four days . . . a man with a life, a world so far from her own.

"Leslie, I'm not the kind of man to take things like this with a grain of salt," he said. "This is real to me and it's important."

What could she say? That she didn't truly believe him? But then, what reason did she have to disbelieve? There was but one thing to do . . . take him at his word and hope for the best.

"I'm hungry," she exclaimed.

For a second, his eyes clouded. Then, like sun breaking through a gray cloud, he smiled and hugged her close.

"And here I thought I did a fair job of satisfying you," he growled.

"Oh, rest assured you did and quite nicely, too." Her arm encircled his neck to bring his lips down to hers. "But, Hollander, there's satisfaction and then there's a cheeseburger with all the trimmings."

His eyes were slumberous on her face when the kiss ended. He cupped her breast in his hand while the other held her against his growing need.

"And even better, there's satisfaction and a little more satisfaction and then a cheeseburger. Don't you agree?"

"Oh, I agree with you one hundred percent," Les whispered huskily.

"You could take some time off and come to Pennsylvania with me."

"You know I can't do that. I have Aunt Josie to care for."

"She's welcome to come along. I have two bedrooms."

"Blaise, it's preposterous and you know it. I have a business, I have that property—"

"You also have me and that's a tall package."

"Do I?"

"Don't you?"

"Make love to me, Blaise."

"The subject isn't closed that easy."

"Then temporarily shelve it. I want you."

"You're insatiable, Angel Eyes."

"I had an incredible teacher."

SEVEN

Radiant morning sunshine spilled into the bedroom. Les awakened slowly and lay for a moment acclimating herself to the strange but plush surroundings. Then stretching leisurely, she grimaced as a twinge of pain from sore muscles reminded her of the previous hours in Blaise's arms.

Blaise had laughed at her rather archaic determination that they would not share the same bedroom. And Les knew, had there been no likelihood of running into Brandon when she opened the door next morning, she'd gladly have slept in Blaise's arms.

In the lavish bath, she splashed cold water on her face, chancing only a cursory glance at her love-swollen lips. Then she pulled on the black undies, retrieved her robe, and slipped quietly from her room.

The pool basked in the awakening morning and chirping birds greeted her from the lush shrubbery. A lizard roused from its nap in the sunshine and scurried into a bed of daylilies as Les approached. She tossed off her robe and then dove deep into the aquamarine depths of the shimmering water.

Blaise watched from the window, having heard her rise in the room next to his. Elation filled his heart as he followed her lithe movements from one end of the pool to the other and then back again. Memories of her in his arms immediately filled his head. Want flooded into his groin. She had been everything he could possibly want in a woman. In her arms, he'd known a completion heretofore lacking in his life. He'd miss her desperately when he returned to Pennsylvania.

But for now? Leslie and all her magnetism were but a few seconds away. Turning from the window, he grabbed his slacks, draped them over his arm, and then secured a towel from the bath. He had plenty of time to luxuriate in the perfection of their new relationship before he would settle her down with the rough figures he'd drawn up after tucking her into bed. That he'd had little sleep was not a problem. A man in love didn't need sleep.

"Good morning."

Les turned at the sound of his voice, swam to the end of the pool, and then grabbed for the tile edging. Reaching up, she shaded her eyes for that first glimpse of the man who'd stolen in and out of her restless dreams throughout what had remained of the night. There'd been no time to consider her response to him this morning, and as he casually tossed aside his slacks and towel and started for the pool, her response was automatic. Her heartbeat escalated; her mouth grew dry; the smile on her lips felt frozen in place as she contemplated the smooth play of muscles as he dove into the water.

"Like having your own little piece of paradise," he gasped when he surfaced next to her. His arms were around her immediately and his fevered lips tasted of chlorine and mouthwash, a combination Les would never have considered aphrodisiac . . . until this moment. Molded to his hard, wet body, she moaned softly as a groundswell of desire swept her from head to feet, eradicating everything but the impatient need to love him again . . . be loved by him.

"I want you," he murmured against her mouth. His

hands coursed slippery smooth along her back and down to grip her buttocks, fingers digging into her taut flesh. "Oh brother, do I want you."

"And if I complain?" she teased in a breathless voice. Her hands curled over his shoulders, kneading the thick muscles she found there; her hips swiveled against him for a more perfect alignment with the eager evidence of his words.

"You won't I hope," he growled as he reached for the clasp on her bra.

In seconds, his hands had divested her of the scant clothing. His dark eyes smoldered as he freed his body of yet another pair of skimpy underwear.

"I woke up aching for you," he murmured as his hands cupped her breasts, teasing the peaks to erection. "You could get to be a delicious habit, you know?"

"No, I don't know," she whispered as excitement raced hot through her veins. Wantonly, she arched her back, pressing her breasts tighter into his possessive palms. Erotic shivers coursed over her. "Why don't you show me, big man?"

Then with a groan of excruciating want only partially smothered by his lips against her mouth, he urged her legs around him until, once more, she was filled with his demanding strength.

Their passion was swift and strong . . . a savage outburst of rekindled hunger . . . a fierce struggle for the last vestige of exquisite torture. And when they again reached that gasping crescendo and plunged headlong into the momentary insanity of total bliss, both were trembling from head to toe.

Long after the storm had abated, Blaise held her tightly against him, her face buried into the curve of his shoulder while the dual rhythm of their heartbeats gradually returned to normal.

For Les, it was again the realization of total surrender. Never had she known such an incredible ache for fulfillment; never had she known such complete satiety. Her arms tightened as a flood of tangled emotions tore through her, and with trembling hands, she cupped his face and took his lips beneath her own.

"I know," he whispered when he tasted the tears on her mouth. "Oh Leslie, I know."

Lifting her in his arms, he carried her to the pool steps and up out of the water. Then lowering her to a chaise lounge, he retrieved her robe and draped it around her.

In awed silence, she watched as he dove back into the pool, gathered up their clothing, and tossed them up over the side.

"Conceal the evidence in case Brandon walks up," Blaise teased as he returned to her side. His lashes were spiked with water, his hair a satiny cap over his head, and in his nudity, he was the most perfect specimen of masculinity Les had ever seen in her life. The gorgeous man was carved in bronze, molded with hard ridges and seductive shadows, and graced with the ability to drive her beyond the limits of her sanity.

Blaise wrapped his towel around his middle, raked his fingers through his hair, and then dragged a chair to her side.

"Now, Angel Eyes, explain that look on your face," he ordered in a tender voice as he leaned forward, elbows resting on his knees.

"There's no look," Les defended as she silently willed her emotions to return to normalcy; entreated him not to recognize what she knew to be so obvious in her eyes. She loved him. Simply and completely loved this man who, in memory alone, would forever overshadow whoever might cross her path in the future.

"I just think we need to talk," Les stated as she raised her chin and fought back the hot sting of tears at the thought of his leaving her.

"Since when has that been a problem?" Blaise teased, and reaching over, he cupped the back of her head in his hand, pulled her forward, and kissed her firmly. "Conversationally and in a lot of other ways, you and I are about as compatible as they come. And whatever it is you're thinking that's making you sad, forget it. What's between us should make you as happy as I am."

"I don't regret making love with you, Blaise," Les whispered around the lump in her throat. "And I'm not sad at all. This has been a wonderful trip—"

"Has been?" he repeated, his eyes twinkling with mirth. "Why, lady, it isn't over yet. Is that all that's on your mind?"

How could she tell him the reason for her depression without sounding poetic and utterly juvenile? She was a grown woman. It was now or never to begin acting like one. She'd told herself earlier in the relationship to roll with the flow. Well, she'd rolled. Now it was a little late for regret.

Les sighed deeply and then fastened a smile on her face.

"Actually, I think it might be a good idea if you and I put on some clothes before Brandon shows up," she said lightly.

If only your words are true, Les thought as she followed him back into the inn and up the winding stairs to the second floor. Once inside his room, Blaise closed the door with his bare foot and then busied himself hanging their wet clothing on the shower rod in the bathroom.

"How about a nice hot cup of coffee to put you in the mood for the day?" he suggested as he slipped his hands beneath the collar of her robe and gently massaged the tight muscles in the back of her neck.

Les nodded, and tilting her head back, she welcomed the delicious confidence of his warm mouth . . . welcomed the momentary assurance that what they shared was not a fleeting thing . . . and cursed the despair that threatened to return when he released her.

"I'll even serve it to you in bed," he murmured as he tugged aside the rumpled blankets. "Here. Crawl in."

Les giggled with compliance, and when she was settled against pillows fraught with his masculine fragrance, he bent, kissed her, and then left the room.

I know what she's thinking and I have no concrete answers, Blaise thought as he made his way to the kitchen. *I only know I've found her and, dammit, I'm not letting her go. But how do I say that to her?*

Blaise smiled as he fiddled with the coffeemaker. Feeling ridiculously adolescent and practically giddy with his newfound happiness, he leaned across the breakfast bar and pulled the house phone toward him. He punched out the three digits for the room in which he'd left her and, moments later, he heard her breathy, surprised voice.

"I'm not letting you go. You hear that, Angel Eyes?" Then, laughing softly at his juvenile actions, he replaced the receiver.

In no time at all, the effects of the hot coffee coursed over her. Tension eased from her muscles. The chill dissipated from around her heart, and soon, they were curled against a bank of pillows, his arm draped around her shoulders, his hand resting proprietarily on the warm cushion of her breast. Drowsy from unaccustomed exertion and dizzy with his nearness, Les listened to his rich, husky voice as he told her how he'd taken over Hollander & Associates after his father's death.

"What about your mother?" Les asked, tilting her head back to gaze up at him . . . watch the movement of his lips as he spoke . . . watch the slight smile curve his sensuous mouth . . . watch the man she loved.

"We lost her when I was a kid," Blaise replied. Then he drank the last of his coffee and placed the cup on the nightstand. "And that's enough history," he whispered as he rolled onto his side and curled her close to him, his hands moving soft as a whisper over her back, urging her against the hard planes of his body. Warm, sensuous lips moved over hers, and for a long, spellbinding moment,

Les knew once more the heady perfection of his strong, dominant kiss.

Against her breast, his heartbeat escalated, and when he finally gazed down into her eyes, she saw the glint of rekindled desire . . . felt his strong throb.

"You make me feel like a love-starved kid, Leslie," he murmured huskily. "All the way to the marrow of my bones."

"And other parts as well," Les teased as she reached down and wrapped her fingers around his fullness, her lips pressed to the crisp, curling hair on his hard chest.

"And you do that so nicely," he breathed, closing his eyes, and for a long moment, he gave himself over to the exquisite sensations her touch inspired, until Blaise knew his body could not stand such erotic torture without a complete loss of control.

With a groan of restless need, Blaise released himself from her grasp, and moved her onto her back. With infinite patience and whispered words of erotic encouragement, he began to work his own magic. Warm hands caressed and kneaded her awakening body. His wet, moist mouth captured and teased her nipples to tingling erection. Knowledgeable, caring fingers found her secrets and coaxed her toward that earth-shattering plateau.

"Oh, Blaise, please—" Les cried out as she struggled to capture his hand.

"No," he murmured, his lips infinitely tender as they brushed hers. "Let me do this for you. Let me watch your face."

Then with a harsh cry of abandonment, she arched toward his hand, welcoming the exquisite torture of his caresses, and Blaise felt a rush of need so strong, it took all his control to refrain from plunging into her warm depths and knowing, again, the gratification of their complete union.

Bending, he took her nipple into his mouth, urging his mind away from his throbbing impatience. Mentally, he forced himself out of the moment . . . willed himself to recede until he'd taken her over the edge in so intimate a manner.

"Oh, Blaise, come into me," Les cried out, and raising his head, he visually feasted on her flushed expression, the glaze of raw hunger in her eyes, the quivering lips that sobbed his name as no woman had ever done before.

Suddenly, the storm was upon him once more and, with a groan of surrender, he moved over her.

"Say it again," he urged as he tentatively eased himself against the junction of her thighs.

"Come into me," she demanded, her wide eyes intent on his face.

"Like this?" Blaise eased forward, then hesitated.

Instinctively, Les arched, her breath coming in short gasps, her nails digging into his back.

"Or like this?"

With a groan of surrender, Blaise buried himself in her warm, moist offering.

"Just a friend, huh?" Brandon teased as he watched his father's unwavering attention to the tall, slender blonde in the lavender sundress who'd just excused herself from the table to go wash her hands. They'd just finished a scrumptious buffet brunch at a hotel nearby.

Blaise glanced at his son and then grinned sheepishly as he carefully folded his napkin and laid it beside his plate.

"Since when did you get so curious about my personal life?" he asked.

"Since it looks like my father might be onto something nice here," Brandon replied. He reached for his wallet and extracted some bills. "Of course, the fireworks between you two will probably rival the Fourth of July. I don't believe I've ever met a more opinionated woman and we won't even talk about your hard head, General."

"She's independent, all right," Blaise agreed, with a

fond sigh. "And please, don't delude yourself into believing you can tell her what to do about anything."

Brandon laid the money atop the check and then leaned back in his chair to finish his coffee.

"What's the financial problem with her?"

Blaise told him. Brandon frowned.

"You don't think she's after your—"

"Are you kidding me?" Blaise scoffed. "I've offered it. She all but slapped my hands. But I do wish she'd take a little advice instead of being so hell-bent on handling everything by herself."

"Sounds familiar," Brandon said with a knowing wink. "You aren't exactly pliant yourself in that department."

Blaise glanced up as Les made her way back to the table. *A woman who's been thoroughly loved*, he found himself thinking as he noted the glow in her face as she sat down. He reached beneath the table and found her hand. When her fingers returned his light squeeze, Blaise felt a rebirth of need for her. How long had it been since he'd been this hungry for a woman? It was early afternoon and already he was contemplating the night ahead . . . a night when there would be no worry of Brandon's precipitate return to the inn. Brandon was leaving soon for a rendezvous of his own.

"Ready to see Busch Gardens?" Blaise asked.

"Sure," Les replied, her eyes warm on his face. *Anything, anywhere, anytime*, she added silently. *Just as long as you're a part of it.*

"You two have fun," Brandon said when they were in the parking lot. "Be seeing you again, Les."

"You bet," she assured him, but the twinge of doubt threatened to overcloud her happiness. *I won't be negative about this*, Les reminded herself as she slid into the front seat of Blaise's rental car. *I walked into this, eyes open.*

"I adore that dress," Blaise murmured when, inside the car, he reached to pull her close. One finger toyed lazily with the tiny straps holding the bodice up over her bare breasts. Possessively, he trailed his finger along one warm curve and hesitated at her cleavage, his eyes hot on her face.

"And even more, I like the lack of that dress," he whispered, and bending, he pressed his lips on the spot his fingertip had found.

Les felt the warm weakening in the pit of her stomach, and closing her eyes, she inhaled deeply. How easily he could arouse her. How completely he could satisfy that arousal. And how hungry she was for more.

His lips on hers were hard and demanding; his hands gripped her shoulders. His fire was as hot as her own.

"We don't have to go to Busch Gardens," Les gasped.

"No, we don't," Blaise groaned against her mouth. "But we do have to stop this or I'm gonna be guilty of making love to you right here in the front seat of this car."

Reluctantly, he released her, and for a long moment, he stared deep into her glazed eyes.

"You've bewitched me, woman," he finally growled, and turning, he started the car's engine.

Don't I wish, Les thought with a sinking in the pit of her stomach as she again recalled the limited time before they must part company. For how long, she had no way of knowing, and fear would keep her from asking when the time came to tell him good-bye. The want on his face was a mirror of her own. In her peripheral vision, she drank in his handsome features now set with concentration as he maneuvered out of the parking lot. Broad shoulders moved easily beneath his pale gray cotton shirt . . . shoulders plenty broad enough for her truck load of responsibilities.

But then, Les knew she could never lean on him . . . or anyone else. It simply wasn't her nature. For all her life, this had been a source of pride. Now it was cause for confusion.

Once inside the gates of Tampa's famed brewery theme

park, Les gave herself over to the visual delights to be had on every turn. Tropical plants and brilliant flowers flanked paths that wandered beneath lush foliage. Exotic and some not so exotic birds called out to their leisurely progress as they wandered.

At a boutique featuring California-styled sportswear, Blaise fondled a daringly brief black bikini, a wicked gleam in his eyes.

"Sixty dollars for that?" Les exclaimed.

"Beats a bra and panties, doesn't it?" he whispered as he jerked it from the rack and then went in search of a pair of men's trunks. Les urged him to buy white ones.

"Shows off your tan," she declared, already envisioning that magnificent body in those skimpy swim trunks.

Back out in the sunshine, a passing park photographer coaxed them to have their picture made. The kiss Blaise gave her for posterity set her heart racing and blood coursing into her cheeks.

Just before they boarded the train that would take them to view the wild animals in their natural habitats, Blaise suggested they leave.

Les couldn't be happier. She'd had enough of people and lines and the joviality of the park. She wanted peace and quiet and the sun on her back and Blaise in her arms. She wanted meaningful time and words she could remember when he was gone.

At the inn, Les left Blaise to concoct a pitcher of margaritas and she went to change into the suit he'd purchased. As she eyed her reflection in the mirror, she sensed skepticism. No, it wasn't much briefer than the bra and panties he'd already seen her wear. But the suit did something for her slender curves underwear could not do.

The dark gleam in his eyes when she joined him poolside said so. The hard crush of his body when he stood to pull her into his arms said even more.

"I can't get enough of you," he whispered against her

lips as his hands cupped her backside, bringing her tightly in line with his firm maleness.

"You don't hear a lot of objections, do you?" Les murmured, and when his tongue delved deeply into her mouth, she savored his mastery . . . savored the taste of him. Desire hummed through her veins . . . love blossomed fuller in her heart. Fear of losing him took a backseat to the beauty of the moment.

Suddenly, he released her and urged her away from his inflamed body. Romancing this beautiful woman in this tropical setting was nice, he thought as he read the disappointment in her eyes. But there comes a time when a man wants a clear picture in his mind as to the next plateau. He'd brought her here for a reason. It was time to see just how much headway he was making.

"Leslie, let's talk," he said as he urged her toward an umbrella'd table on which he'd placed the drink tray.

His expression was solemn as he took the chair across from her. In response, apprehension crawled in her gut. The fear returned.

Blaise filled two glasses and urged one in her direction. He took a sip of the icy drink and then leaned back in his chair, the drink balanced on his knee.

"How did you end up with all the problems of River's Edge on your shoulders?" he asked. "Where does your mother fit into all this?"

"She doesn't," Les replied, her eyes intent on his face. "Dad borrowed money when they divorced and bought out her fifty percent. When he died, I inherited. What's so complicated about that?"

"No insurance, no nothing in case of hard times," Blaise stated.

"His insurance took care of the funeral," Les said. Her eyes narrowed; she could feel annoyance growing in her middle. "I really don't care to talk about all this, Blaise," she added.

"I know," he said with a scowl. "It's none of my business, but I'm worried about you, woman."

"Don't be."

"Oh, for Pete's sake," Blaise exclaimed. He reached over and placed the glass on the table. Cool liquid sloshed over his hand. Taking his time, he retrieved a cocktail napkin and dabbed at it.

"Blaise, why are you getting so angry?" Les asked in surprise.

"I'm not. I'm frustrated," he returned. "And your Aunt Josie? Is she your mother's sister?"

"No, she's a Braddock and—"

"You support her now," Blaise finished.

"Mother helps."

"You can't make it like this, Leslie," Blaise stated flatly, his ebony eyes boring into her own as though willing her to understand without this turning into an argument. "It's time to consider an alternative."

Les's lips tightened. Slowly, she replaced her drink on the table, settled back in the chair, and folded her arms over her breasts.

"I've done just fine long before you walked into the picture," she reminded him. "And if this is another pitch for ownership of River's Edge, I might also remind you it's wasted effort."

"I don't want your damned property," he declared in exasperation. "I want to help you hang on to it. I care for you, Leslie, and I care what happens to your home."

For a long moment, Les stared at him. Exactly what had started this tirade? They'd been having such a good time and all of a sudden he's jumped on the soapbox.

"Shall I ask the questions one by one or would you rather I settle back and let you spit it all out?" Les asked, carefully enunciating each word in an effort to control her rising anger, born from an upsurge of disappointment. It was as if the sun seemed to have gone behind a cloud, leaving the air chilled.

"Renovate River's Edge and open it as a bed and breakfast inn," Blaise said. "You've already admitted it's an idea worth considering. But you don't have forever to make a decision. If the bank forecloses on you, it'll be too late to weigh your options."

"Lovely idea," Les exclaimed with forced enthusiasm. "On what? My looks?"

For a second, his eyes softened and a hesitant smile curved his mouth.

"You probably could, but that's not what I have in mind," he murmured.

"What do you have in mind?" she demanded.

"I'll back you financially," he said.

Les stared at him in disbelief. How many times did she have to tell the man she didn't want his money?

"Thanks but no thanks," Les replied tightly. "Your idea has merit. But it's up to me to figure out the how-to's."

Blaise leaped to his feet, frustration tearing at his gut.

"Why do you have to be so damned independent?" he demanded. "I have plenty of money, plenty of time to help you, and all the willingness in the world. What's your problem, Leslie?"

Les leaped to her feet, hands jammed against her hips as she glared at him across the table.

"If it was your intention to ruin a lovely day, you've accomplished your mission, Blaise. And as for my independence, I'd have been up the creek without a paddle if I hadn't had the ability to think for myself. Why couldn't we have had a lovely little affair and kept personal problems out of the picture?"

"Because I told you from the beginning, lovely little affairs aren't my speed," he told her flatly.

"Oh, really?" Les demanded. "Well, what have we got going here, Hollander? A one-man crusade to save the world?"

"No, not the world. Just you," he said quietly, and

folding his thick arms across his chest, he tilted his head to one side as he contemplated her angry face. "Does that tell you something, Braddock?"

"Yes," Les retorted. "It tells me you really love running the show. Your show, my show, and everybody else's too. Well, I don't operate that way."

"Why does being dependent scare you so badly?" he demanded.

"Being weak scares me," Les replied. She turned and grabbed her towel from the chair. "If you'll excuse me, I think I've had enough of the pool."

Long after she'd gone inside, Blaise sat in the shade of the umbrella, his thoughts intent on her last statement. So that was behind the steel-woman facade. So simple. At an age when she should have been experimenting with lipstick and fawning for some adolescent kid, Leslie had been forced into the position of leading a weak father around by the nose. And then she'd married a man even weaker and the end result was a woman, cushiony soft on the inside, wearing a cast-iron shield of self-sufficiency. Failure scared the hell out of her. In her eyes, relying on another person was admitting failure.

"Stupid philosophy," Blaise growled as he eyed the condensation puddled around the base of his untouched drink.

Well, he had his work cut out for him. If he wanted Leslie, he simply had to be stronger than she was. *Not an easy feat*, he mused as he stood and piled their glasses back onto the tray. *But she's worth it.*

Blaise left her to her own devices for a while longer as he showered and changed into soft white slacks and a matching pullover. As he laced his sneakers, he listened for sounds from the room next to his. But no sounds were forthcoming.

A quick inspection of the house revealed its emptiness, and finally, he wandered out onto the wide screened porch.

Leslie reclined in a chaise lounge, her eyes closed. They did not open when she heard him approach.

"You look nice and fresh," he said as he lowered himself into a chair opposite her.

"The Jacuzzi was heavenly," she murmured.

Blaise took his time appraising her clingy black tube top and the seductive curve of calves revealed by her short white skirt. She'd coiled her hair on the crown of her head and the breeze through the screen had tugged enticing tendrils down onto her neck. Desire moved in his groin and he was on his feet, bending over her.

His minty breath was warm on her face as his lips drew nearer. Les made no move to encourage or discourage the firm pressure of his mouth. Instead, she remained inert, secretly savoring the delicious aroma of his after-shave, the delicate fragrance of soap, and the incredible heat emanating from his kiss. Inwardly, she reprimanded her earlier anger, scolded that part of her that demanded she respond in kind when someone tried to play the heavy, and browbeat herself for the love she'd been so sure would not erupt should she allow herself a few days in his company. Insane that she should ever have believed that. Blaise was all a woman could want or need. Blaise was the answer for the ache that had lain in her soul for so many years. And Blaise was now kissing her as though he could not satiate himself with the taste of her.

"Oh, Blaise," she moaned, and eagerly, she wrapped her arms around his broad shoulders and allowed him to draw her from the chair to mold her tightly to his awakening body.

"Why do you have to be so pigheaded?" she gasped as his hands sought the firm flesh beneath her top, urged her nipples to tingling erections, incited that volcanic disturbance deep in her loins.

"And why can't you just let me worry—"

"Why can't you stop talking for a few minutes?" he murmured against her mouth and then his tongue was delving deeply into her warmth, urging her participation. Gladly, she gave it until her head was reeling and strength fled her knees and all her anger dissolved beneath a cloud of feverish desire for him.

His rigidity probed at her and she arched toward it, wanting the delicious pressure that made her quiver inside . . . burn inside . . . ache for fulfillment. His hands were bold on her backside, cupping and squeezing and urging the short skirt higher until his hot hands encountered banded silk. His fingers slipped beneath the elastic of her panties and he sighed with pleasure as he kneaded her flesh, rocked her against his hardness. He pushed the panties lower.

"I never—thought—a—person—could—oh, damn, Blaise," Les stammered as she felt herself in danger of achieving that crescendo of delight, precipitated by the hard thrust of his maleness exactly where she needed it most.

Eager hands wormed between their straining bodies, found his zipper, released it, and, with his help, released him. The panties slid down to her ankles, and impatiently, Les kicked them aside.

Strong hands gripped her waist, lifting her. Ebony eyes burned deep into her own. His breath was hot and ragged as he silently conveyed his intention. Inhibition dissolved and silently she nodded.

Blaise gasped with almost uncontrollable pleasure as her long, bare legs encircled his waist, her warm, womanly flesh brushing and teasing. Leaning back, he braced his own legs and urged her assistance in completing the union.

And when he finally shoved himself deep into her grasping body, Blaise groaned deep in his chest and then bit hard on his lower lip to delay his release. Her moist warmth encompassed him; eagerly she rode him, bucking and urging him with a fever that had not been in their prior lovemaking.

He felt her quiver start deep and Blaise knew there was

no longer a need for restraint. Savagely, he thrust into her, his lips devouring her gasping mouth, and when the explosion came, he filled her with the last vestige of pent-up need waiting deep in his soul.

They lay on a pile of cushions before the fireplace. Empty cartons from the Chinese food he'd ordered bedecked a TV tray beside them. On the hearth, a small fire crackled, its blaze teasing the darkness in the room with wavering shadows and turning the wine in their glasses to burning amber.

Les wore his robe. Blaise was content with those sinfully brief undies that continually drew her eyes like a magnet to his magnificence.

"I love it here, Blaise," she murmured as she idly traced the hard muscles defining his broad chest.

He was stretched out beside her, propped on one elbow, one hand lying on her stomach. His eyes were fixed unseeingly on the dancing fire. The glow from the flames warmed his sharp features, accentuated his wonderful mouth, and Les knew she would never love him more than she did at this precise moment. The knowledge both thrilled and frightened her. That he felt something for her, Les was certain. Just what it was, she wasn't certain. But not by nature a negative person, Les knew she would bide her time and believe in the best.

"What are you thinking about?" she asked softly, her fingernails lightly grazing his firm stomach.

"Riverboats," he replied, his gaze still fixed on the fire. "I always wanted to live on one."

"Aren't there rivers in Pennsylvania?"

Blaise made no reply. A slight smile curved his mouth. Les could have sworn at that moment there was a devilish gleam in his eyes.

"Did you hear me?" she teased, reaching up and turning his head as though impatient for his full attention.

"I heard you," Blaise murmured and, bending, he

kissed her tenderly. "And yes, sweetheart, there are rivers in Pennsylvania. But not behind my apartment."

Then he sighed happily. "You're going to love River's Edge when you get it fixed, Leslie."

"I love it now," she murmured. "Even if I can't see me lying on the floor in a den like this," she added playfully as she ran her fingers up into his tousled hair.

His eyes glittered with excitement. "So do we get started?"

Les smiled slightly and removed her hand from his hair.

"Blaise, I thought I made it clear I don't want your help."

"Then find someone else to help you, but get moving on this."

"Let me speak to Mother," she hedged. Inwardly, she doubted she would. She'd never asked her mother for anything. Not even after the divorce when life was hard for a lonely fourteen-year-old girl with a father contented to rest his load on her shoulders. Les had managed without the maternal side of parental assistance for so long, it would be difficult to reach out for help now. She wasn't certain how Sherry would react to the unexpected. She wasn't certain she had the courage to find out.

"Who knows?" Les mused. "She might be interested in another hobby besides griping and shopping."

"You don't want my help?" Blaise asked. Disappointment was obvious on his face.

"Oh, I'll probably need you to hold a ladder or something," Les teased. "But money, no. But thanks anyway, Blaise."

She grew thoughtful.

"Do you really believe it'll work?" she asked. "River's Edge a bed and breakfast inn?"

"Of course," he exclaimed, pushing himself into a sitting position. "You have an even better area than we have here. All you need are good accommodations, good advertising, and a good chef in the kitchen. Can Aunt Josie cook?''

"Sure, but I wouldn't expect—"

"You should," Blaise interrupted, excitement dancing in his dark eyes. "She'd love it."

"I wouldn't put that kind of responsibility on her," Les argued. She sat up and smoothed back her tangled hair.

"Why not? You need all the help you can get and I really think you might underestimate your little aunt. She appears to me as someone who's been so sheltered, she's never been given the opportunity to exercise her own abilities. You'd be doing her a great favor, Leslie."

Les laughed with uncertainty.

"I don't know, Blaise," she said as she fiddled with the ends of the robe's tie belt.

"I do," he replied emphatically.

"Yes, I know," Les exclaimed in mock exasperation. "You seem to know just about everything, don't you, Blaise?"

At this, he frowned, and reaching out, he pulled her into his arms.

"Not quite," he murmured against her mouth. "But I'm learning."

EIGHT

It was the most incredible feeling she'd ever experienced in her life. Struggling up from deep sleep with her body aflame, Les moaned as one in the throes of sweet pain.

His tongue fluttered on her wet, tingling nipple as his hands cupped her breasts. Against her hip, she could feel the warm pressure of his arousal. His breathing was deep and fast.

His mouth moved to her other breast and Les laced her fingers in his hair, her body arching eagerly.

"Like that, huh?" he whispered huskily. Hands slid down, thumbs trailing lazily along her sides. His mouth continued the painstakingly slow exploration of her nipples.

"I'd have to be made of granite not to," Les breathed.

"You taste good," he mumbled against her flesh.

"I'm on fire," she cried out.

"Then let's make it burn hotter," he growled.

Les writhed with fiery impatience as his mouth moved from her breasts to taste the satiny flesh on her rib cage. Nails dug into his back but the pain was nothing compared to the agony of wanting her. Blaise closed his eyes and willed patience into his aching body. But beneath his touch

. . . beneath his questing mouth, she was a woman about to come undone . . . a woman losing herself in the magic of his giving. It thrilled him to the marrow of his bones to hear her sighs of delight, to feel the quiver in her taut muscles, to know how easily he could bring her to such heights.

His fingers moved lower, lingering on her belly button and then dipping still lower until he found her damp and ready for him. Lips moved to replace questing fingertips, and when he pressed his mouth to her most secret sector, Les gasped out against her own torrid reaction to such a delicious sensation. No one had ever made love to her in such an all-encompassing manner.

Les closed her eyes tightly, her hands gripping his shoulders, her body aching for fulfillment while her selfless mind urged her to wait and share his pleasure.

"No," Blaise murmured as he felt her struggle to withdraw. "I want to drive you crazy with my love."

Lost out there somewhere beyond reality, Les gave herself to him . . . opened all sensations to experience him . . . let go completely. Muscles tensed in readiness, contractions started slow and built to a crescendo, and in the midst of her delirium, when her whole body was on the verge of the most dynamic explosion of her life, Les sobbed out the feelings in her heart.

His body was slick with perspiration as he slid up over her.

"Oh Blaise," she murmured as she parted her legs, welcoming him inside. When he slid deep into her waiting tenderness, she wrapped legs and arms around him, drawing him tightly to her.

His thrusts were long and deep and incredibly slow. His eyes burned down into her own. His breath was hot and ragged.

And when she arched up to meet his lunges, his lips curled back from his beautiful white teeth and a thrill of raw power washed over her as she saw the look of exquisite enjoyment contorting his features.

Beneath her hands she felt his muscles grow taut, and gripping him tightly within her, she silently urged him toward fulfillment.

"My sweet Leslie," he gasped, and then with one last powerful thrust, his hot wetness filled her.

Slowly, still tingling in the aftermath of complete satiety, Blaise rose on his elbows. His lips were salty with perspiration. His kiss was slow and tender and, oh, so wonderful.

"I'm too old for this," he groaned as he buried his face in the damp curve of her neck.

"You'll never prove it by me."

Her arms, her legs were still looped around his broad back and involuntarily they tightened. She kissed the side of his head, nipped gently on his earlobe, and then held him gently. A few moments later, she heard his soft, even breathing and only then did Les lower her legs to the bed, close her eyes, and rest in the secure warmth of his weight bearing her down.

She awoke to the fragrance of hot coffee and a gentle hand smoothing the tousled hair from her brow. Opening her eyes, Les was instantly bathed in the contentment radiating from the handsome face of the man who had eased himself down beside her on the bed.

"I didn't even hear you get up," Les murmured, her voice husky with sleep.

"I didn't intend you to," Blaise replied, and reaching over, he lifted the tiny bud vase. "Brought you something."

A miniature rose seemed to greet her with its blood red petals still moist with dew. Les reached out and touched the lovely flower and then raised her eyes to his beaming expression.

"Thank you," she whispered around the constriction in her throat. No man had ever given her a rose in bed. But then, no man had ever brought her morning coffee either.

Taylor didn't even drink the stuff and Tony had been prone to asking her to serve him.

"You have till the fiftieth of July to stop spoiling me like this," Les murmured as she laid her palm against his smoothly shaven cheek.

"A beautiful woman should be spoiled," he replied. Turning his head, he kissed her hand and then reached over for her mug of coffee. "Drink up and then I have some figures I want to show you."

"Figures on what?" Les asked. She plumped her pillows high on the headboard and then pushed herself upright. Sunshine spilled through the open window, warming her shoulders, bared as the sheet fell away. Les reached to lift it back into position, but Blaise's hand stopped her.

"I can't think of a more inviting sight while I have my coffee," he drawled as his hand cupped around her fullness. Bending, he planted warm kisses on her nipple, immediately encouraging it to stiffen.

"You keep that up," Les murmured, "and you'll be drinking cold coffee, Mr. Sexy Eyes."

"You think I have sexy eyes?" he asked as he raised his head to peer at her.

"Of course," Les replied. "And don't tell me you haven't heard it before."

Blaise grinned sheepishly and pressed her cup into her hand.

"Okay, can I tell you it hasn't meant anything for quite a long time?"

"You may." She took a sip of the coffee and then asked, "What figures?"

"Yours," he growled and, bending, he kissed her breast before continuing. "Seriously, Leslie, I've worked up a financial plan for River's Edge."

Les frowned at him over the rim of her cup.

"You object?" he asked.

"You really do believe in advancing the action, don't you?" Les asked. She knew her annoyance was childish, but his take-charge attitude had a way of grating on the nerves sometimes.

"Yes, I do," he admitted, a frown creasing his forehead. "And that goes against your grain, doesn't it?"

"Just a bit." Les sipped again from the cup and told herself that it was his nature to lead and direct just as it was her nature automatically to challenge leadership.

"Well, get used to it, Angel Eyes," he murmured as he bent and kissed the tip of her nose. "Oh babe, you look gorgeous with the sun turning your hair to silver like that."

"Here we go with the compliments again to cover an awkward moment," Les teased.

"There's no awkward moment," he told her honestly as he again reached for his coffee cup. "I'm simply anxious to get you on the road to financial independence."

"Suppose I'm not ready to get started?" Les asked curtly.

"You don't have much choice," Blaise reminded her. Then his eyes narrowed as he contemplated her tight expression.

"What are you afraid of, Leslie?"

"I've never feared anything in my life," she exclaimed.

"Never? As in past tense?" he challenged. "What about the present?"

Before she could reply, Blaise covered her mouth with a possessive kiss and then rose from the bed.

"Get moving, gorgeous. I can't wait to show you what I've drawn up."

There's no reason to feel sad, Les told herself as she coiled the electric cord around the base of her blow-dryer and then shoved it into her suitcase. *You've had a wonderful time, you ninny. You're in love. You're happy even if you are a little apprehensive. And aren't you convinced that what you have going here is much more than a vacation romance?*

So the weekend's over. You have the rest of your life and there is good indication that life includes Blaise. Somehow, you'll work out the distance, the diversified responsibilities, his tendency to domineer. He said it would work out, didn't he? Has he lied to you yet?

Les tossed in the rest of her clothing and then zipped the bag closed. She was just lifting it from the bed when the phone on the nightstand jangled.

For a moment, she stared at it. Then she remembered that cute little phone call from Blaise when he was only down in the kitchen.

With a smile on her face, she laid the suitcase back on the bed and then picked up the receiver.

Les felt the sick pull of dread the moment she heard her mother's voice.

"Okay, what's wrong?" she demanded as she sank down on the side of the bed, one finger coiling and uncoiling the phone cord.

"You know I wouldn't call you unless it was an emergency," Sherry said quietly.

"Yes, I know that, Mother. What's wrong?"

"Well, I just thought you ought to know a little something about that man you're with."

The sick pull of dread became a dull ache.

"Unless, of course, you already know this," Sherry went on.

"Mother! Will you please tell me what's wrong?" Les demanded. Her heart was now knocking against her breastbone.

"You've been bought," Sherry said. "Ben called just now from the bank and said to tell you Hollander & Associates has purchased your loan and you'll be contacted in a few days as to the repayment procedure."

The information went down like ice cubes, cold and solid, and settled painfully where, only moments earlier, happiness and luminous hopes for the future had dwelled.

"You're sure?" Les asked pointlessly. Of course her

mother was sure! She might be a lot of things, but Sherry Weston was not confused!

"Ben said if you have any questions, just give him a call," Sherry told her in a voice filled with commiseration. Then she sighed heavily. "Les, I'm sorry to have to tell you this. But I figured you ought to know what kind of person you're dealing with down there."

Then her voice brightened.

"Of course, you were never too fond of Ben Trainham anyway and maybe doing business with this Blaise person—"

"No," Les protested into the phone. Then realizing her involuntary reaction was directed at the wrong party, Les cleared her throat and inhaled deeply for a measure of composure.

"Sorry, Mother," she said softly as she closed her eyes against the growing horror of this enlightenment. "Look, I'll be home this evening. We'll talk then. And—uh— thanks for calling me."

Quietly, Les replaced the receiver and sat for a moment, her icy hands clutched together in her lap, her eyes fixed on the weaving palm fronds outside the window.

What an idiot, she silently raged. *What a scatterbrained airhead I've been!* She closed her eyes and forced back the hot tears that threatened . . . tears of indignant anger, tears of scalding disappointment in the man she loved, tears of honest self-pity for the beating her heart was going to take again. All in the name of River's Edge.

Feeling the onset of tears gradually subside, Les opened her eyes and immediately spied the lovely red rose Blaise had picked from the garden.

There has to be a mistake, she argued.

But deep in her heart, Les knew there was no mistake. She'd known all along Blaise wanted River's Edge. Why had she been stupid enough to believe several bouts of red-hot lovemaking would dissuade that want? He was a businessman and his business was land. Now he had what he wanted . . . her land if she couldn't make the payments as agreed.

Like hell he will, Les muttered between clenched teeth. Purposefully, she rose from the bed, straightened the leather belt that cinched in the waist of her yellow jumpsuit, dabbed the moisture from the corners of her eyes, and reached for her suitcase.

She found him in the office, impeccably dressed in white slacks and a soft blue cotton pullover, his thick black hair brushed into order and a thick ledger spread open on the desk before him. Brandon lounged in a chair facing the desk, the rubber tip of a pencil between his teeth. A yellow pad lay on his lap, and even from a distance, Les could see the scribbles there.

At the door that stood ajar, she had hesitated, giving her heart a chance to slow its dangerous pace, giving her mind a chance to dismiss his aesthetic appeal and concentrate on his double-dealing other self.

Apparently, both men were so intent on the figures over which they labored, neither had heard the sharp click of her high heels on the polished floor outside the door. Nor could they see the determination on her face or feel the twist of emotions that turned her soft mouth into a grim line. But neither had difficulty reading the anger in her blue eyes as she shoved the door completely open and stalked inside.

"Brandon, I'd like to talk to your father, if you don't mind," Les said, her eyes like daggers on Blaise's face, the expression of which had changed from happiness at seeing her to surprise as he immediately perceived the cloud of doom hanging over her head.

"Sure," Brandon said. He laid the tablet aside and rose. "I need to stretch my legs anyway."

When he was gone, Les folded her arms across her breasts. One foot tapped out a rhythm of suppressed anger about to be released.

"So the Hollanders will be contacting me, huh?" she seethed. "Is that what you call passionate forays under the stars? Contacting?"

Blaise leaned forward, his entire posture one of undivided attention. *Okay, she's furious about something,* he told himself while at the same time realizing now was not a good time to visually caress those enticing curves packaged up so well in that form-fitting jumpsuit with its inviting front zipper.

"Did I forget the sugar in your coffee?" he asked lightly, opting for the casual approach to this storm that had blown into his office just when Brandon and he were making some headway in finalizing the figures for the River's Edge renovations.

"No, and you didn't forget the sugar in your kisses or in your arms or in any of your other downright disgusting means of getting exactly what you want. You're full of it, Blaise Hollander, and I'm not sure it's sugar I'm talking about. How dare you think I'll stand by and let you pull something like this on me."

Uh oh, she's getting up a full head of steam now, Blaise decided and his brow furrowed with concern. What had happened between the time he'd left her arms and her appearance downstairs? They'd had a beautiful weekend together and now, for no reason he could possibly think of, she was off on a red-hot tangent. *Disgusting means of getting what I want? Heh, lady, I thought we'd made some lovely headway quite mutually.*

Blaise sank back in the chair, his eyes intent on her face.

"Would you mind telling me what you're upset about, Leslie?" he asked quietly.

"No wonder you were so worried about Ben Trainham," Les shot back. She shoved her hands deep into her pockets and began pacing as her anger grew. How could he sit there looking so damned implacable? "Oh, his little bottle of wine and suggestion for friendship didn't stand a chance against your methods, did they, Blaise? Poor guy. I should offer him some advice seeing as how I got it firsthand from an expert.''

Blaise folded his arms across his chest. Obviously he was going to have to ride this one out if he wanted an explanation for her behavior. She was armed and ready for battle, and since he didn't know exactly what he was battling, maybe he'd best keep his mouth shut.

Les whirled to face him, her cheeks now mottled with what appeared to be pain. Compassion instantly melded with the confusion in his middle, and he was on the verge of rising to his feet when her next words froze him to the seat.

''You might think you're in the driver's seat just because Hollander & Associates had the money to buy me out, but as I've told you before, Blaise, I've had a lot of experience with those reins. I'm not beat yet.''

Now he was really confused!

''What in the hell are you talking about?'' he demanded as he came around the corner of the desk. ''Buy who out?''

Les scoffed and glared up at him. So tall, so arrogantly good-looking, so sweet, and so devious. The pain that shot through her was almost her undoing.

Her shoulders sagged and she inhaled another deep breath. Then she leveled bright blue eyes on his face and smiled tightly.

''I don't know at whom I'm more angry,'' she said softly as she felt that remarkable Braddock composure slip into place. ''You for being such a cad or myself for believing you. You'd think when a woman's been through one experience like this, she'd learn. But I have to hand it to you, Blaise. You're good. In and out of bed. You're top of the line, mister.''

''Stifle the insults, Leslie, and tell me what you mean,'' he demanded. ''Who bought you out?''

''I'd just like to know when you found the time,'' Les

said with honest amazement in her voice. "I mean, we've spent almost the entire time here in bed in one form or another. Was it in between times preparing coffee, or maybe while I was showering, or could it have been while I was getting my breath after that session in bed this morning?"

Blaise opened his mouth to speak, but Les was beyond the point of listening to his rationale. Heaven help her, she was remembering the romantic words he'd whispered in the moonlight . . . the eroticisms she'd shared in his arms . . . and she was swallowing a bitter pill. Just a very clever piece of maneuvering a woman's affections only to serve his selfish interests.

No, she hadn't known him at all. She'd made him out to be something perfect, and all along, he'd wanted her property, not her, the woman.

Well, for all practical reasons, he had what he wanted . . . or at least he thought he did.

Les knew she could not tolerate his presence another minute without turning into a shrieking banshee. Turning on her heel, she stalked from the room, her heart thundering in her breasts, her breath coming in hurting gasps.

"I can't believe she did this," Blaise exclaimed, raking his fingers through his hair in exasperation as he prowled back and forth across the spacious office where Brandon watched in silence from his post by the window. "Her suitcase is gone, my return ticket is gone . . . she just up and went home."

Brandon smothered the grin that tugged at his mouth. He'd never known his father to allow a woman to unshelve him like this. Obviously, that little slip of a blonde had even more going for her than he'd imagined, even though his opinion had been exceedingly high. No one . . . absolutely no one left Blaise Hollander in the lurch! No one, that is, except Leslie Braddock.

"She's probably waiting for you at the airport."

"I called and checked," Blaise thundered. "Miss Braddock had her flight changed to an earlier one. She's scheduled to depart Tampa airport in exactly ten minutes."

"You could have her paged," Brandon offered.

At this, Blaise scoffed.

"You, my son, don't know Leslie Braddock. It would take a sizable army to deter her from getting on that plane."

"Excuse me for saying so, Dad," Brandon said with a chuckle, "but I think you've met your match this time."

But Blaise was not listening. Jerking the phone to his elbow, he dialed information. Brandon watched as he jotted down the phone number.

"Who are you calling?" Brandon finally asked as he watched the storm clouds gather on his father's face.

"The bank in Williamsburg for a little information."

Ominous storm clouds darkened the sky as Les's flight from Tampa rocked and bounced and finally bumped onto the runway at Richmond airport. Her heart was as heavy as her carry-on luggage as she deboarded the plane and joined Sherry, waiting inside the terminal. Her mother's face was a mask of curiosity and annoyance at having been asked via phone from Tampa to meet her daughter's returning flight.

After the perfunctory trip to the baggage claim, they lugged Les's bags out into the early evening gloom.

"It was beautiful in Tampa," Les commented as they made their way toward the parking area.

"We were having a terrible storm when I left Williamsburg," Sherry said. "I just hope Josie's all right there by herself."

"Don't sound accusatory, Mother," Les said with a sigh. "A forty-mile trip in a taxi was a little out of the question."

As they piled the luggage in the trunk of Les's Datsun, a dusty maroon jeep bearing Pennsylvania license plates seemed to beckon from the long-term lot where Blaise had left it such a short time, but seeming such a lifetime, ago. The knot in her throat tightened as they drove past where he'd parked. Involuntarily, her eyes wandered once again in that direction and she could almost visualize his handsome bulk filling the driver's seat.

"I guess you don't want to talk about your trip," Sherry commented when, after they'd been driving for nearly fifteen minutes, Les still had not said a word.

"Not really," Les admitted, and then for her mother's benefit, she managed a weak smile. "I had a good time. Up to a point and you know the point."

"Did he tell you why he bought you out?"

"Actually, I don't remember what he said," Les said with a tinny laugh. "I was too busy raking his buns over the coals."

They lapsed into silence until Les reached the exit for Route 5. As she turned onto the rain-slicked highway, thunder rumbled in the distance and jagged lightning illuminated the skies on the southern horizon.

"I guess the storm's moved out to sea," Sherry commented.

Les did not answer. Her thoughts had somehow managed to drift southward; bittersweet memories were already tearing at her gut.

At the entrance to River's Edge, Les turned into the driveway and immediately glanced toward the rooftop in the distance as though seeking solace for the ache inside her. But even her love for the historic mansion was no balm for the misery of losing Blaise.

"What in the world is Josie doing?" Sherry exclaimed as they pulled to a stop in front of the house. Les shut off the engine and followed the direction of her mother's pointing finger. At one of the towering windows near the corner of the house, Josie stood on a stepladder struggling with a narrow piece of plywood.

"Nailing up the window?" Les asked in amazement. "Why? The storm's over now."

They crawled out of the car, extracted the luggage from the trunk, and started for the front door.

"Aunt Josie, what are you doing?" Les called, and just as she uttered the words, she saw the shattered glass littering Aunt Josie's petunia bed at the base of the ladder. Les dropped her suitcase on the sidewalk and hurried over to her aunt.

"What happened, Aunt Josie?"

The little woman peered over her shoulder. The board slipped and clattered to the ground.

"Drats," Josie exclaimed and short legs brought her back down the ladder.

"A limb broke and hit the glass," she said, her eyes wide with excitement. "So I was nailing boards over the window. I dragged the limb behind the barn if you want to see."

"No, that's okay," Les assured her. She glanced up at the remaining shards of glass in the window, a yawning mouth filled with ugly broken teeth. Then she shivered. "Darn it, Aunt Josie, you shouldn't have messed with that window. What if some of that glass had fallen on you with you here all by yourself?"

"I wanted to help," Aunt Josie explained in a contrite voice.

"I know," Les replied and Blaise's words regarding Josie filled her head. *Jeez, Les,* she thought. *She was only trying to help and you gripe.*

Turning, Les bent and gave her aunt a strong hug. "You had a great idea, Aunt Josie. But we need a bigger sheet of plywood. Come on. I think there's one in the shed."

Darkness had fallen by the time the window had been sealed and the ladder and toolbox returned to the shed. Aunt Josie went inside to clean up. Les busied herself picking up the broken glass and dumping it into the wheelbarrow, her misery threatened now that no physical activity remained to banish hurting thoughts from her mind. Rationally, she fought back memories and struggled to concentrate on the practical.

Tomorrow, she'd have to arrange for someone to come and fix the window. Those sheets of glass would not be cheap. It looked as though the sash was cracked. That would have to be replaced. But then on the other hand, she could buy the materials and Bernie could repair the window. He was, after all, the handyman at River's Edge. That would save a few dollars but if the glass broke and Bernie got cut or fell off the ladder. . . .

The magnitude of it all swept her from head to feet. Les sagged to the ground, uncaring that her backside, cushioned by the lush stand of purple flowers, would suffer unremovable stains. Drawing her knees up, she cradled her face in her hands and gave in to the sobs choking her.

"I can't do this anymore," she cried out against her dirty palms. "I just can't handle this by myself. Damn you, Blaise. It's all your fault. Why did you have to come along and spoil my life? Why did I fall in love with you? And why do I feel so helpless all of a sudden?"

Tears flowed down her cheeks and wet her hands. Les swiped it all away, her body jerking with the force of her crying. The tears had been half a lifetime in coming. There were many to shed.

Tears for an aborted childhood she hadn't even realized she missed . . .

Tears for a too weak father she had loved so completely . . .

Tears for that miserable husband Taylor who'd ruined her best sheets with his lusty shenanigans . . .

Tears for poor, sweet Aunt Josie who tried so hard to please . . .

Tears for the beauty of the man who'd broken her heart . . .

Tears for that stupid window and the anxiety that had cramped her stomach when the flight was rough and the lonely nights ahead . . .

Tears of disappointment because she had honestly believed Blaise might care for her.

And when finally there were no more tears, Les snuffled a couple of times, swiped at her face again, and raised her eyes to the dark sky.

"I was so stupid," she said aloud, the words like sandpaper on her raw throat. "So incredibly vulnerable and here I thought I was Miss Tough."

Les heaved a deep sigh, waited for a recurrence of the waterworks, and then sighed again when she realized the reservoir now was dry. For a long time, she studied the black heavens, decided there would be no stars tonight on which to make a childish wish, and then slowly rose to her feet.

"It's okay now," she murmured as she brushed the crushed flowers from her backside. "Everything works out. I woke up in heaven. I'm going to sleep in hell. All in the name of love."

For a second, her eyes burned. She bit hard on her lip.

"Dammit, dammit," she muttered.

Not one prone to swearing, somehow the adamant utterance of that simple expletive made her feel better. Not good . . . but better.

NINE

Uncaring that her mouth had dropped open in shock, Les gaped at Bernie, the gray-haired caretaker who'd been so much more than an employee at River's Edge for nearly forty years.

"Why didn't I think of that, Bernie?" she finally managed. A broad smile of relief curved her mouth and brought light back into her blue eyes, a light that had been missing for the past three days as she'd explored first one avenue and then another in search of a resolution for the overwhelming financial problems facing her home.

"Well, you're a woman, Miss Leslie," Bernie stated in his blunt manner. "Running a show like this is man's work. Pardon my sayin' so."

The smile broadened, and stalking across the hard clay floor of the stable in which they'd been cleaning stalls, Les gave way to the impulse. She threw her arms around his frail but still squared shoulders and gave him a resounding kiss on the cheek.

"It's a wonderful idea, Bernie," Les exclaimed, paying little heed to the flush that rose in his cheeks. Turning on her heel, she began to pace, hands jammed deep into her dusty jeans pockets, plans formulating in her head. "If, like you say, you can get some help from the Hanley boys and I can get that old truck running again, I'll let Wayne and Mike handle the Car Doctor and we can start cutting and hauling first thing Monday morning.''

"Soon as I'm done here, I'll head on over to the Hanley place," Bernie said.

"Okay," Les exclaimed. She reached down for the pitchfork she'd propped against the wall. "And I'll go talk some sweet, loving words to that antiquated GMC truck that's done nothing for the past five years but grow rust.''

Les suddenly felt as light as a feather as she bounded out of the stable and into the bright morning sunshine. For three nights as she stared out, watching as darkness settled over the thick forests on either side of River's Edge, why had it not occurred to her she was staring at the answer to her money problems? Thick virgin forests that had never seen a chainsaw . . . thick virgin forests that could use thinning . . . acres and acres of timber to be cut and sold at the lumber mill only fifteen miles up the highway.

She'd awakened earlier with little care for the blue jays arguing outside her bedroom window or the rich smell of coffee or even the recurring thoughts of the man who, in her opinion, had figuratively placed a dagger between her shoulder blades. Bought her note, huh? Well, that piece of paper did not entitle him to one square inch of River's Edge and she'd be damned if she wouldn't make sure it stayed that way. He might bleed her dry where the almighty dollar was concerned but loans got paid.

All of this, she'd told him in no uncertain terms when he'd had the gall to telephone her from Pittsburgh early Wednesday morning. Then with a rush of perverse satisfaction bordering on euphoria, she'd slammed down the receiver, giving him no chance to state the reason for his call.

As for the two subsequent phone calls, she'd flatly refused to come to the phone. To hell with Blaise Hollander! He'd wooed her and he'd cajoled her with dynamite kisses and skillful lovemaking and then he'd grabbed the old dagger. Of all the things Les might have neglected to tell him about a Braddock, why had she forgotten the main thing? Why hadn't she told him that Braddocks, when wronged, got even!

By the time the sun had dropped low over the James River, Les's enthusiasm was suffering a bit of a letdown. There was simply no way around it. The 1952 three-quarter-ton truck that had belonged to her father needed a lot more than loving care. It needed the transmission rebuilt, four new tires, and a multitude of dents beaten out of the oil pan to say nothing of a major tuneup. If the truck was to be ready to go into the woods on Monday, Les had two days to do a job that, even for the experienced, was horrendous, unless she could scrape up a few dollars and bribe Carl to come over and give her a hand. Bernie, bless his soul, was a lot of things, but Bernie was not a mechanic.

Later, in a hot tub of soapy water, Les closed her eyes and struggled to push aside her troublesome thoughts. She'd get the truck running and they'd cut the timber. Bernie had the help they needed and Carl had begrudgingly agreed to come by first thing in the morning and give her a hand with the truck . . . to the tune of six bucks an hour.

Closing her eyes was a mistake, for immediately her mind was filled with Blaise's face, her body reacting immediately to memories of his smile, his luscious mouth, his touch.

Why, Blaise? she thought. *Why the con game? And why was I such a pushover?*

It had been difficult to refuse talking to him, even though the anger, born in Tampa, had not abated. She'd ached for the sound of his voice . . . silently prayed he'd say the words that would make everything right again. And then she'd remember his subterfuge and the anger would return in full force.

I'll survive, Les told herself firmly. With the tip of her toe, she released the drain and then rose from water that had grown lukewarm. Braddocks were a hardy bunch, she decided as she reached for the towel. A hardy bunch with acres and acres of tall, lush hardwood timber to be cut and sold for beautiful green dollars that would get one certain Yankee off her back permanently.

Disappointment and disillusion were not unfamiliar emotions, Les told herself as she pulled on a pair of pink plaid shorts and teamed them with a white strapless tube top. Taylor had introduced her to both emotions. But in the time following her disastrous relationship with Taylor, Les had prided herself on the maturity she'd gained . . . a maturity that certainly should have enabled her to resist charm and polish and overwhelming masculinity.

Well, Les thought. *It didn't and now the only thing I can do is pull my heart up by the bootstraps and forget him!*

Not a simple task, Les knew. Blaise Hollander, for all his underhanded, double-dealing machinations for the purpose of acquiring River's Edge, was the most exciting man ever to have crossed her path. No, he would not easily be forgotten.

She ran a brush haphazardly through her long, tousled hair, flipped it back over her shoulders, and then allowed herself to be drawn by the delectable aroma wafting up from the kitchen below. She and Aunt Josie would be dining alone; Sherry was paying some last visits to old friends before her flight back to Miami on Sunday.

They were just settling down to dinner out on the patio when Les heard the chime of the ancient doorbell. With one lingering look at the food before her, she rose from her chair and headed for the front door.

As she swung it open, her heart leaped into her throat. His handsome features were cast in shadows and the light evening breeze played freely with his thick hair, tossing it onto his forehead. Absently, he brushed it back as he moved closer to the open doorway.

"You have a lot of nerve coming here," Les said flatly even as her fingers curled into damp palms and she struggled to breathe normally with her heart thundering double-time in her chest. "If it's to collect money, I still have a few more days until you can legally toss me out on my ear."

"You talk too much, Leslie," Blaise replied, his dark eyes roaming hungrily over her face. "And you know exactly why I'm here."

"I thought I made it clear I didn't want to talk to you."

"Yeah, when a woman refuses to answer the phone, a man tends to get the impression she hasn't anything to say. But since I'm here, do you invite me inside or do we talk out here on the porch?"

Thinking only of her aunt in the kitchen whom she would not want to subject to her anger, Les stepped out onto the wide veranda, leaving the door ajar. Then turning, she crossed her arms over her breasts and glared up at him.

"Okay, buster, talk."

For a long moment, Blaise contemplated the anger on her lovely face and struggled against the urge to pull her into his arms . . . temper the ache of wanting to kiss her, feeling her warmth against him.

Then he sighed heavily and tucked his fingertips into his hip pockets. His eyes drifted beyond Leslie's demanding expression and came to rest on the gray ribbon of water flowing silently past River's Edge. Even in the gathering dusk, it was beautiful here, so quiet, so peaceful, so much home. Though his visit to River's Edge had been brief, it had left a mark . . . a mark that had gone with him when he'd returned to Pittsburgh to spend endless nights missing and yearning with an intensity that was surprising to a man who'd given up on the love lottery.

"Will you say what you came to say so I can go back

to my dinner?'' Les demanded. But before Blaise could open his mouth to speak, she continued in full force. "You had no right to buy that note, Blaise."

"Oh?'' His thick brows arched in surprise. "Would you have preferred dodging the piranha's passes? Perhaps sharing a dinner or two when you couldn't make a payment, Leslie?"

"What would be the difference?'' Les demanded, the heat of anger surging into her cheeks. "At least Ben Trainham was up front about his wants. Not so with you, huh, Blaise? Picnics in the park, kisses in the moonlight, trips to Florida. My goodness, I'm surprised you haven't gotten around to slipping me a few bills for services rendered."

"I didn't hear the first complaint from you," Blaise replied tightly as his own anger began to grow. He'd missed her so badly, and as he'd waited on standby in the Pittsburgh airport, he'd told himself repeatedly the timing for this trip might be all wrong. Well, dammit, he'd come anyway because this little slip of a woman had grabbed hold of his heart and the past three days without her had been as miserable as any he'd ever spent in his entire life. Besides, he had to level with her.

"That's because I had no idea I was being wined and dined for the purpose of getting your hands on anything that has to do with River's Edge.''

"I told you before,'' Blaise muttered. "I don't double deal, Leslie. Anything we shared was genuine on my part."

Les ignored his comment.

"But don't you think for one minute, Blaise Hollander, that note you hold will ever do you any good."

Les's head lifted in defiance.

"I'll make those payments and I'll make them on time. And I don't need you traveling all the way to Williamsburg in an attempt to intimidate either. Because, I assure you, you don't.''

"That, I honestly believe," Blaise retaliated. "Not that I'd even try."

"For what purpose did you buy that note then?"

Blaise was about to reply. Les cut him short. "But then it really makes no difference why you did it. For all practical purposes, you have your hands on what you wanted all along. But you didn't fool me. I knew all along you weren't to be trusted. Now, if you'll excuse me, my dinner's getting cold."

"No, I won't excuse you," Blaise growled, and before Les could guess his intention, strong hands closed around her shoulders to draw her tightly against him. "Now stop carping and kiss me, dammit. I've missed you."

Les fought desperately to prevent the upsurge of tangled emotions when his warm, moist mouth moved over her own. For a breathless moment, she swayed in the euphoric splendor of lips so perfectly fitted, arms that bound her to that exact place she longed to be, a heart thudding beneath her splayed hands, a masculine echo of her own heartbeat. His aroma surrounded her, filled her senses, momentarily eradicating all but the bittersweet enticement of this magnetic man who had stumbled into her life and now held her heart in the palm of his hand.

A chill touched her lips when the kiss ended and, silently, she withdrew from his arms.

"Go home, Blaise. As I've told you before. You fooled me once. It won't happen twice."

"You're contradicting yourself, Leslie," he said mildly. "According to you, I didn't have you fooled for a single moment."

His eyes were intent on her face, and in the dim lighting, Les thought she saw a sadness there. But as quickly as her heart responded, she slammed a mental door. Her head jerked up, her chin jutted forward in defiance.

So she liked kissing him? So he'd thrilled her senseless with his lovemaking? She was in no way incapacitated by either. He was a man. She was a woman. Chemistry had been at its finest.

"Leslie, your stew's getting cold," Aunt Josie said behind her. And when she spotted Blaise, she blushed and shoved her hands deep into her apron pockets.

"Hello, Miss Josie," he greeted.

"Hello. Did you eat yet?" she asked shyly. "I made a lot of stew."

"No, I haven't had dinner," he replied, glancing at Leslie's face. It was on the tip of his tongue to refuse what was certain to be an offer to share a meal. But Leslie's defiant expression was too annoying to ignore. Her coldness on the phone couldn't be forgotten. Her distrust of him was unforgivable. To annoy the heck out of her, he'd stay as long as he wanted to.

"I haven't had stew for a long time," he said abruptly.

"Would you like me to fix you a plate?" Josie asked. "I made bread, too."

"I'd love it," Blaise replied, and when Leslie glared at him, he simply brushed past her, tucked his arm across Aunt Josie's shoulders, and urged her toward the kitchen, all the while inquiring as to how she'd been since he'd seen her last.

Damn him, Les fumed as she followed behind. And even as her anger toward him raged, a strident voice reminded her that her love for him came with needs affixed, the satisfaction for which would not be found in fighting with him.

I need him like another hole in my head.

I need him more than I need air to breathe.

Les toyed with her food and watched and listened as Blaise gave equal attention to charming her aunt and consuming two bowls of the rich, hearty stew, three chunks of French bread, and a mammoth salad. And over a thick wedge of peach pie, he elicited more than a few girlish giggles from her normally reticent aunt with his lavish praise of Aunt Josie's cooking.

What am I to do about you? Les thought with growing alarm when Blaise leaned back in his chair and pulled a mug of coffee toward him. As though in daring response to her silent question, dark eyes drilled her from across the table . . . compelling eyes . . . hungry eyes.

"So, how's business with the Car Doctor?" he asked, his idle question in direct contrast to the blatant messages his intense eyes were delivering. Les swallowed around the immediate constriction in her throat.

"Busy," she managed.

"We're cutting wood on Monday," Aunt Josie interjected.

"Oh?" Blaise commented politely. Damn, Leslie was so beautiful with the soft candlelight flickering in her blue eyes . . . blue eyes filled with the same yearning that rendered his pants uncomfortably tight in places, brought a sheen of perspiration across his upper lip, and made him wish for just a few moments that he was alone with her in a place more compatible with the erotic thoughts passing through his mind.

"Firewood?" he asked, not out of curiosity, but out of a growing need to keep his mind occupied with something other than the torrid memories of the previous weekend when he'd known the satiny perfection of those breasts so lovingly swathed by that tube top.

"No," Les murmured, tearing her gaze from his face and concentrating on the steam swirling up from her coffee. "Timber. To sell."

Suddenly, Blaise's mind was indeed occupied. He sat forward in the chair, his eyes intent on her face.

"You're not talking about the timber on River's Edge, are you?"

"Of course," Les replied. She glanced up, surprise etching her features at the intensity of his response.

"For Pete's sake, why?" Blaise demanded. "Why would you even consider spoiling the virgin forests on this place?"

Her eyes grew cold and filled with determination as she returned his intent gaze.

"To pay my bills, Blaise," Les replied tightly. "The note, remember?"

"There're other ways," Blaise told her.

"Yes, like renting out the bedrooms to a bunch of strangers," Les retorted. "This is my home, Blaise. It's not a damned hotel."

"It's a lucrative business, Leslie," he said. "The prospect of which I thought appealed to you."

"The idea gives me indigestion."

"Yeah?" he snapped. "Well, what you're contemplating doing to those forests out there is pure insanity."

"I could do the cooking," Aunt Josie said quietly, her eyes darting between their angry faces. "And make the beds."

Blaise looked at her and smiled. Then, reaching over, he patted the back of her hand, realizing what a wonderfully sweet lady Aunt Josie was.

"Yes, and I told Leslie you'd be darned good at it, too, Aunt Josie," he said softly. Then he glared at Les. "Why is it you're the only one around here who can't see past the end of her nose?"

"Oh, I can see one thing crystal clear," Les said smoothly. "You steadfastly refuse to accept the fact this is my property, Blaise, and your input as to its management has not been solicited. As long as you get your money once a month, I believe I can safely assume your nose belongs on your face and not buried to the hilt in my affairs."

"I won't let you cut those trees," he exploded.

"You have no say-so in the matter."

"You're the most hard-headed woman I've ever met in my life."

"And you just wore out your welcome," Les shot back. She rose to her feet and stood glaring down at him. "I believe you know your way back to Williamsburg."

"I can fix the guest room," Aunt Josie offered.

"No," Les said. "Mr. Hollander won't be staying."

"Thank you, Aunt Josie," Blaise interrupted. "I'll get my suitcase out of the car."

"Blaise, you can't stay here," Les exclaimed, reaching out to clutch his arm.

"Can't I?" he drawled. "Watch me."

"It's no use, Les," Carl growled as he wiped sweat from his grimy face. "The housing is cracked in two places. You need a new transmission for this relic, kid."

After tossing aside the grease rag he'd been using to clean his hands, Carl glanced at his watch and frowned. It had taken less than a half hour to pull the transmission out of the truck, two minutes to see the hopelessness of his endeavors, and it would take days to forget the look of adject misery on his employer's young face.

"What's lying around the shop we can use?" she asked, her eyes narrowed in speculation.

"Nothing except what's left of a Datsun transmission," Carl replied. "What're you planning to do with this truck anyway, Les?"

"See that?" Les motioned with a sweep of her hand, the broad stretch of oaks bordering the property.

"You're taking up logging?" he exclaimed in disbelief. "How?"

"I know," Les sighed. "You along with everybody else thinks I'm crazy." She plopped down on the running board of the truck. "I just don't know what else to do, Carl. Daddy left me holding one heck of a loan at the bank and I'm barely making enough with the Car Doctor to pay taxes on this place."

Carl pulled a cigarette pack from his shirt pocket and took his time lighting up. It was a rare time when Les Braddock took anyone into her confidence. Somehow, he was compelled to give her answers. But what answers? He had a wife, four kids, and a grade school education.

He knew about being up against it; he knew about trying to stretch a dollar.

"You know, Les," he said, exhaling loudly, "if it was me, I'd quit leasing the land and farm it myself."

"Carl," Les exclaimed. "I'm no farmer."

"Then I'd be looking at some other way of making this place pay for itself," he drawled as he gazed up toward the sprawling mansion, solid and arrogant in the bright sunshine.

"Yeah, like turning it into a bed and breakfast place," Les mumbled.

"That's an idea."

"That's what I'm told," Les muttered. She jumped to her feet and stood for a moment glaring down at the disassembled transmission. "Well, without a truck, I sure won't be cutting wood in the morning."

"It'd be a shame to ruin the looks of those woods," Carl commented. "What's wrong with the other idea? The bed and breakfast?"

Les whirled to glare at him.

"Do you have any idea how expensive it would be to get this place ready just so I could secure a license? I'd have to completely redo the kitchen we just got through doing. I'd have to rewire and replumb and resand and then there's the furniture. Oh Carl, even if I liked the idea—which I admit I do—we're talking one whopper of a bankroll here. And that, I don't have. So we're right back to square one. I guess I'd be better off—"

Her words trailed off as she saw a tall, dark-haired man with massive shoulders, ebony eyes now shielded by sunglasses, and the most infuriating way of making her heart leap at the most inopportune moments amble out the back door and head in her direction.

"Good morning." His eyes swept over her greasy coveralls before coming to rest on her upturned face. "Why up so early?"

"Good morning, Blaise," she retorted. "I trust you slept well."

"Like a baby," Blaise lied. In fact, he'd spent more than half the night telling himself he'd likely start World War III if he gave in to his wishes and invaded the room into which she'd locked herself immediately after dinner.

"Anything else you need me for, Les?" Carl asked as he immediately sensed the vibrations darting between the tall stranger and the woman for whom he worked.

"No, I guess not, Carl," Les said. "I'll go ahead and pay you—"

"You don't owe me nothing," Carl said with a wave of his hand. "See you tomorrow."

"I was hoping we could bury the hatchet and go for brunch," Blaise said as he contemplated the various pieces of metal at his feet. "I didn't know you'd be—what is it you're doing anyway?"

"It doesn't matter," Les said with a sigh. Without considering his presence, she jerked down on the zipper tab, and even as his eyes widened in surprise, she shrugged out of the heavy coveralls and took her time folding them before laying them atop her toolbox. Beneath, she wore ragged cutoff jeans and a simple white T-shirt. "And I've eaten, thank you."

Blaise shoved his hands into his pockets and mentally considered the extent of her anger should he jerk her in his arms and kiss those luscious lips. The immediate calculation made him shove his hands a little deeper into the pockets.

"I've been thinking about what you said," Les mumbled, carefully keeping her eyes averted as she prepared herself to eat crow. "And maybe you're right."

"I usually am," Blaise replied. "What about this time?"

"The trees on River's Edge."

"You aren't cutting them?"

"No."

"May I ask why?" Blaise persisted. "Not because I was opposed to it, I'm sure."

Les smiled wryly. "You're right there. I can't fix the truck. And I don't think I'd come out ahead to hire someone to haul them for me. Anyway, I still have a few days before I owe you a payment," Les continued as she began gathering up her tools and returning them to the box. "Maybe the sky'll open and a sack of money will fall through."

For the first time since his arrival, Blaise noticed the dark circles beneath her eyes and the grim lines etched around her soft mouth. His earlier compassion seemed to triple in size.

"Leslie, for Pete's sake, give it up, will you?" he demanded, moving forward and gripping her arms.

"You wish," Les murmured, raising blue eyes to meet his intense gaze. "Blaise, my grandfather worked himself into an early grave to keep this place going. And when he died, we all thought my father would fall right into place doing just what Grandfather did. Well, he didn't and all you have to do is look around you to see the result. And Mother couldn't care less."

She hesitated a moment, her eyes now subdued to the point Blaise wondered if she was on the verge of tears. That he couldn't take.

"Every man I've ever met in my life took one look at this place and then at me, immediately assumed helplessness, and started making his pitch to get his clutches of River's Edge."

"Don't place me in that category, Leslie," Blaise told her.

Les ignored his comment. She moved free of his hands, and turning her back, she squared her shoulders and continued, "Once, the Braddocks were a proud, successful lot. It seems I'm the only one left to preserve that dignity. Mother's married and has her own life. Aunt Josie depends on me. It's not stupid pride. It's being proud of who you are and willing to work your buns off to that end. What is so difficult to understand about that?''

"Because you aren't facing the truth, Leslie," he said quietly. "It isn't so much your love for River's Edge as it's your determination you won't be like your father. You saw him as weak. I see him as a strong man for having the guts to face his limitations and go on in spite of them. He was no farmer. That didn't make him wrong.''

"You didn't even know my father," Les scoffed. "How can you make judgments?"

"The same way you do," Blaise replied. "It's a human failing. Not admirable but, nonetheless, actual.''

"It's weak to depend on another person," Les said contritely. "And that's what you want from me, isn't it?''

"Is it weak? You depend on Miss Josie. You depend on your mechanics. You depended on me to a certain extent this weekend. Are you weak, Leslie?''

"Oh, Blaise, you aren't making sense at all.''

"Oh yes, I am," he corrected, moving around to face her. "I think you're secretly ashamed of your father for being what he was. And I think that's why you're so hellbent on being all he wasn't. In short, you seem to think you're a Miss Atlas or something, determined to set the world straight on its axis. But you have your own limitations, kid. Face them.''

Les smiled coldly into his face.

"I wasn't aware the world was crooked on its axis.''

"No, but your whole outlook on existing within the confines of the human race is," he shot back. "Excuse the cliché, Leslie, but no man's an island and that includes you whether you want to believe it or not. You need help here. All I did was offer that help.''

"Are you finished?" Les asked, ice dripping from her voice.

"No," Blaise retorted. "Actually, there is another thing I'd like to say. In the end, you'll end up taking on a business partner. I intended it to be me. But I realize that won't be the case and that's perfectly fine with me. I honestly don't think I could tolerate your incessant need to be in the driver's seat even when you're operating outside your field of expertise."

"No, that's a role you reserve for yourself," Les snapped. "I've never met anyone in my life who had to take charge of it all the way you do."

"Have you looked in the mirror lately, Leslie?" he drawled. "I'd like to think it's a man's prerogative to take care of a woman. In your case, that's next to impossible."

"Well, I suppose what we have here is a case of too many chiefs and too few braves, huh?"

"Next to zero," he replied tightly.

"Isn't it amazing how these little problems didn't come to light when I was in your bed?"

"It takes two to go to bed," Blaise said coldly.

Bending, Blaise reached for the toolbox, and ignoring her protests, he lifted it and started toward her van. Meekly, she followed.

"I brought you those figures on River's Edge," he stated flatly as he hefted the heavy box into the rear of her van. "Before you throw the idea out the window, at least consider it meritoriously. Serving breakfast to a honeymooning couple is a heck of a lot easier than rebuilding engines or sawing logs. And a heck of a lot more ladylike."

"Chauvinism should be your middle name," Les snapped as she shoved the sliding door closed on the van and then locked it.

"Who says it isn't? But then, I am what I am, Leslie," Blaise said as he regarded her stony expression. "And among other things, I'm not a swindler or a liar or a gold-digger. I'm sorry you think otherwise. By the way, I have something for you."

Digging deep into the rear pocket of his jeans, he came up with scraps of paper. These he shoved into her hand.

"I won't stand around while you piece those together

for clarity. It's the note on River's Edge. You don't owe me diddly squat. And that's what I really came here to tell you.''

''Payment for services rendered?'' she snapped even as the finality of his words brought the taste of fear to her mouth. She was losing him . . . she'd really lost him.

''Call it whatever you want to. I'd prefer to think of it as washing my hands of the whole mess.''

Then turning on his heel, Blaise headed for his car. Okay, so he'd suffered this trip for nothing. Dammit, a man had his limitations. If she chose to spend her life looking back over her shoulder, distrusting anyone who reached out a helping hand, there was nothing he could do about it. Her wounds were deep. He wasn't a doctor. Besides, he had a few wounds of his own, not the least of which was his pride.

Reaching inside the car, he withdrew the small notebook and carried it back to where she stood silently watching him.

''Read it at your leisure,'' he instructed. ''If you decide you want to discuss it, I'm sure Brandon will be most cooperative.''

And leaving her with her mouth hanging open, Blaise stalked back to the house. In moments, he came back out the door, crawled into the rental car he'd arrived in, and all too soon, only a cloud of dust settling slowly over the driveway evidenced his having been there at all.

TEN

"I think it's a good idea," Aunt Josie said as she swished soapy water over the dinner plates that evening while Les pored over the figures Blaise had given her. It was a struggle to maintain concentration, for as she studied his broad, decidedly masculine handwriting, she continually had a clear mental image of him bent at a desk, hair tousled, brow furrowed, lean fingers gripping a pen as he worked out a plan for saving River's Edge. The ache inside her had grown to the point of being almost unbearable.

As they'd sat in the airport waiting for Sherry's flight to begin boarding, Sherry had urged her to call Frank for advice. Then, on the trip home, as a means of dissipating the unexpected sadness at being separated from her mother, she had idly mentioned Blaise's suggestion to Aunt Josie.

"Aunt Josie, please," Les exclaimed in exasperation. "You keep saying that. But just because he has that so-called charm you like so much doesn't mean he knows everything. These figures are so far over our heads, they might as well be clouds."

She shoved aside the notebook and then slouched back

in her chair, her eyes fixed on the coffeemaker that had nearly finished its cycle.

"Besides, I don't know the first thing about undertaking a project like this."

"You could let him help you," Josie suggested. A skillet clattered as she dropped it into the dishpan.

"He'd love that," Les muttered. She rose, stretched her tight limbs, and then moved to the cabinet where she extracted a couple of mugs. "Come on, Aunt Josie. Let's have our coffee outside. I'll finish the dishes later."

Les fixed a tray and carried it out to the patio. When they were settled at the table, Josie took her time stirring cream into her coffee. Her eyes were downcast; her lips pursed.

"Okay, Aunt Josie, what's on your mind?" Les said with a laugh. "You always purse your lips like that when you're getting ready to chew me out about something."

"I was just thinking," Josie replied in her little girl voice. "He's a nice man and a good-looking man and I suppose he's pretty smart. He wants to help us and I think you ought to let him. Sometimes you hurt a person's feelings when you don't want their help. Like when Sherry didn't ever want me to help her fix stuff and serve when we had company."

"Aunt Josie, that's not the same thing," Les assured her, love for her sweet aunt flooding her heart. "Mother was just being impatient and nervous and you know how she liked to control her little social affairs. But Blaise is not our family. He's a businessman looking to turn a buck. Now, you quit fretting about our situation. I'll take care of us just like I've been doing." Reaching over, she gripped her aunt's hand and coaxed a smile from her.

"But you aren't happy anymore."

"I'm happy," Les exclaimed. "I'm just at my wits' end right at the moment. Heh, is there any of that chocolate cake left? I'm hungry again."

Aunt Josie bustled to her feet.

"You're gonna get fat," she teased and Les was relieved that she'd managed to put her aunt's mind at ease, at least temporarily. It was just too darned bad there was no one to put her own mind at ease. With Josie, it took a few kind words; with her, it would take a miracle. *And who possesses miracles of the magnitude I need?*

Blaise, a little voice whispered in her head. *He's loaded with whatever it is you need, including answers. You just don't want to listen, hardhead.*

"It wouldn't bother you having the house full of strangers all the time?" Les asked as she moved her elbows so that her plate could be placed before her.

"No," Josie exclaimed. "I like to have people around. I like to talk to them and show them my flowers and make them nice lunches. I'd have lots of things to do then."

Her simple words touched a soft spot in Les's heart. All her life, Aunt Josie had been sheltered . . . had lived on the parameters of other people's lives, having no responsibility and having no one expecting anything of her except her presence. And now the thought of waiting on a horde of strangers honestly thrilled her. It saddened Les more than she could show, for any negative emotional displays disturbed Aunt Josie. How right Blaise had been about her little aunt.

"Oh, Aunt Josie," Les said, reaching over and patting her hand again. "You make it all sound so simple."

"Then we'll give it a try?" Aunt Josie said hopefully, her eyes dancing with excitement.

"Let me sleep on it," Les replied, her mind discarding first one and then another reason why she shouldn't call Frank for his advice as her mother suggested. Maybe she would.

Leslie was saved the trouble when, two days later, Frank called.

"Hey, why don't you and Josie come on down for a visit?" he exclaimed. "Looks like you and me have some talking to do and we could do it a lot better face to face than over the phone. Besides, your mother's already missing you two.''

''Thanks, Frank, but I don't see how—''

''I'll take care of the reservations. After all, what's a stepfather for anyway?''

''Frank, thanks, but we can't right now. Besides, Aunt Josie's up to her eyeballs in fresh vegetables. She's decided to set up a stand out at the end of the road. Maybe we can make it down for Thanksgiving.''

''Sounds good,'' Frank said. ''Anyway, Sherry told me about your idea for River's Edge. Then we took a drive over to Tampa and checked out that Hollander fella's place. Nice.''

Les's stomach momentarily dropped into her shoes. And then she realized it was Brandon to whom Frank was referring. The chances were slim that Blaise would have been at Hollander House.

Even though his presumptuous nature galled her, she could see the plausibility of Frank's idea to, as her grandfather would put it, have a look-see. In fact, even though she hated to admit it, the idea was a good one. If she decided to go ahead with the inn idea and he decided to invest, then of course, he'd want some firsthand information as to what he was getting into. Who better than Brandon to furnish that information?

''Okay, now in a nutshell,'' Frank said, and from the tone of his voice, Les knew the social side of the conversation was finished. It was now down to business. ''I have a little money that needs to be doing something besides growing moss. And I know you're in dire straits up there, so what say we get this show on the road?''

''Frank—''

''No, I'm not of a mind to hear all your petty little reasons. I want something concrete like there aren't any contractors in the area, or all the carpenters and plumbers are on strike or there's a law against private enterprise in your neck of the woods. Got any of those lying around?''

At this, Les had to laugh. Frank was easy to like with his down-home wit and outgoing personality. Quite a difference from her mother's rather staid outlook on life. They made quite a pair, Les thought.

"No, I guess not," she replied.

"Well then, let me get on the horn in the morning and line you up a few contractors, start getting some bids together, and see what we have here," Frank said. "Meantime, if you're gonna run the show around there, I'd suggest you find yourself a reliable manager for the car business. Sherry says you turn a neat profit so it'd be in your best interest to keep that little endeavor going for a while longer. At least, until you get River's Edge back on its feet. I'll get back to you in a couple of days. Oh, and there'll be a check coming to get those tax people off your back. Consider it your Christmas present in advance. Hug Josie for me and find out about the licenses you'll need."

"Frank, slow down a minute," Les exclaimed, feeling a tug of irritation at his take-charge attitude . . . so like Blaise's. Was it a common malady among men? How should she know? She certainly hadn't been exposed to that kind of attitude in her lifetime.

"Ain't got time, girl. I'm turning sixty-three next month."

It was only after she'd replaced the receiver that Les realized she could not even pinpoint the exact moment she knew she would try Blaise's idea. Perhaps it had been when she'd seen the excitement and hope in her little aunt's eyes.

She debated calling Blaise. In fact, for thirty minutes after she'd hung up the phone, her hand rested on the receiver. And when she finally took it away, having made a negative decision, the rationale was good. She didn't have the foggiest idea where he was and that knowledge hurt like a knife in her heart.

The racket on the second floor was giving her a brain-buster headache! With a sigh of exasperation, Les threw down her pencil and rose from the desk where she'd been working since early afternoon. At the window, she folded her arms over her breasts and stared out at what was summing up as a gray, overcast September day. A misty fog shimmered just above the river's surface and a drizzling rain glazed the leaves on the oak trees. Even though Les knew there would be plenty of unseasonably warm days before summer was gone, today she imagined she could feel the sadness of winter in the air.

Perhaps that's because it's been six weeks since I last saw Blaise, Les admitted as she watched two tiny brown wrens searching diligently for worms on the damp lawn. A squirrel scampered across the walk, a peanut from Aunt Josie's feeder clamped in its jaw. Six weeks and not even one phone call.

I suppose I was right about his mercenery interests, Les decided as she turned from the dismal scene. When it didn't pan out, he flew off to better territory.

"Miss Braddock?"

Les turned an inquisitive face toward the carpenter looming just inside the doorway of the library.

"Yes, Phil?"

"Just wanted you to know we're knocking off for the day," the man told her. "If you or Miss Josie go up on the second floor, watch out for that stack of paneling in the hall."

"We will and thanks."

She listened to the men filing out of the house, and when they'd gone, Les sighed with relief. For the past month, the workers had come and gone six days a week, sometimes working a half day on Sunday. Now with only three weeks left before her preopening party, Les was growing apprehensive about their scheduled completion. So far, the bathrooms had been remodeled, the furnace replaced, and furniture sent out for refinishing. Now it remained to finish the paneling and then lay the rugs.

Turning from the window, she crossed to the fireplace and tossed in another log. From the rear of the house, she could hear Aunt Josie's off-key humming as she prepared dinner.

She returned to the desk and the last task to be performed before she could call it a day. As she scribbled out the check to Hollander & Associates, the dormant ache inside her surged to bristling life. It happened so often, and even though Les had told herself in time she'd get over him, time did not seem to be on her side. In fact, if anything, the misery grew more intense each day.

Well, Les told herself, *at least with this check, he's paid in full.* It was a debt she'd resolved not to ignore for reasons that went far deeper than simple integrity. Just because he'd torn up a piece of paper did not negate the debt's existence. The figure was emblazoned in her mind! So she'd sent him a terse note informing him of her intentions, enclosed a check for what she considered a month's payment, and then advised that the balance would be forthcoming. Frank's financial contribution had included that stipulation. The deed had to be free and clear if he was to be in partnership with her in this new venture.

The extent of her enthusiasm for the refurbishing of River's Edge had honestly surprised her once the work was under way. And there was no denying she wished with all her heart that pride did not stand in the way of her sharing her enthusiasm with the man she loved . . . a man who obviously did not return her feelings.

According to her bank statement, the check she'd sent to Blaise was still undeposited. And last week when she'd tried phoning to ask if there was a problem with the check, she'd been told he was out of town for an indefinite period of time.

Days she stayed too busy to realize the extent of her loneliness; nights nearly drove her insane as she lay in her cold bed remembering all the reasons why she should put him out of her mind . . . and realizing she was so desperately in love with him.

If only he'd call, Les told herself over and over again. *If only I knew where he was so I could call him. Just to hear his voice would be a balm for this crazy ache inside me.* And yet, Les knew she would not call him.

The next two weeks sped by in a flurry of activities. When the renovations were completed, Les set about hiring the minimal staff she considered adequate to run the inn. Aunt Josie would supervise Willa in the kitchen, she would handle the reservations, a maid would take care of the housecleaning, and Bernie assured her he could handle the rest.

But as opening night drew nearer, the panic within her grew. Suppose she bombed; suppose River's Edge drew no guests; suppose she was forced to stand by and watch the money she and Frank had invested go up in smoke. She'd posted notices all over town; she'd taken an ad in the local newspapers; and she'd even advertised on the radio.

Frank and Sherry flew up from Miami the night before the opening, and their praise as they strolled through the refurbished mansion was a soothing comfort, albeit short-lived. Over drinks in the spotlessly clean parlor, Sherry patted her daughter's hand and urged her to relax.

"Oh sure," Les exclaimed as she resumed her pacing. "I'm scared out of my wits and you tell me to curl up and deep breathe. Don't forget, we've all three sunk a lot of money into this place, Mother. If it goes down the tube, we all go together."

"So much for thinking positive," Sherry teased.

"I suppose I'm that rare person with her neck in the noose who can't think happy thoughts," Les muttered as she collapsed into a chair. "Just keep a spare room available for me in Miami. I might be needing it."

"Have you heard from that lovely man you were seeing?" Sherry asked.

"What man?" Les asked, her blue eyes intent on her mother's face as she firmly delivered a silent message. Sherry asked nothing more.

Blaise's eyes narrowed in speculation as he fiddled with his dinner fork and listened to the enthusiasm in his sister's voice. And when he'd heard enough, he sighed heavily and then shook his head from side to side, again negating an idea that was being presented to him for the fifth time in as many weeks.

"Okay, be pigheaded," Celia exclaimed in exasperation.

"Look, if a subsidiary office means so much to you, go for it," Blaise told her. "You don't need my help or my consent. You have money; you have know-how. And you're the one taken with Williamsburg. Not me."

"Oh rubbish," Celia scoffed, plopping back in her chair and motioning for the waiter in the little coffee shop where they were dining to bring her more coffee. "Don't tell me you haven't been a wounded bear ever since you came back from Virginia. I can't imagine how, but it would seem one little Southern gal did quite a number on both your heart and your confidence. And it just isn't like you, brother dear. I've never seen you mope over a female in my life."

"About the only thing I'm moping over is the time," Blaise replied, glancing at his watch. "If you don't hurry up and finish your dinner, I'll have to leave you to dine alone. Have you forgotten I have a plane leaving for Tampa at nine?"

"No, I haven't forgotten," Celia assured him. Reaching over, she clamped her hand over her brother's. "At least, give another office some thought, Blaise. It's not like you to let a love affair interfere with good business judgment.

You said yourself there's a gold mine down in Williamsburg and at one time you wanted to tap into it. Condos, apartment buildings, hotels . . . you name it. I mean, it's strictly a tourist town and hardly subject to fluctuations in the economy. I mean, we could—"

"I'll think about it," Blaise interrupted with a disgruntled sigh. "Any particular location, Miss Advance the Action?"

"Oh, anywhere out on Route Five that would make you smile again," Celia teased. Then she winked and squeezed his hand. "Why don't you stop off on your way back and see how the little lady is doing?"

"No," Blaise replied curtly as he extracted his hand and reached for the check. "Miss Braddock and I have said our farewells. You know I don't have a tendency to repeat myself. I'll call you from Tampa."

It wasn't until Blaise was buckled into his seat in the first-class section of a plane lifting into the dark sky did he take out and read, once again, the pink message slip that he'd picked up at his office when, earlier that day, he'd returned from an extended trip to upstate Pennsylvania. Just seeing her name scrawled there, with a notation only that she'd called with reference to an undeposited check, made his stomach knot with the dull ache of missing her. But she'd hurt his pride . . . thrown rocks at his integrity and even should he do as Celia suggested and drop in to see how she was doing, he'd be constantly on guard for the slightest indication she honestly believed him a smooth-talking opportunist. How could she possibly know that of all the things in the world of which he could be accused, that one cut deepest?

Blaise laid his head back against the headrest and closed his eyes. He and his father had never been close. Blaise had been told countless times by an admiring grandfather that he'd inherited the Hollander brains and the dashing good looks. Obviously, as much could not be said for Blaise's father, Aaron. Therefore, from the time he was old enough to know the difference between the warmth of a father's embrace and the chill of his denial, Blaise had accepted what was common knowledge. His father resented him . . . resented the fact Blaise was the pride in his grandfather's life . . . resented Blaise's college education . . . resented the self-assurance with which he dealt with the world around him.

When in high school, he'd fancied himself in love with the football coach's sexy daughter, and when he'd managed to make first string even though his grades were not up to par, his father had enlightened the entire neighborhood with his shouts.

"You're nothing but an opportunist," Aaron had shouted over and over again in the ensuing years . . . so much in fact there had been times Blaise had honestly believed him.

Especially when after college he'd been quite taken with the only daughter of a prominent banker. By then, his father's business was on the verge of collapsing for lack of funds. For reasons Blaise chose not to analyze, he found it relatively simple to obtain the loan that bailed him out. Of course, he'd married Elaine and he'd repaid the loan, but his father had never let him forget the fact that Hollander & Associates would have ceased to be if Blaise with his eye-catching good looks and smooth charm hadn't managed somehow to be in the right place at the right time with the right person. Aaron Hollander had gone to his grave without ever knowing how deeply his neglect and his accusations had hurt his son . . . never knowing how wrong he was . . . never having faced the fact that it was poor business judgment that had resulted in Aaron Hollander's having to turn to his son to bail him out.

And now, to hear those same accusations from the woman he loved?

No, Celia, I won't be stopping by for another dose of salt on the wound, Blaise told himself firmly. *I've put my*

*cache of pain from Aaron Hollander to rest. I don't feel
like having to do it a second time.*

In an effort to erase the memories from his mind, Blaise
opened his briefcase and extracted a stack of mail he'd
collected from his office along with his telephone messages. Sorting through, he mentally prioritized by means
of the return address, returning each to his briefcase.

He hesitated as he noted the return address on a rather
odd-sized envelope. River's Edge. Something leaped in
his stomach and Blaise frowned as he studied the handwriting. It was not the same as what he'd seen on the
check received from Leslie. Her handwriting was a scrawl;
this handwriting was precise and almost looked as though
it had been meticulously drawn.

Slipping his thumbnail beneath the flap, Blaise opened
the envelope and removed a white card. When he'd read
the simple invitation, he slowly returned the card to the
envelope and sat for a moment, simply staring down at
the address scrawled on the outside.

So, she'd taken his advice. Leslie Braddock, with a
head of granite, had actually taken his advice and was
opening River's Edge as a bed and breakfast inn. And
someone on her new staff had chosen to invite him to the
opening party.

Blaise smiled slightly and then he tucked the envelope
in the inside pocket of his sports coat. Two days away!

*Well, Celia, I might be taking you up on your sugges-
tion after all. Dropping in unexpectedly at River's Edge
and arriving by invitation were definitely animals of a
different species. Besides, I want to see what Les has done
with my ideas.*

Sure, his heart ridiculed.

Les was just stepping out of the shower when she heard
a light tap on her bedroom door.

At her yelled out invitation, Aunt Josie stole quietly
into the room and laid a box on the bed. She was retracing

her steps to the door when Les came out of the bathroom, knotting the belt of her robe.

"What's this, Aunt Josie?" she asked as she eyed the box.

"I ordered you a present," Aunt Josie said, her face beaming. "A surprise. I got it from that catalog you look at sometimes."

Les lifted the lid and folded back the edges of the tissue paper. Black sequins winked at her.

"Aunt Josie?" Les exclaimed as she drew the gown from the box. "Oh goodness, Aunt Josie. It's gorgeous." Rushing to the mirror, she held the dress before her as she tried to gauge the effect.

Bless you, Aunt Josie, Les thought with tears burning in her eyes. *How could you possibly know this is far too formal for the purpose intended? But dammit, I'll wear it anyway. There's no way on this earth I'd hurt your feelings.*

"You'll have to try it on," Aunt Josie explained as she moved over and sat down on the bed. "I looked on your other dresses for the size and it looks like it'll fit. But you can't tell how pretty it is until you put it on."

"Aunt Josie, you're something else," Les exclaimed as she crossed to the bed and bent to wrap her arms, black sequins and all, around her tiny aunt. "Thank you so much."

"I wanted you to look especially pretty tonight," Aunt Josie said, wringing her hands in a fluster. She rose to her feet, patted her hair into place, and then rushed toward the door. "You better get dressed. It's almost time for the party to start."

The dress fit as though it had been tailor-made. Of an elasticized fabric, the strapless top hugged Les's slender body from breasts to mid-hip before falling in glittering folds to just above her knees.

As she examined her reflection in the mirror, some of her confidence returned. Digging into the back of her closet, Les found a pair of decidedly sexy black slingback heels, and after pulling on silky black nylons, she strapped on the shoes.

The reflection in the mirror had grown even more seductive. For a second, Les envisioned how Blaise might react were he to see her in this alluring outfit.

But, immediately, Les shoved the thought aside. It simply hurt too much to ponder what she knew would be an approving reaction. She'd spent enough time in his presence to know that his preferences leaned heavily toward sophistication with a blatant undercurrent of sexuality. It was his basic nature. But then, he'd made her aware that her nature in the bedroom was not unlike his own. The fire was there; the chemistry was there; that seemed to be where the compatibility stopped.

After piling her hair in a tousled topknot, Les fastened silver earrings in her earlobes and then sat down at the dressing table. An elaborate dress called for just a touch more makeup than she normally wore.

Well, Les thought when at last she was ready to go down to greet what she hoped would be a roomful of guests. If her party was a bust, at least she'd have the satisfaction of knowing she looked her best when her ship of hopes went down the tube.

His flight out of Tampa was delayed and by the time Blaise arrived at Richmond airport, he was an hour behind schedule. With yet another hour's driving time ahead of him once he'd secured a rental car, he'd be lucky if he made it to River's Edge in time to bid Leslie a quick good night.

On I-64, the traffic seemed to be moving at a snail's pace. The last of his patience slipped. Muttering under his breath, he stomped down on the accelerator and whipped over into the lefthand lane . . . just seconds before he saw the dark object in the road ahead.

*   *   *

On a scale of one to ten, her grand opening party would
have to be classed a fifteen, Les thought with elation as
she roamed through the boisterous crowd, exchanging
small talk, accepting compliments, and doling out thanks
for the many good wishes bestowed for her future success
with the River's Edge Bed and Breakfast Inn.

In the kitchen, Aunt Josie was in her element as she
refilled a tray of finger sandwiches and was about to carry
it back to the boisterous gathering.

"Are you having a good time?" Aunt Josie asked, peering at her.

"Wonderful," Les exclaimed. Then her brow furrowed
with curiosity. "Why are you looking at me like that,
Aunt Josie?"

That mischievous smile on her aunt's face was a dead
giveaway.

"Okay, what's up?" Les asked.

Aunt Josie shrugged and then giggled. "Did he come?"

"Did who come?"

"Mr. Hollander."

Les shook her head. "Was he supposed to?"

"I think so," Aunt Josie replied.

"You invited him," Les exclaimed as her heart leaped
with anticipation. She'd considered sending Blaise an invitation, but she'd lacked the nerve. Apparently, her tiny
aunt was not so timid after all.

Aunt Josie nodded vigorously.

"Oh, Aunt Josie," Les said with a small sigh. "What
am I gonna do with you, lady?"

And until the last of the guests vanished through the
heavy front door, Les's head felt as though it was on a
swivel, her eyes constantly flitting over the milling crowd.
But all in vain. Blaise did not come.

As she sat in the kitchen sipping a cup of hot tea and
discussing the party with her mother, Les fought back the
disappointment. Okay, so Aunt Josie had invited him.
That did not necessarily mean he had to come. Obviously,

Blaise Hollander had lost all interest in River's Edge . . . and everyone involved.

In her bed, she tuned out thoughts of him by contemplating the numerous reservations she'd taken that night. But even as she considered the potential success of her labors, thoughts of him returned. After all, it had been his idea . . . his figures that had initiated the entire project.

Oh Blaise, she thought as she flipped onto her stomach and buried into the pillows. *I just wish you'd found time to be here tonight. You would have been pleased, I think. But mostly, I just wish you and I . . .*

ELEVEN

Les fought upward through a thick cloud of sleep and when finally she managed to force her eyes open, she lay for a moment contemplating the dark confines of her room. Silence lay heavy, broken only by the sound of her own harsh breathing.

But what had awakened her? Les was certain she'd heard a noise . . . not an ordinary noise, but one indefinable enough to rouse her from a deep sleep.

After a few moments, she shrugged and then closed her eyes. Perhaps it had been a dream. Anyway, she was much too drained emotionally to lie here analyzing those inexplainable bumps and thuds so common when the nerves are raw and the body is crying for rest.

Something pinged against the windowpane and Les shot upright in bed. Blood thundered in her ears, and reluctantly, she shoved back the covers and swung her legs over the side of the bed. Not at all a coward by nature, however, there were times when it took a lot of mental shoving to go in search of the mysterious.

Through a slit in the drapes, she saw a shadowy form move just beyond a thick clump of hydrangea bushes. Les hesitated. By the clock it was after two and everyone had gone to bed hours before. But then, that form was no figment of her imagination. As she debated opening the drapes to get a clearer view of her prowler, she heard a distinct "Ouch, dammit" and relief was as sweet as honey in her mouth . . . relief and a heady dose of downright surprise.

Les jerked open the drapes and then slid the window open. Leaning against the screen, she peered out into the darkness.

"What in the name of high heaven are you doing?" she demanded.

"I'm trying to get my pants leg out of this barbed wire," Blaise hissed, and at that moment, she heard a telltale rip, followed by another muttered expletive.

"What are you doing in Aunt Josie's collard patch in the middle of the night, Blaise?"

"Ruining a seventy-dollar pair of pants, what else?" Blaise retorted, and with that, he ambled up to the window and raised his face to her. "I never heard of putting barbed wire around plants in my life."

"It's chicken wire and Aunt Josie does it to keep Bernie from mowing—" Les gasped as moonlight touched the thick swathing of bandages adorning the side of his face.

"Blaise! What happened to you?"

Gingerly, Blaise touched the padding and visibly flinched.

"Long story," he replied and then he smiled that endearing smile that had never been far from her mind since she'd last seen him. "You wouldn't happen to have a nice tall bottle of scotch tucked under your bed, would you?"

"No, but the liquor cabinet's full," Les replied. "I'll meet you at the front door."

Not until his eyes swept the length of her, scantily clad in a peach-colored satin teddy, did Les realize, in her haste, she'd forgotten her robe. She grinned sheepishly and folded her arms across breasts all but bared by the plunging neckline, edged in lace.

"I'm afraid you missed the party," she said inanely,

all the while wishing his eyes would find the safe vicinity of her face before the goose bumps popping up all over her body became permanent attachments.

"I'll wait while you get a robe," he offered as heat flooded his groin.

As though unwilling to leave his side for a moment, Les turned, jerked open the newly installed coat closet, and withdrew a slightly wrinkled, slightly musty-smelling raincoat. Just as she was about to slip it on, strong, warm arms slid whispery smooth around her narrow waist and drew her back against his awakening body.

"This is stupid but a man would be a fool not to touch something as enticing as you are right now," he growled as he buried his face into the curve of her neck. "Lord, I've missed you, Leslie."

Les turned in his arms, and rising on her tiptoes, she fastened her arms around his broad shoulders. Satin murmured as his hands coursed down over her back and came to rest on her backside.

His kiss was hard and demanding and she returned it with equal fervor. His next kiss was slow and moist and thorough as he expertly fanned her smoldering desire.

"We aren't alone, are we?" he asked in a voice husky with need.

"Only if you don't count my mother, my stepfather, and my aunt," Les murmured. Slowly, he released her and stepped back. Les pulled on the raincoat and belted it over her shivering body.

"Let's go back to the kitchen so we won't wake the others," she whispered. En route, she confiscated an unopened bottle of scotch from the supply cabinet in the dining room.

"How was the party?" Blaise asked as he eased his bulk into a chair at the table. Bruises made their presence known as he straightened his legs.

"Terrific turnout," Les replied. She dropped ice cubes into two glasses and carried them to the table. "I'll let you serve." Then noting the grimace on his face, she reached for the bottle. "Maybe I'd better do it. What happened to you, Blaise?"

He told her of the piece of metal in the road, how he'd struck it, the front tire had blown, and the car had landed up against a guardrail.

"I think I cut this on my ring," he finished, again touching the bandage. "It's not so deep, just ragged and ugly."

"Oh jeez, now you'll have a devilish scar to enhance your good looks," Les teased even as a chill ran up her spine. He could have been seriously hurt . . . even killed. The thought was sickening and, visibly, she paled.

"I shouldn't have been speeding," Blaise admitted. "Now a toast . . . to River's Edge."

Les touched her glass to his and smiled slightly.

"Drink up, lady," he urged softly. "You look like you need it more than I do."

His dark eyes were warm on her face over the rim of the glass and Les felt the impact to her toes. Even with the bulky bandage covering half his face, he was the most gorgeous thing she'd ever seen in her life and love for him welled up hot and strong. She gulped more of the liquor, choked slightly, and then lowered the glass to the tabletop.

"Blaise, I—"

His hand covered hers as he slowly shook his head from side to side.

"I didn't come here to compromise you, Leslie," he said quietly. Then he rose to his feet and stood gazing down at her. "I came because I was invited. I'm only sorry I missed your party. Tomorrow, I have a little time before my flight home. I'd love to see what you did with this place."

"And tonight?" Leslie asked, returning his gaze, her heart in her eyes.

"Tonight we get some rest. You here. Me at the hotel." His meaning was clear. His meaning cut like a knife.

Les followed him to the front door and out onto the veranda, confusion roiling in her middle. Had she lost him completely? Then why had he come? Surely not out of simple obligation.

"You don't have to leave, Blaise," Les said pointedly. "There's plenty of room here."

His expression was unreadable as he stood in profile, his eyes fixed on some object only he could see. If she only knew how badly he wanted to stay. But somehow, he'd gotten off the track with her, and until he rectified that situation, he had to keep a tight rein on a raging libido. In separate beds beneath the same roof? Nope, it wouldn't work . . . not tonight anyway.

Then he smiled slightly, and turning, he draped his arms over her shoulders.

"We tried it once, Leslie," he said softly, his fingers trailing impersonally along her arm. "An occupied guest room with a bed that wasn't used could be a dead giveaway."

Before she could respond . . . promise him his virtue was safe with her, he released her and started to walk away.

"Blaise—"

"We'll talk in the morning," Blaise promised. "About a lot of things."

"Breakfast is normally served at eight," she murmured, her heart aching as his hand closed around the doorknob.

"I like my eggs over easy," he replied and then with a wink, he was gone.

Okay, so cooking isn't one of my specialties, Les thought as she stumbled into the kitchen the next morning. Especially not the kind I plan to serve to Blaise Hollander.

She'd set her alarm for six, had showered and washed her hair, and was now powdered, perfumed, and coiffed in readiness. Form-fitting navy slacks and a striped silk blouse concealed a body that had burned restlessly throughout the night. Blond hair spilling freely over her shoulders covered a mind fine tuned to rectify the mistakes she'd made with Blaise. And heaven help her, there had been a few . . . starting with her ludicrous character analysis of a man possessing a heart as big as the sky.

Now to convince her trembling hands it was possible to concoct a delicious morning feast capable of soothing the savage beast her stupid pride, her immaturity, and her hard head had created.

"What in the world are you doing up so early?"

Les dropped the skillet she'd just extracted from the cupboard. It clattered to the floor.

"Mother! Don't slip up on me like that," Les wailed as she bent to retrieve it.

"Leslie, it's only seven o'clock . . . on a Sunday morning, I might add. Most people in their right minds sleep in when they've been up half the night."

"Not when they're having guests for breakfast," Les corrected as she placed the skillet on the stove burner and then started prowling through first one cabinet and then another.

"Oh. So that's what your man Blaise was doing here at two in the morning," Sherry said with a knowing smile. "Inviting himself to breakfast."

"Of course not," Les scoffed. "He came for the party. Aunt Josie invited him."

She turned a guilty expression toward her mother. "We tried to be quiet. I'm sorry you were awakened."

"When a man's standing out in the middle of your aunt's garden cussing God only knows what, I tend to be awakened. What, may I ask, are you looking for?"

"He was cussing the wire and I'm trying to find where Aunt Josie keeps the recipe for hash brown potatoes."

Sherry sighed. "Suppose you pour yourself a cup of coffee and I'll make breakfast."

"I can do it, Mother," Les protested and suddenly she recalled her solemn vow only moments after Blaise had left. No more would she refuse a helping hand. No more would she demand always to ride in the driver's seat. And besides, she loved her mother's cooking almost as much as she did Aunt Josie's.

Smiling sheepishly, she moved away from the stove.

"Let me know if there's anything I can do," Les offered as she took two coffee cups from the cabinet. "Want honey in your coffee this time?"

For a moment, Les experienced an overwhelming sense of déjà vu. Before her parents had divorced, it had been Les's way of saying good morning on Sundays when they chose to sleep in. She'd make a tray with toast and coffee and a little pot of honey. The sudden memory brought a hot sting of tears and she wondered why she was retreating into the past just now.

Turning slowly, she faced her mother. The bright gleam of tears in Sherry's eyes told Les their thoughts paralleled.

"I haven't had that since your father and I—" Her words trailed off.

"I love you, Mother," Les said huskily.

"I've always loved you, Leslie," Sherry replied. "I have wished a thousand times you'd chosen to go with me instead of remaining with your father. I guess in the long run, Corrigan needed you more than I did."

Quickly she turned away and busied herself washing her hands at the sink.

"Honey and coffee coming right up," Les managed around the constriction in her throat.

After tying one of Aunt Josie's aprons around her, Sherry took a pound of sausage from the refrigerator. The smile on her face spoke of an inner happiness that had not been there when she'd entered the kitchen.

"Honestly, Leslie, at the risk of insulting your delicate sensitivities where advice is concerned," she said as she began forming patties, "I think a woman in love ought to learn a little something about the mechanics of a kitchen.

Just knowing how to overhaul an engine or throw together a bologna sandwich won't get it, girl.''

Les laughed and handed her mother one of the coffee cups. "You're right, but in this instance, I think I'll wait until I know if the man returns that love. Wouldn't want to waste my time, you know.''

From the corner of her eye, she saw movement through the patio door that stood ajar. Excitement leaped in her veins. Blaise! He'd come early.

Bounding to her feet, Les raced out to unlock and open the screen door for him. His enticing fragrance enveloped her. The bulky bandage on his head had been replaced with a narrow adhesive strip.

"Good morning," she greeted, ushering him inside, her heart thudding with joy at seeing him again.

"I'm early, I know," he said. Glancing past her, he nodded a hello to a hovering Sherry. Then taking her arm, he urged her toward the door once more. "I was hoping we might have a chance to talk in private.''

"Okay," Les replied. "Mother's cooking so I'm free. Would you like to walk or maybe go in the den?''

"Let's walk," he said. "I love the fresh morning air.''

Walking tall beside her with the wind in his dark hair, Blaise projected an untouchability that silenced the happy small talk forming on her lips. She matched his stride, her mind discarding first one and then another supposition as to the reason for his being here . . . what he might want to talk about. Most of them, she didn't like at all.

In the orchard, he paused momentarily to wrench a winter apple from the limb.

"They aren't quite ripe," Les offered.

"I like them green," he replied, and with a loud crunch, he bit into the firm green skin.

"My father did, too," Les said. "With salt.''

"I put salt on grapefruit, but not apples," he said.

He tossed the fruit aside and stopped in his tracks. Turning, he pulled her into his arms and kissed her roughly.

"Coming here wasn't easy," he said gruffly, his eyes burning into her own. "I don't grovel, Leslie. Believe that before you start jumping to some of your insane conclusions. I came only because Miss Josie asked me, and as I told you before, she's a deserving lady."

"I love you, Blaise," Les murmured as she laced her fingers up into his silky hair.

His eyes grew cloudy. A muscle jerked in his jaw. He released her and jammed his hands into his pockets, his eyes drifting past her with that unseeing glaze in his eyes.

"Leslie, I love you, too. But I have some problems with this relationship," he said in a low voice.

Les's heart soared and then sank a little. Not knowing what else to do with her hands, she duplicated his posture by shoving them into her slacks pockets.

"Like what?" she asked, her voice a mere whisper.

For a long moment, he stared off into space. Then his gaze shifted to the slow-moving river.

"I always wanted to live on a houseboat," he murmured and his eyes narrowed a bit. Then as though realizing he was in the midst of a conversation with her, he turned and grinned slightly.

"Sorry. This place gets to me a little, I guess. Kind of like your father. It's so easy to stand here and daydream."

"You were wrong about one thing, Blaise," Les said. "I wasn't ashamed of my father. I guess I wanted him to be a stronger man, but I loved him too much to resent him in any way."

"Maybe," Blaise replied. "Celia thinks we should open an office in Williamsburg."

Hope leaped again in her breast.

"Are you?" she asked.

At this Blaise chuckled. "Celia's smart and most times I trust her ideas. Of course, when she took it upon herself to buy the note on River's Edge she didn't collect any accolades from me."

"Celia bought the note? But why?"

"She knew I wanted the place and thought she was doing me a favor."

"So will you open an office here?"

"One of us will." He grinned again. "The trouble will be deciding which one."

Les said nothing. She didn't dare ask if his choice would be to remain in Pennsylvania.

"Anyway, that's in the future," Blaise went on. His eyes drifted over her face and settled again on the dimple in her left cheek. "Right now, I have to decide something more pressing. What to do about you."

"I thought you saw for yourself I'm doing fine now," Les said, knowing full well it wasn't her property to which he referred.

"I've always admired independence in a woman, Leslie. Until I started butting heads with you," he said, his eyes moving back to the river. "You make me feel so unnecessary."

"I don't mean to," she said contritely.

"Not only me, but your Aunt Josie, too. I don't know about the other people with whom you associate, but it'd be my guess, your spots would be harder than a leopard's to change. People need to feel needed. I need to feel needed."

I'm different now. I need you so desperately, Les wanted to cry out.

Instead, she kept silent, waiting for the ax she knew was headed for her neck . . . her heart. The wall was there . . . the wall he'd erected. She'd seen it last night. She'd refused to acknowledge it. But it was there, each brick carefully in place, cemented firmly by his determination.

"I guess what I'm trying to say is that even though I love you and I want you so bad it's killing me, I'm wondering if I'm not just too tired for you. With my business going as well as it is and given the competence of my staff, I'm ready to slow the hellish pace that's been my whole life. You, on the other hand, are just getting warmed up for the big run."

"Age again?" she blurted out.

His eyes were almost sad as they returned to her face. "No. In a lot of ways, you're as old as me. In a few ways, I can hold my own with your age."

His eyes momentarily darkened as they both remembered the fever when they touched, his amazing stamina, and the voracious appetite for one another that refused satiety.

"Blaise, I do love you," Les murmured.

"And I think I've loved you since that day you embarrassed the pants off me with the gas can," he said with a laugh.

"I didn't mean to embarrass you," Les defended. "I was doing my job."

"Perhaps embarrassed wasn't the right word," he corrected. "More like bested?"

"Are you telling me it's over, Blaise?" she finally asked.

He studied the toe of his sneaker for a moment.

"It'll never be over," he murmured and then he sighed heavily. "You know, I'm not getting this said right. Maybe I need to mull it over for a while longer."

In silence, he took her arm and urged her back toward the house.

"Would it be an inconvenience if I didn't stay for breakfast?" he asked when they reached the porch. "I have some things I need to do while I'm in town."

"No, not at all," Les assured him, her heart breaking.

"I'll call you," he murmured and leaning forward he kissed her cheek, delicately touched the dimple, and then turned to go.

"Blaise?"

His bland expression broke her heart. Her words froze on her lips.

"See you," she said simply.

* * *

The doormat was a nondescript shade of brown without one single redeeming feature that would prompt a discriminating shopper to select it above others on the shelf. But as Leslie lugged it toward the cash register and proceeded to pay for it, she knew her choice was perfect.

In the stationery store, she bought a roll of red gift paper, and a bag of chocolates for her Aunt Josie. Then she headed home to arrange for Wayne to handle the Car Doctor, shower and change clothes.

At the airport, she boarded her flight while giving little notice to the fact that the gift she carried was drawing considerable attention from the other passengers. Looking for the world like a giant stick of dynamite, why shouldn't it?

As she settled back in her seat, Les inhaled deeply and closed her eyes to ward off misgivings. She had his address; she knew from Celia he'd be home. Just how he'd receive her, she had no idea. But in the four days since he'd gone off to mull over his problems, she'd made her own decisions. If it backfired, then she could put him to rest in her mind.

A taxi delivered her to the address on the west side of Pittsburgh, and when she stood outside the low-slung, rambling duplex apartment, nerves gnawed in her stomach. One window boasted light. The rest of the apartment was dark. She surmised at nine o'clock he must be watching television.

It was a surprised face that greeted her when the door swung open to her knock . . . a surprised face with a shadow of beard, circles beneath ebony eyes, and a slight quiver in lips made for kissing.

"Leslie?" Blaise exclaimed.

"Last time I checked," she teased.

For a moment, he stood staring down at her.

"Well," she said, shifting from one foot to the other. "Do I get invited in or do we talk out here on the sidewalk?"

Immediately, he gripped her arm and urged her inside. The oversized gift banged the doorjamb in the process.

"What the devil is that?" he asked when they were in his overcrowded but exceptionally neat living room where a hockey game was in progress on the television. "I'm surprised they let you bring that on the plane."

"It isn't dynamite," Les assured him and then pressed the package into his hands. "It's a gift for you."

Blaise eyed the offering and then her implacable expression. "Is it safe?"

"You'll have to decide that for yourself," Les said. She motioned toward a portable bar in the corner. "Do you mind if I make myself a drink? It was a tiring flight."

"I'll get it," he started to say and then halted when she flashed him a tolerant smile. "Sure, help yourself. I'll have one with you."

What the devil is going on? Blaise wondered as he studied the unconscious sway of enticing hips beneath the slim black skirt of her one-piece dress with its inviting front buttons, the mouth-watering curve of leg to be viewed through the sexy slit in the back, her slender ankles made even more pleasing to the eye by high-heeled black pumps. With her hair swept up on her head, she was class and elegance and the most desirable woman he'd ever seen in his life.

God, he was thrilled to see her, but where was her nervousness to match his? Where was her annoyance that he hadn't called during this sojourn into his own mind? What was she doing here?

"I've missed you," Les said brightly as she handed him a scotch on ice just the way he liked it. And without waiting for a response from him, she motioned toward the red package he still held like a shield before him.

"Open it."

It annoyed Blaise that his hands fumbled with the ribbon. It further rankled when she smiled at his rather inept way of ripping the paper. The brown doormat slipped free of its confines and fell at his feet.

"What the devil is this?" he muttered as he bent to pick it up. It dangled from his fingers as he extended it in front of him, searching front and back for God only knew what.

Quizzical eyes met her amused expression.

"It's a doormat," Les said, and then moving to the sofa, she sank down, crossing one shapely leg over the other, knowing well how high her skirt rose in the process. Jeez, could she go through with this?

His eyes flitted over her exposed thighs and she saw a hint of color rise in his dark cheeks. *Well, it's for sure I can't stop now,* Les thought as she saw the want on his face.

"I know it's a doormat, but why?"

"To help you with your mulling," Les replied and then she took a sip of her drink for added courage. After dabbing at her lips, she raised sultry eyes to meet his once more. "That you can fling in a convenient location, walk on it, even wipe your feet. If you choose another spot, there's no complaint when it's moved. It doesn't argue, talk back, or voice an opinion."

She took another sip of the drink, already feeling the potent liquor warming the pit of her stomach, softening the knot there, increasing her susceptibility to the magnetic man who was now staring at her as though she'd become witless since last he'd seen her.

"However," Les continued, her voice dropping an octave, "if you'll notice, the surface is rough to the touch, it has no lips to kiss you, no arms to hold you, and it really isn't all that attractive to the eye even though the wrapping was rather interesting."

Moving foward, Les placed her glass on the coffee table and then rose slowly to her feet. *Here we go,* she thought as she stepped clear of the table and smiled at him.

"On the other hand . . ." She ran her fingers up the

buttons on the front of her dress, seductively fingering each before slipping it free of the buttonhole.

". . . you have the antithesis of a doormat . . ." The dress swung open.

Blaise's mouth grew dry as his eyes swept the length of her. Beneath the dress, she wore a skimpy black garter belt to support silky black hose. A vision straight out of his most erotic dreams of her.

". . . which won't be flung wherever you please . . ." The dress fell at her feet. Firm, bare breasts with hard nipples caught the soft lamplight, beckoning him. Heat flooded his groin and tightened the fabric of his sweatpants.

". . . won't be walked on, won't tolerate feet wiping, talks back, argues at will . . ." Slowly, she reached up and drew the pins holding her hair atop her head. Blaise moistened his dry lips and swallowed hard.

". . . but promises lips to kiss, arms to hold . . ." Thick blond hair tumbled onto her shoulders. She slid her hands slowly up her hips and then rested them on her narrow waistline. Her eyes glistened with suppressed excitement as she read the desire so evident on his face . . . in his body.

". . . and more love than you'll ever need in this lifetime." Moistening her lips with the tip of her tongue, she then tossed her head arrogantly and smiled the calm, poised, ultra-seductive smile she'd been practicing for four days while her heart drummed against her breasts.

"The choice is yours, Blaise," she murmured huskily.

_____ TWELVE _____

Blaise exhaled the breath he'd been holding while two months of suppressed desire tore free of its restraints, flooding his body, threatening his rationale.

"You do believe in getting a point across, don't you?" he finally growled as his eyes again traveled the length of her delectable offering.

"It's an old habit with me," Les murmued. "However, in this instance, it's putting it all on the line."

"Am I supposed to carry on a conversation with you or come over there and vent one huge load of sexual frustration?"

"I came with the hope you'd do both," Les replied. "But do something. I feel like a stripped mannequin in a department store window. Besides the fact that it's cold in here."

In truth, the chill was only skin deep. Inside, the fire burned with a greedy voracity. She had grown weak with its consumption; she was light-headed with the heat of need for him. And the obvious fullness so pronounced in the front of his own body was added fuel.

"Cold?" he challenged as he dropped the doormat on the floor and then stripped away the sweatshirt covering his muscular torso. Then he moved toward her, his glide as purposeful as a stalking cat, his eyes blazing with intent. "You look about as cold as an erupting volcano. Come here."

Les wanted to sag with relief as he jerked her against his bare chest. Urgent fingers gripped her backside and urged her hips tightly against his hardness. His lips hovered inches from her own, his breath hot and sweet with the aroma of the scotch he'd sipped.

"Lovely," he murmured, his tongue flicking out to moisten her mouth. "Sinfully, wickedly, deliciously lovely."

And when he fastened his mouth possessively over her own, the dam of her restraint broke. Her arms whipped around him, nails digging into his back. Her deep moan of pleasure was an echo of his own as her mouth warred hungrily with his demanding lips. Against her, he throbbed with impatience, each pulse teasing her with delicious pressure.

"We've tried beds and chaise lounges. I opt for the couch next," he mumbled as he urged her backward. The edge of the sofa brushed her calves and still he did not release her. He raised his head to gaze down into her eyes. "Unless you have a better suggestion."

"Oh, can it, Blaise," Les protested as she attempted to lower herself to the cushions. "Make love to me."

Their passion was explosive. Somehow, he managed to divest himself of the constricting sweatpants. Fumbling hands fought with the garter belt, the stockings, and then the minuscule panties. And when his arching maleness found the warm, bare flesh of her lower body, Les sobbed with happiness.

Blaise caught her sob beneath his mouth. His tongue plunged deep as his hands covered her breasts, torching his palms with those hard nipples for which he'd ached for so long.

A hot shaft of hunger ripped through her, and impatiently, Les parted her thighs, silently urging him.

"I love you," he mumbled and then he thrust deep and hard into her writhing body.

Like someone in the throes of sweet torment, she arched and bucked, blindly hurrying for relief from the agony of want. With driving force and heated words of encouragement, he drew her higher . . . farther from sanity . . . closer to that delicious explosion of mind, body, and senses.

And in that moment when she began to contract around him, Blaise knew he would never want anyone except this delicious devil with the power to incite all types of rages within him. Her passion was as genuine as her honesty; her love for him as demanding as the warm, tight loins he filled. And he wanted that passion, that love . . . he wanted Leslie for his own. He needed her desperately.

"Give it to me," he panted as he felt his control slipping. "Give it all to me, babe."

In answer, her legs tightened around him, her trembling body moving with a fierceness as never before when he'd loved her.

And then with an ecstatic groan, he gave himself over to the sweet delirium, plunging deep, gripping tightly, and then filling her with his hot explosion just as she quivered with her own release.

Some time between the insanity of climax and the downy softness of sated reality, he'd found a multicolored afghan to cover their damp, drained bodies.

"Tell me about the last affair you had," Les murmured as she idly stroked the spattering of hair in the middle of his chest.

"No," Blaise replied. "And I don't want to hear about yours either. I want to know present things, like what do we do about your hard head."

"The same thing we do about yours, I guess," Les drawled, closing her eyes and relishing the warm press of his body on the narrow couch. "We do our best to live with it."

"Compromise, you mean? You don't know the meaning of the word."

"Neither do you, but we love each other." At this, Les opened her eyes, rose on her elbow, and peered down into his tired face. "Don't we?"

"Either that or we're gluttons for punishment," he replied and then he smiled and gently touched the dimple in her cheek. "I love you. Plain and simple. And I'm glad you're here."

"We need to talk."

"I know, but isn't it more fun to just lie here and hold each other?"

Les snuggled back into his arms. Blaise stared up at the ceiling, the slow birth of dread forming in his stomach. Could they ever learn to compromise? Would she ever learn the meaning of the word?

He smiled to himself. Would he?

Yes, they had to. He couldn't let her go now. She'd managed to fill the last vestige of space left in his weary heart.

Involuntarily, his arms tightened around her, and closing his eyes, he drifted off to sleep.

"The doormat was priceless," Blaise said as he jerked on his sweatpants and then went to get his robe for her. "I'm not so sure I like the underlying message, but I have to applaud your ingenuity."

Les slipped her arms into the sleeves and then belted it around her. As she attempted to restore some order to her tangled hair, she smiled in retrospect.

"Good routine, too," he teased. "Must have taken some practice to perfect."

"Are you kidding? I'm a natural-born stripper," she murmured as she went to him, lifted her arms around his neck, and waited for the wonderful pressure of his lips on hers.

"I don't want a doormat in my life," Blaise told her gently. "I wouldn't respect a woman like that."

"So you want me," Les declared. "I knew it all along."

"But could you relinquish the reins once in awhile?" he asked in a mock plaintive voice. "The passenger seat gets cramped after long periods."

"I've learned a lot these past weeks," Les admitted as she pulled free of his arms and started for the front door. At his questioning look, she explained.

"My suitcase. It didn't fit the image I wanted to make, so I left it outside."

After retrieving it, she settled herself on the sofa.

"Especially about Aunt Josie," she continued. "You were so right about her, Blaise. I've never seen such a transformation in a person. Or such energy. And Mother and I have a rapport I never thought would exist. I even like her now that she's quit griping all the time."

Les smiled as she recalled the night in the petunia bed.

"But mostly, I've learned how vulnerable love can make a person." At this, she raised her eyes to meet his. "And I do love you, Blaise, with all my heart. Oh, I don't promise I'll ever be able to completely relinquish the reins. It was instilled so long ago, but I can understand and accept the reason now. My father was a beautiful person born into the wrong situation for his nature."

"But I'm not like your father," Blaise told her as he joined her on the sofa. His eyes were warm and intent on her face. "I suppose I'm more like you."

"You're exactly like me," Les said with a hearty laugh as she moved into his arms. "That's the problem."

"I thought it was opposites that attracted."

"See what I mean? We were born to test the rules. Gives us a common ground on which to build."

"Oh brother, such philosophy from one so young," Blaise mumbled teasingly. At this, his stomach rumbled. "Did you have dinner?"

"Nope."

"Can you cook?"

"Nope."

"Can you scramble eggs?"

"I can try."

"Good. That's all that's in the refrigerator."

Later, in the kitchen, Blaise made toast while she scrambled the eggs.

"So we put a chart on the front of the refrigerator," Les teased as she sloshed scrambled eggs onto his plate and then added two slices of the toast.

On the television, the final moments of the hockey game reminded her how little time had passed since she'd walked in his front door, heavy with anxious anticipation. Now, she was light enough to float.

"One day it's your turn to call the shots. The next, it's mine."

Bending, she planted a kiss on his forehead. Then she tightened the belt on the robe she wore and settled herself in the chair next to him.

"Lousy idea," Blaise drawled as he sprinkled pepper over his food. "I told you you didn't know the meaning of the word compromise."

"Then why don't we just play it by ear? Blaise, there are no guidebooks, you know."

"Yeah, but a man should be king of his castle," he said, feigning a pout.

"We don't have a castle."

"That's another point." He scowled handsomely. "Where would we live?"

"At River's Edge, of course," Les replied. She swathed a dollop of butter over her toast. "You can open an office in Williamsburg, turn in the key to this apartment, and we live happily ever after."

"No, you could turn management of River's Edge over to someone and you could move up here."

"No, that's impossible, Blaise," Les exclaimed as she

gazed at him. "I just opened my inn and you expect me to leave it?"

At this, Blaise threw back his head and laughed.

"You think I'm being facetious?" Les demanded.

"No, I think you're being Leslie, the driver." Reaching over, he drew her from the chair and onto his lap. "Look, Miss Braddock, you keep River's Edge and run it just like you planned. Celia can open an office in Williamsburg and yours truly could retire."

"And do nothing?" Les exclaimed in disbelief.

"Are you afraid we'll starve?" His eyes were playful on her face. "I assure you we won't. A good workaholic is also good at stashing his profits aside."

"You'd last in retirement about three days," Les scoffed as she raked his tousled black hair back from his forehead.

"Probably less than that," Blaise admitted. "I'd have to find myself some hobbies—"

"Or you could help me with River's Edge," Les declared.

"And have you bossing me around all day?" Blaise hooted. "No way, lady. I'd rather open a fruit stand. Come on. Eat your eggs so we can get some sleep. Tomorrow promises to be a busy day."

"You're working on Saturday?" Les asked as she leaned over to kiss the pulse beating softly in his neck.

"In a manner of speaking," Blaise replied, his eyes twinkling. He reached for her hand and then shoved his heavy class ring onto her middle finger, where it hung loosely. "It'll have to do until we finish combing the jewelry stores tomorrow. Just don't lose it."

Les stared down at it in disbelief. Then she peered at him.

"You haven't asked me to marry you yet," she protested.

"Oh?" Blaise teased. "Sorry. I thought it was your day to call the shots."

Les laughed gleefully and then kissed him.

"So it is. Will you marry me, Blaise?"

"Only if you promise to eat your eggs," he murmured against her mouth.

The living room at River's Edge was a flurry of activity two weeks later as Les and Sherry struggled to rearrange the heavy furnishings in preparation for Blaise and Les's engagement party. Aunt Josie was making table arrangements from the bundles of chrysanthemums, holly, and pyracantha she'd collected from her beloved gardens.

"Where is he?" Les fumed as she glanced at her watch for the fourth time in ten minutes. "He's been gone since seven this morning. It's nearly three now."

"Calm down, Leslie," Sherry admonished as she removed a priceless antique cut-glass candy dish from a low table and moved it to a safer location on the massive hearth. "The party doesn't start until eight."

"Yes, but he said he'd only be gone a little while."

"You can't carry him in your apron pocket, for Pete's sake."

"I would if I could," Les admitted as she felt a swift surge of overwhelming love for the man she would marry at a lavish wedding to be held in two days at River's Edge.

"Maybe he's at his new office," she decided. "He's working so hard to get it opened before Christmas. I could call and see when he's coming home."

"You have a lot to learn, Leslie," Sherry said with a smile. "Your father might have been putty in your pretty little hands, but I don't believe for a moment Blaise Hollander will be."

"Oh, Mother," Les exclaimed in exasperation. She flopped down on the sofa and extended jeans-clad legs before her. "I don't want him like putty. I just want him here. Some of this furniture is too heavy for us to move alone."

Sherry turned and stared at her daughter in amazement. In the few days she'd been at River's Edge awaiting Frank's return from Boston so they could commence the first vacation they'd had together in years, she'd come to see some startling changes in her feisty, iron-willed offspring.

"I can't believe it. Leslie Braddock actually needs help."

Les smiled and was about to respond when the front door opened and the reason for her childish agitation entered.

"Damn, it's cold out there," Blaise exclaimed as he stripped off his gloves and then shrugged out of his heavy parka. His eyes came immediately to rest on Les's luminous face as he raked order into his windblown hair.

"Hello, Braddock."

"Hello, Hollander."

Sherry sighed in fond remembrance of a time when she'd gazed at Les's father with such burning love in her eyes. She'd loved Corrigan. She just hadn't respected him enough. Les would not encounter that problem with this hunk of a man now bending down to bestow on her waiting lips a kiss filled with possessive passion. Discreetly, Sherry left the room to go help Josie with the flowers.

"I need your help with the furniture," she murmured as she rose to her feet and hugged him tightly.

"Just tell me where you want it," he drawled. His eyes moved over her upturned face, and though he hadn't begrudged the lack of privacy in the past week when he'd been like a fixture around River's Edge, he wished for about fifteen minutes of the precious commodity so he could satisfy the lust mirrored in those beguiling blue eyes.

"Do you realize it's been seven days since I made love to you?" he murmured. "The pressure's killing me."

"My door's been open every night," she replied softly as she felt a surge of her own hunger for him.

"Yeah, and if it hadn't been for my ridiculous respect

for Miss Josie and now your mother, I'd have barged in like a rutting dog.''

"Two more days," she whispered as she traced his lower lip.

"Oh, I think sooner," he whispered in return and another kind of excitement drew near to bursting inside him. He could hardly wait till she saw it. But he'd planned the presentation as carefully as he'd planned the surprise. It had taken him all day to get it here. Now he had to wait for the perfect opening to show it to her. Knowing his precious Leslie, it wouldn't be that long a wait.

"We'd better get to work or I won't be responsible for my wicked body's demands," he growled.

For the next few minutes, they labored with the heavy furniture until Les was satisfied with the results. The room could now accommodate the impressive number of guests who had been invited without having them bump into tables or trip over each other.

"I see a future project for the contracting side of Williamsburg's new Hollander & Associates," Blaise said as he feigned concentration on the curving stairway leading to the second floor. "That flight of stairs needs to be reversed to provide more room here."

He turned and peered at the fireplace, his brow furrowed with interest.

"And that could be widened. And those windows—"

"Blaise, this is my home," Les reminded him. "I like it just the way it is."

Relief surged through him. Perfect opening! Leslie had swallowed the bait!

With his heart thundering with happiness, Blaise grabbed her shoulders, spun her around, and urged her ahead of him to the wide windows on the side of the house facing the river.

"This might be your house," he said in a husky voice. Then he slipped his finger through an opening in the sheers and shoved them apart.

Les stared out, her eyes widening in disbelief as he pointed to the river where a riverboat, large enough to do Samuel Clemens proud, bobbed in its new moorings.

"But that, my love," he whispered in her ear, "is OUR home."

"But how?" Leslie exclaimed as she gazed out, easily remembering that day in the orchard when he'd told her of his secret desire.

"That's where I've been all day. Trying to get this thing home where it belongs," he said proudly. Then he turned her in his arms. His eyes were glazed with hunger. "I'd consider it an honor, Miss Braddock, if you'd allow me to give you the guided tour and everything that entails."

"Now?" she teased as her heart escalated with anticipation of being totally and completely alone with him.

"Right now."

SHARE THE FUN . . .
SHARE YOUR NEW-FOUND TREASURE!!

You don't want to let your new books out of your sight? That's okay. Your friends can get their own. Order below.

No. 125 COMMON GROUND by Jeane Gilbert-Lewis
Blaise was only one of her customers but Les just couldn't forget him.

No. 7 SILENT ENCHANTMENT by Lacey Dancer
Was she real? She was Alex's true-to-life fairy tale princess.

No. 8 STORM WARNING by Kathryn Brocato
Passion raged out of their control—and there was no warning!

No. 9 PRODIGAL LOVER by Margo Gregg
Bryan is a mystery. Could he be Keely's presumed dead husband?

No. 10 FULL STEAM by Cassie Miles
Jonathan's a dreamer—Darcy is practical. An unlikely combo!

No. 11 BY THE BOOK by Christine Dorsey
Charlotte and Mac give parent-teacher conference a new meaning.

No. 12 BORN TO BE WILD by Kris Cassidy
Jenny shouldn't get close to Garrett. He'll leave too, won't he?

No. 13 SIEGE OF THE HEART by Sheryl McDanel Munson
Nick pursues Court while she wrestles with her heart and mind.

No. 14 TWO FOR ONE by Phyllis Herrmann
What is it about Cal and Elliot that has Leslie seeing double?

No. 15 A MATTER OF TIME by Ann Bullard
Does Josh *really* want Christine or is there something else?

No. 16 FACE TO FACE by Shirley Faye
Christi's definitely not Damon's type. So, what's the attraction?

No. 17 OPENING ACT by Ann Patrick
Big city playwright meets small town sheriff and life heats up.

No. 18 RAINBOW WISHES by Jacqueline Case
Mason is looking for more from life. Evie may be his pot of gold!

No. 19 SUNDAY DRIVER by Valerie Kane
Carrie breaks through all Cam's defenses showing him how to love.

No. 20 CHEATED HEARTS by Karen Lawton Barrett
T.C. and Lucas find their way back into each other's hearts.

No. 21 THAT JAMES BOY by Lois Faye Dyer
Jesse believes in love at first sight. Will he convince Sarah?

No. 22 NEVER LET GO by Laura Phillips
Ryan has a big dilemma. Kelly is the answer to *all* his prayers.

No. 23 A PERFECT MATCH by Susan Combs
Ross can keep Emily safe but can he save himself from Emily?

No. 24 REMEMBER MY LOVE by Pamela Macaluso
Will Max ever remember the special love he and Deanna shared?

No. 25 LOVE WITH INTEREST by Darcy Rice
Stephanie & Elliot find $47,000,000 *plus* interest—true love!

No. 26 NEVER A BRIDE by Leanne Banks
The last thing Cassie wanted was a relationship. Joshua had other ideas.

No. 27 GOLDILOCKS by Judy Christenberry
David and Susan join forces and get tangled in their own web.

No. 28 SEASON OF THE HEART by Ann Hammond
Can Lane and Maggie's newfound feelings stand the test of time?

No. 29 FOSTER LOVE by Janis Reams Hudson
Morgan comes home to claim his children but Sarah claims his heart.

Meteor Publishing Corporation
Dept. 193, P. O. Box 41820, Philadelphia, PA 19101-9828

Please send the books I've indicated below. Check or money order (U.S. Dollars only)—no cash, stamps or C.O.D.s (PA residents, add 6% sales tax). I am enclosing $2.95 plus 75¢ handling fee for *each* book ordered.

Total Amount Enclosed: $_____.

____ No. 125	____ No. 12	____ No. 18	____ No. 24
____ No. 7	____ No. 13	____ No. 19	____ No. 25
____ No. 8	____ No. 14	____ No. 20	____ No. 26
____ No. 9	____ No. 15	____ No. 21	____ No. 27
____ No. 10	____ No. 16	____ No. 22	____ No. 28
____ No. 11	____ No. 17	____ No. 23	____ No. 29

Please Print:

Name _____

Address _____ Apt. No. _____

City/State _____ Zip _____

Allow four to six weeks for delivery. Quantities limited.